Drive-By Shouting

DRIVE-BY SHOUTING

Mark Chase

Drive-By Shouting

Drive-By Shouting

Text Copyright © Mark Chase 2016

Mark Chase has asserted his right in accordance with the Copyright Designs and Patents Act 1988 to be identified as the author of this work.

All rights reserved

No part of this publication may be lent, resold, hired out or reproduced in any form or by any means without prior written permission from the author and publisher. All rights reserved. Copyright © 3P Publishing Ltd

First published in 2016 in the UK

Set in Giovanni 11pt

3P Publishing Ltd
C E C, London Road
Corby
NN17 5EU

A catalogue number for this book is available from the British Library

ISBN 978-1-911559-12-2

Cover design: Jamie Rae

Drive-By Shouting

For Jacqueline, and all my kith and kin

Drive-By Shouting

Contents:

Part One – Overture	7
Chapter 1	8
Chapter 2	18
Chapter 3	31
Chapter 4	48
Chapter 5	52
Part Two – Bridge	61
Chapter 6	62
Part Three – Verse	79
Chapter 7	80
Chapter 8	100
Part Four – Bridge Two	119
Chapter 9	120
Part Five – Chorus	129
Chapter 10	130
Chapter 11	136
Part Six – Middle Eight	161
Chapter 12	162
Chapter 13	172
Chapter 14	187
Chapter 15	196
Chapter 16	200
Part Seven – Double Cross	215
Chapter 17	216
Chapter 18	240
Chapter 19	256
Chapter 20	267
Part Eight – Coda	277
Chapter 21	278
Chapter 22	304
Part Nine – Fade Out	317
Chapter 23	318

Part 1

Overture

Drive-By Shouting

"Waiting while you have your fun,
You'd think by now that maybe I'd have learned,
I'm sitting like a loaded gun,
I carried a torch 'til my fingers burned."

World of Leather – 'When Saturday Comes'

Chapter 1
London 1999

Staring forlornly through the window of the W7 bus as it made its tortuous journey up the hill from Finsbury Park to Crouch End, Gram Kane was vaguely aware of the mixture of smells emanating from his clothes and body, a faintly nauseating mix of sweat, smoke and last night's sex.

A group of black teenagers thumped each other in the seats ahead of him, one appearing to point Gram out to another. Gram tried to melt into his seat whilst clutching his gig bag closer to him. The teenager's interest wandered elsewhere, but Gram continued to grip the padded bag tightly between his knees. Inside was his sunburst Gibson Les Paul, his one possession

Drive-By Shouting

of value, but also, he thought ruefully, the agent of his mounting disappointment with life.

He vaguely remembered reading somewhere that a man who willingly rode on a bus over the age of 30 was a self-confessed failure. Gram was fast approaching 36. That he also carried a guitar seemed to further cement his growing feeling of being a loser. When he'd been younger, in Maghull and Northampton, someone who had a guitar, especially a Gibson, was accorded an almost mythic status. A guitar was a passport to local glamour and, usually, sex. You were an artist, a creator, someone going somewhere. You'd find yourself in flats, bedsits & student halls of residence late at night, quietly working through your repertoire, before the inevitable clinch and burst of passion. Oh, how those girls had loved an artist; now, guitars were carried by buskers and out of touch wannabes, while guys who couldn't play a note, but called themselves DJs, got laid every night.

He was pulled from his comfortably bitter reverie, by a hideous tinny version of *Smoke On The Water*. He fumbled for his pay as you go mobile. The screen said '*Matt M.*' He winced.

"Yeah?"
"Gram? It's Matt."
"Yeah. Hi."
"You sound shit."
"Thanks…" (God, right now, he despised Matt).
"You hungover?"

Drive-By Shouting

"A bit… I was gigging last night." Gram tried to sound casual, but knew where this was heading.
"Where?"
Gram paused, desperately wanting to say anything other than the truth.
"Er, you know, the usual."
"Christ, Rock'n'Roll! The Arsenal Tavern eh?"

Gram rubbed his temple wearily, willing himself to end the call and curtail the torment, but almost despite himself, found himself replying: "Hey, it's a gig and it's regular."
He heard Matt force a laugh: "Hey, I'm not knocking it, don't get me wrong mate. It's just… well, you know. You're better than all that"

Gram recognised this as Matt's usual attempt at a middle ground, located somewhere between being sensitive to his plight and being simultaneously condescending (a favourite trick). What Matt was really saying was, 'You know that *I'm* better than all that, these days.'

"So anyway," Matt continued, "get laid?"
Gram sighed audibly and mumbled: "Hmmm…, yeah…"
Matt picked up the cue: "Obviously not the usual supermodel then?"
Gram glared and reddened at yet another slight. He deflected: "Anyway Matt, you're six weeks early. What's up? Why the break with tradition?"

Drive-By Shouting

Soon after first meeting each other, Gram and Matt had discovered that they shared a birthday. In the days when their lives and dreams were intertwined, they had readily fallen into a pattern of celebrating together. Since their paths had diverged so dramatically however, it was with increasing reluctance that Gram had continued with the arrangement. Now it represented their only real contact. Matt would call a week or so before the date, they would meet and re-tread the past together, before Matt moved on to his favourite subject: his current burgeoning health, wealth and good fortune. They would part hours later, both drunk, with one of them confident and triumphant and the other; bitter, resentful and wallowing in self-loathing at the injustice of it all. After all, without Gram, Matt would be… where?

The bus braked violently, throwing Gram and his co-travellers forward. No one cursed or complained, all London buses were seemingly now driven with attitude by angry young men (or angry middle-aged women). His attention returned to the call. He could hear children screaming in the background and an off-phone Matt trying to placate them.

"Gram, sorry mate, the kids are kicking off and Jen is doing her fucking Pilates. Can I call you in a bit? I've got something I want to put to you?" Eager to get off the phone, Gram readily agreed and clicked the red button.

He rode sullenly through Crouch End Broadway, before getting off. As the bus pulled away, the smallest

Drive-By Shouting

of the black kids gave him the finger, apropos of nothing. He walked up the long side street to the communal front door. Ignoring the junk mail and buff coloured envelopes, presumably containing bills (and possibly summonses), he creaked up the stairs to his rented flat, home for the past seven years. Colin, his old friend, turned landlord, was out so he immediately turned on the bath taps, studying himself in the mirror while it ran. The familiar gaunt face stared back at him. His former luxuriance of hair had thinned and showed signs of receding. He had lately opted for a short crop, but no one, least of all him, was fooled. He was going bald.

He had never really qualified as handsome, but, in his youth, had ridden on a wave of imperturbable charisma and, ironically, great hair. No, he hadn't been handsome, but somehow, he'd snuck in as a 'looker' through the back door. He'd merely been quietly confident and assured, and that had counted for a lot. He wondered now where that version of Gram had gone. It seemed that he was left with only the ageing shell.

Peeling off his clothes, he sank into the bath. As he lowered himself into the water, the waft of odours carried him back to the previous evening. As usual, Matt had touched a nerve; Gram hated admitting that he was still turning up to play to drunks in the back room of the Arsenal Tavern for fifty quid a time.

Some seven years earlier, the issue of playing there had been the catalyst for Matt to change his life. The two of

Drive-By Shouting

them had been the singer and guitarist in a good band. They'd got a management deal, signed a record contract, made a couple of decent albums, been viciously reviewed, and eventually been 'dropped' from their record label. By this time, Matt had acquired a wife, a child and had another baby on the way.

Both he and Gram were reduced to subsisting on the meagre cash payments available from working as casual van drivers for a music hire company, reduced from 'nearly popstars' to roadies. Then, a regular gig came up at the Arsenal Tavern. £200 a night, split four ways, with a guarantee of every Friday. Gram had put together a band and offered the vocalist slot to his mate Matt, certain that he'd be pleased, or even grateful, to get some guaranteed cash. Matt's wife, Jen, had had other ideas.

Jen had supported Matt throughout his still born career. She had then abandoned her own aspirations to have the first baby and had gone cap in hand to her parents when times were hard, which had become a permanent state of affairs. The Arsenal Tavern was a leap of faith too far for Jen. That their lives should depend on cash from casual van driving and now, playing to drunks in a late night bar was too much for her to bear. Life had become a series of humiliations. The constant need to ask her parents for money, their dearth of a social life whilst all of their (moneyed) friends remained childless and free to plan spontaneous nights out, with no comprehension that babysitters couldn't be conjured up at an hour's notice (and even then, couldn't be afforded), all had

Drive-By Shouting

conspired to bring Jen to her pivotal moment. She drew the line at the Arsenal Tavern. If Matt wanted to grow up and become a real husband and father, he had to become a real provider. The boy/man who still thought he could be a rock star had to go. So, Matt turned the Arsenal Tavern down.

This came as a shock to Gram, as indeed, it had shocked Matt. Matt didn't know what he was going to do to earn money, but it was evident that the fun was over. This was the beginning of the end for Matt and Gram. One of them, like it or not, was about to grow up.

Indignantly, Gram had drafted in another singer and started doing the dates. It was immediately dismal. The rear bar had a late licence, so the band wouldn't start playing until 11.30 at night, by which time the crowd were too plastered to care. The material was all cover versions; it was futile to be creative, they only wanted standards, followed by slowies to finish. The last 10 minutes were when the dregs and wallflowers would pair off with whomever they could. Sexual favours and infections were shared liberally at the Arsenal, and in a rarely changing crowd, almost everybody had paired off with almost everybody at some point.

Seven years on (my God, where did *they* go?), the pattern was well-established and last night was no exception. Gram was the only constant band member, the bass, drums and singer changing constantly as people moved on to better (or worse) things. Last night had been particularly bad. Bob, the current regular bass

Drive-By Shouting

player, had gone down with the 'flu. At the last minute, Gram had found Roland, a friend of a friend who, he was assured, had played with loads of big-name artists (although none had actually been named, merely hinted at). After one song, it was immediately apparent that they were in the middle of a musical disaster movie, with the bass playing in numerous different keys and time signatures, none of them relating to those employed by the rest of the band. It was a shockingly bad mess.

From Gram's perspective however, what was much worse than the embarrassing shambles, was the fact that nobody noticed. Too drunk to employ any critical faculties whatsoever, the audience loved it, cheering and jeering enthusiastically, as the band stared at each other in panic. Gram took solace in beer as his self-disgust enveloped him. He knew that he was selling himself cheap, but tonight the sensation was unbearable. By the sixth song (the most chaotic version of *The Summer of '69* that Gram had ever experienced), he was starting to feel as drunk and oblivious as the 150 or so audience members colliding with each other in front of him.

Through his alcoholic haze, he had recognised a plump girl who he'd slept with a couple of weeks before that the band had nicknamed 'Tank'. Last week a pre-flu Bob had gone home with her. After the last song, while the apparently tone-deaf Roland lay down on the sticky carpet (possibly to hide his shame), the girl stumbled over to Gram.

Drive-By Shouting

After a good ten seconds where she made unusual and strangely fascinating shapes with her mouth, she had managed to utter a phrase "Hello, big boy," before stumbling forward and hanging onto Gram, her breath reeking of cheap booze.

Naturally, he'd gone home with her. With something approaching shame, he remembered them rolling naked on the bed, her too drunk to co-ordinate, him manfully attempting to keep the image of Bob doing precisely the same thing a week previously out of his head, Bob hadn't spared any details. It was loveless, emotion free, drunk sex, and its only saving grace was that it was over quickly.

Gram had gone to the loo. Upon returning, the light from the hallway had illuminated her large pink behind, still sticking in the air. He'd climbed into bed and gone to sleep. Lying in the bath, he winced at the memory. The morning had been embarrassing, she'd remembered little and the conversation had been stilted, so he had dressed quickly, grabbed his guitar and headed for the bus station. Dunking his head underwater, he tried to think if he'd forgotten her name or simply never known it.

Ten years ago, Gram had looked forward to a life filled with possibility. Right now, he felt numbed by the brutal treadmill of a horrible, hand to mouth existence. He knew that his life was going nowhere, but he simply had no idea of how to alter the hopeless trajectory that he was on, with no notion of which lever he could pull to switch tracks. So he relentlessly ploughed on, a sense of futility pervading his every action. He felt useless and discarded by life, a feeling once more accentuated by comparison with Matt's success. A wave of self-loathing rose up and, before he knew it, he began to weep, initially attempting to suppress the sobs, until his resistance collapsed and he shook, hugging himself in misery.

Drive-By Shouting

Chapter 2
Hurstwood, East Sussex

Aware of the futility of trying to quieten his children, Matt Mann finished his phone call. He shouted the usual remonstrations anyway, while the children skipped, giggling down towards the paddock. He was seated on a large York stone patio, an umbrella sheltering him from the June sun. To his surprise, Jen appeared from behind the bushes, carrying a glass of water.

"Hi. Heard you on the phone. Who was that, Gram?"
"Oh, didn't think I'd see you so soon. But yes, it was him. I'll have to ring him back, too bloody noisy here. Anyway, I thought you'd gone to pilates?"
"Cancelled. Got the call when I was nearly bloody there. Anyway, what are you talking to him for? Is he still all bitter and twisted?"
"Oh, he's okay, you know, he's had a hard time?"
"Yes, all of his own making." She turned and headed towards the house. "Why d'you want to see him anyway? It's a bit early for your birthday thing."
"No reason really, he's just my touchstone with reality..."

Drive-By Shouting

Jen gave him a disapproving look and continued up the lawn towards the house, commenting over her shoulder. "Well, you know my opinion. The only people, who hang out with losers, are other losers." He watched her depart, before turning to survey the scene beyond the pool, with something less than his customary unalloyed pleasure.

Beyond the garden and paddock with its cavorting children, the rolling hills of East Sussex shimmered in the heat haze. Everywhere you looked there was greenery, and for the first thirty-two acres, it was greenery that he owned. He had rarely tired of reminding himself of this; it had been as delightful as it had been unexpected. He had gone from wannabe popstar, to van driver and roadie, to landed gentleman and celebrity in just a few heady years. The only diversion from what had been his former daydream was that he didn't occupy the role of 'Squire' of the village (his imagination had used to indulge itself with fantasies of bowing serfs tugging their forelocks). As it was, he merely 'fitted in' with the other landed & wealthy men in the village. Though, in fact, he was indeed lorded in some ways, celebrity went a long way amongst the bankers & city traders who occupied most of the other large houses in Hurstwood.

Combined with his former life as a 'rock and roller' (with all of its inherent suggestion of excitement and wildness), Matt's TV celebrity status now opened every door in the village. And why not? The Mann's had money, prestige and glamour. They had been embraced and could fill every night with dinner at one

Drive-By Shouting

of the numerous vast houses or converted farms that made up the affluent areas of Hurstwood. Their decision to enroll the children at the local private school had certainly helped Jen establish contact with the other mothers (something that had been sadly lacking in the lean London *Cymbal* days), and her wide armed acceptance from the 'ladies who lunched' had certainly had a healing effect on her. As had the soft top Audi and the credit cards. Yes, they'd had money in the latter days of London, but by then, it had become tainted - friendships that had died from poverty were hard to resuscitate when the money started to flow, but the fresh start, with brand new people in Hurstwood, had been wonderfully life-affirming.

Matt was stirred from his daydream by the sound of footsteps to herald Jen's return to the pool area. He watched as she walked into the pool house, and the cloud that had been following him for the last three days rolled back into his consciousness and blocked out the sun once more. He'd dragged himself from the brink of annihilation some seven years ago, to end up exactly where he'd always wanted to be. So how could he have been so stupid, to have made such a banal mistake, and one that could cost him everything?

He thought back to 1992 and the brutal end of the RGA record contract. He and Gram had been the key partnership in the band *Cymbal*, co-writing two albums of (admittedly, heavily influenced) English Rock. Without doubt, they'd worn their joint David Bowie adoration clearly on their sleeve, but the songs

Drive-By Shouting

were good, and the live audience had built on word of mouth support.

Crucially though, the music press had hated them. Or, more specifically, any aspiring music journalist had discovered that their career tended to progress much faster if they could conjure enough vitriol to pour onto *Cymbal*. It became a blood sport, with rival papers vying to write the most damning reviews of them. Individual writers would readily apologise in pubs ("nothing personal mate, it's just what you have to do to get noticed at the paper. It's the game."), but the relentless barrage of negative press had effectively finished them before they had even really started.

By the second album, even the quality music press had got in on the act and he recalled the 1992 Scandinavian tour and the moment he'd known it was all over. After a riotous two weeks, the band had crossed from southern Sweden to Copenhagen, to be met by the Danish record company rep at that night's venue. Before even introducing herself, she had held up a new copy of *Q* magazine, saying: "Have you seen this? It's a really shit review. You won't sell any records in Denmark after this... Hello, I'm Brigid." And with that, the death knell began to toll. They had finished the tour, crisscrossing back to Sweden before taking the 24-hour crossing from Gothenburg to Felixstowe.

The boat had been full of hen and stag parties, treating the 48-hour round trip from the UK as a 'cruise,' and the drunken party had swayed noisily from on-board bar, to club, to casino, to bunkbeds. It was typically

Drive-By Shouting

English alcoholic carnage, with numerous casualties lying prone on various floors throughout the boat.

The revelry couldn't, however, lift the gloom in the band's camp. The realization had sunk in. When even the higher brow music papers like *Q* were putting the boot in, they really were finished.

Back in the UK, they had halfheartedly completed their outstanding UK college tour, before getting the inevitable call to the manager's office from where they had exited barely twenty minutes later, minus their management and record deal and effectively unemployed. Matt had dreaded telling people, but did his best to present it positively: "We're looking for a more supportive label. We really wanted more control, so this is a really good thing...!" But nobody had been fooled.

What he hadn't been prepared for, was Jen's reaction. She'd been relieved. "Finally, you can stop messing about and get a proper job..."

He'd been shocked by this. The veneer of Jen's support had cracked and she sensed that they may finally be able to move on in their lives. Moving on, however, didn't prove easy.

Matt put out feelers for work, although his CV, comprising a below average economics degree, followed by six years of odd jobs and being in bands, didn't make him the most employable prospect and so, in tandem with Gram, he had once again fallen back

Drive-By Shouting

into doing casual work, driving vans for the very same companies that had recently been employed to shift equipment for *Cymbal*.

Financially, things were desperately tight until, out of the blue, Matt got a call one evening from Annabel Lee, the promotions girl at RGA records. Annabel had always had a bit of a thing for Matt and after some phone flirting she got to the point of the call. "Listen, Jasminder is coming over to do some TVs, you know; *Top of the Pops*, *Wogan*, *Number 73* and a couple of European TV shows, and I need to put together a TV band; you're still in the MU aren't you? Do you fancy it?"

"Well, I'd love to, but doing what? You don't need a singer."

"No, but you could play bass. I saw you doing it a couple of times when I came to the studio. And anyway, you're only miming. The money is pretty good too."

Matt didn't have to think too hard. Three months of the *service* side of rock 'n' roll had made him fully appreciative of the joys of record company promotional budgets. There'd be limos, nightclubs, dinners, flights, glamour, and to cap it all, money. Stacked against an airless van and two weeks of lumping equipment in and out of studios and venues, it was a no brainer.

"I'm in! A hundred per cent! That's fantastic, thank you for thinking of me Annabelle, it's really nice to know I'm not completely forgotten at RGA!"

Drive-By Shouting

Annabelle giggled: "Not by me, you're not, handsome!"

Matt, aware of Jen eavesdropping (while she chased the baby around the floor), avoided being overly flirty in response: "Listen, I don't know if you've filled the whole band yet, but Gram from *Cymbal* would be up for this too, and even though it's mimed, he's a really fabulous guitarist."

"Afraid the guitar slot is already filled. Actually, with you on board, we're almost sorted. Unless..., I don't suppose Gram can play sax? Although, as long as he can mime well, and doesn't tell the musicians union, obviously; he could do that. But you're going to have to let me know quickly. I asked around with a couple of other guys, so it's first come, first served."

"Give me your number Annabelle, I'll ring Gram now and I'll call you back, give me half an hour!"

Matt came off the phone and ecstatically broke the exciting news to Jen, who looked thoroughly underwhelmed.

"Oh brilliant, two more weeks of you playing the pop star before we return to our reality... I thought we'd discussed all this kind of thing." She turned and walked out. Peeved, he'd nonetheless enthusiastically picked up the phone and dialled. He'd barely spoken to Gram in the eight weeks since he'd turned down the Arsenal Tavern gig, a distinct frostiness pervading their few chance meetings at the *Rox Rentals* offices. This was a chance to rebuild bridges between them.

Drive-By Shouting

"What's up Matt? Decided you want the Arsenal gig after all?"
"No, it's a bit better than that! You remember Annabel from RGA? You know, promo girl?"
"I think you got to know her rather better than I did if I recall correctly... but yes, what about her?"
"She's just called, she's putting together a TV band for Jasminder, and we're in! I've got you on board as well, Gonna be doing *Wogan, Top of the Pops,* a few kid's shows and a couple of European jaunts, how brilliant is that?"

The truth was Matt would have leapt at it if it was a trip to Crewe. He was beginning to feel dangerously bored and claustrophobic since the band broke up. Dark fantasies were running in a tight loop in his mind; escape, escape, escape! He was absolutely certain that Gram would be feeling the same.

"Er... Okay... I suppose that does sound quite good. But I thought *Zodiac Mindwarp* were doing her backing band stuff?"
"They're out, too wild apparently, but we're in!" Matt was already really getting into the swing, visualizing a packed bag swung over his shoulder, a rushed kiss at the door, taxi waiting, Jen frowning her goodbye as he skipped down the steps to the pavement. Some proper 'A' list treatment.
Gram seemed to be thinking along the same lines: "Well then, better start practicing my guitar miming, make sure I'm convincing."
"Oh, actually, no need for that. She's already filled the guitar slot, but I managed to get you in on the sax."

Drive-By Shouting

Gram hesitated briefly. "But I can't play sax."
"Oh, who cares? It's all bullshit anyway. Don't you want to get out there?' Matt lowered his voice as he spoke into the handset. "I'm going up the wall here and we'll have a great couple of weeks, it'll be like the old days." Matt could hear Gram moving around at the other end of the line as he paced around his lounge. Eventually, he spoke.
"Oh, come on Matt, you're kidding! No way... I mean, fuck that! I'm not pretending to play the sax! It's bad enough miming guitar, I do have *some* pride. I'm not tarting myself out to look like a total dick. I'm a guitarist, and a good one, and that's that."
"Gram, you're joking aren't you? You're not seriously turning this down? You'd rather drive a van? Fucking hell Gram, I'm trying to help you here."
"It's not about driving a van, this is about integrity."

Matt was incredulous and threw his free arm up in frustration. He spat sotto voce into the handset.
"Fuck integrity...! Where's that ever got us? My fucking bin-man has a better sodding life than me right now, at least he gets out every day. If I don't get any driving work, I'm rotting here; watching fucking *Neighbours* and getting my arse kicked by Jen fifty times a day."
"And why is that my problem?"
"It's not; but what are *you* doing that's so scintillating today that you don't see this as a better option? And rolling a joint and lying on your back in Highbury Fields doesn't count! It's up to you, but I've got to phone Annabel back and confirm in the next ten minutes.' There was silence on the line. "This isn't about the Arsenal Tavern is it? You know I turned that

Drive-By Shouting

down because it was going nowhere, but this is! It doesn't make sense for you to say 'no' just to pay me back. It's cutting off your nose to spite your face."
"It's not about that."
"Well, what is it about?"
Pacing the floor in Crouch End, Gram's resolve was hardening. "Matt, you can sell out if you want, I'd rather not. Tell you what, I might say yes, but only if I can play bass, and you play the sax? At least that way I'm doing something I actually can do?"

Matt paused momentarily to think. "Well..., no. She's asked *me* to do the bass and you to do the sax, so let's not fuck the whole thing up by being contrary."
"Ahh, now I've got you! Because you don't want to look like a knob miming the sax, but it's ok for me! Just as I thought. No Matt, you need to count me out."

Matt was struggling to contain himself and keep his voice low, aware as he was, that Jen could hear through the walls. He spoke slowly and deliberately:
"Gram, you're just not making sense. You're prepared to play the Arsenal Tavern and compromise in all the ways that that involves. You're prepared to drive a sweaty van all round town and lump heavy gear all day long, but you're not prepared to take a chance that will actually give you good money and a lot of fun? Where's your integrity while you're doing all that shit?"

"That stuff is still *me* being *me,* at least I can look myself in the mirror. And anyway, there's other stuff that complicates matters."
"Like what?"

Drive-By Shouting

"Well, like going abroad for the European part. That'll be a real hassle with the Arsenal Tavern gigs, and it'll probably fuck up me *signing on* as well."
"Whaaaat? You're on the dole? Whilst working? Are you mad Gram? It's one thing doing that when we were kids, but we're older now, and they're looking out for guys like us."
"Well, you're the one glued to your sofa watching *Neighbours*. So don't lecture me on being a grown up, and anyway everyone else at Rox does it. What it does depend on is you being in the country to sign on in the first place. It's easy to fit in with the van driving; you just make sure you're roughly in the area at the time you need to sign on. But it'd totally screw things up if I'm abroad and miss my sign on day. It's just not worth it for two weeks."

Matt was, once again, incredulous: "Integrity! Can you hear yourself? Bloody hell Gram, I can't believe you're doing this and I can't believe that after all the bullshit, that this is the real reason you're turning this down!"
"It's a combination of the two things Matt. I might have been prepared to take a risk if I was at least playing guitar because that's who I am, but I'm not risking it for this crap."
"That's who you are? I don't think you've had a good look lately at *who you are*? I may be festering on a sofa, but at least I'm not choosing to rot there. I actually thought you'd jump at this, that we'd have a laugh; but fine, stick with the integrity. I didn't think you had the capacity to surprise me after so many years of your utter stubbornness, but hat's off to you mate, I'm

Drive-By Shouting

flabbergasted. I think you're insane..." Matt slammed the phone down.

After knowing Gram for years, he was aware of how intransigent he could be, but was still shocked at his refusal. Gram had always detested 'selling out,' an arbitrary label ascribed to any decision not based on Gram's narrow definition of 'musical integrity,' but this was probably his dumbest moment. Matt wondered what state Gram had got into, where driving a van for cash, while illegally claiming benefit, had more integrity than being well paid to drag your backside onto a stage for a few numbers. Yes, it was miming, but it was still being up on stage with a top US singer. "The world's gone mad" he said out loud, before picking up the phone and dialling Annabelle.

A mile away, Gram put down the phone. He felt justifiable anger at Matt, thinking that he could be picked up like a puppet, and by the very record company that had discarded them. There had also been a certain satisfaction in saying 'no' to Matt, after Matt's rejection of his Arsenal gigs. He picked up his half smoked joint and re-lit it, before sinking back into the worn sofa.

Back in 1999 and in his Sussex idyll, Matt reflected on how that short run of dates in Jasminder's band had changed his life. How a chance meeting with the notorious impresario, Steve Coombes, had given him a whole new start in music and led directly to his current TV success. He'd seen an opportunity and he'd

Drive-By Shouting

grasped it, and that was the difference between him and Gram.

He mused on Gram's stubborn nature and unpredictability. He was, in many respects, the last person that Matt should be calling in an appeal for help. However, he was also possibly the only person who was au fait with Matt's circumstances, while being sufficiently distant from most of the other people in Matt's life, and this made him pretty much the only candidate for the task in hand.

He'd wait for Jen to go out again and call Gram back. He wasn't sure if he could swing his co-operation, but Gram's legendary need for cash might just work in his favour. Whilst they were no longer close friends (they had been once) and surely *a friend in need* deserved a helping hand? He hoped Gram would see it that way, because Matt certainly needed help. On the plus side, he knew that after all the years of exclusion, Gram was still a sucker for a bit of celebrity glamour, he'd invite him to Groucho's that should make him more compliant.

At his core, Matt Mann was scared. Everything hung in the balance and, given Gram's volatility, the plan was risky, to say the least. But maybe, just maybe, getting Gram onside could save him.

Drive-By Shouting

Chapter 3
Three days later. The Groucho Club, Dean Street, London

Ignoring the panhandling beggar outside Groucho's, Gram slunk through the doors and approached the desk directly in front of him, his sense of unworthiness hanging over him like a grey cloud.

"Hi, I'm here as a guest of Matt Mann."
"Of course sir, he's just through the bar. He said he was expecting someone."
Ignoring the receptionist's rather obvious critical evaluation of his appearance, Gram followed the pointed finger through the glass doors and sure enough, immediately saw Matt slumped in a large red leather sofa by the window, cradling a drink. Matt looked up and greeted him: "Gram! Good to see you mate, what do what you want to drink?"

Gram looked doubtfully at the red concoction in Matt's glass, "I'll just have a beer, they have Budvar?"
"Of course they do. Cathy, can we have a Budvar please, and some of those nice pretzelly things?"

Drive-By Shouting

The two men exchanged pleasantries and, given the infrequency of their meetings these days, some slightly awkward banter, before the waitress returned with the cold beer. After a further few minutes, Matt's demeanor altered and he looked meaningfully at Gram and addressed him, quietly and solemnly:
"Listen Gram, I need to tell you about something. I've done something really stupid."
Gram laughed out loud, still caught in the lighthearted atmosphere that had pervaded their talk so far.
"Well, there's a surprise. You spend your whole life doing stupid things!"
Ignoring the barb, Matt pressed on, lowering his voice further, despite there being nobody immediately nearby: "No, really. I've really screwed up this time." He looked imploringly at Gram. "What I'm about to tell you is rather embarrassing. I know it's very wrong, and I actually knew it was wrong when I started. This is in total confidence, yeah?' He blew his cheeks out and braced himself to speak. "There's no easy way to phrase this... but I've been..." He paused, "I've been 'seeing...'" Again, he corrected himself. "Well actually, shagging, Kate Craw."

Gram gasped. "You are joking aren't you?" He flopped back on the seat, shaking his head in a mixture of indignation and amusement. "Let me get this right. The same Kate Craw who's married to your hard-nut manager? The same Kate Craw who used to eviscerate us every week in the *NME*? The one who said you danced like Noddy Holder's less talented, half-witted cousin, and that, let me remember, wasn't she the one that wrote that your "unbearable, fey Bowie

Drive-By Shouting

impersonations left her dreaming of a rock 'n' roll suicide?' *That* Kate Craw?"

Matt shifted uncomfortably and shrugged. "Yes, the one and only. But that's all ancient history, we'd put all that behind us. When Steve got her slotted in as guest co-presenter on the show, y'know, while Faith Lerner was off having the baby? Well, we discussed all of that stuff, everything that'd happened in the past all of which she was actually very sorry about. And, unlikely as it was, we ended up becoming pretty good mates. Well, like I said, rather more than that..."

Gram sucked in the air and laughed: "You total knob! So when your manager and best buddy slots his wife onto the 'Live at 10!' sofa, you think that you should a). Forgive the entire career ending shite that she heaped on us and b). Fuck her, despite her being your nutter best mate's wife?"
Matt gave a resigned sigh. "You make it sound calculated and sordid, or like it's some sort of foolish comedy. It's not like that. I really like her a lot..."
"Oh, this is getting better! Not only is it not 'dingdong the witch is dead,' it's dingdong I've fallen in love with the fucking witch!' You're unbelievable. Even for you Matt, this is a new low! You're a total, total knobhead."
"I know.... You're right, but the thing is..."

Gram collected himself and tried his best to look serious. "Yes, let's discuss the *thing*; why are we here, with you telling me all of this out of the blue?
Matt look up at Gram. "The thing is Gram, it's worse than that.' He looked up again and forced himself to

Drive-By Shouting

speak: "She's pregnant."
Gram gasped for a second time: "Idiot."
Matt sighed: "Ok maybe I am, but this is the end of my 'effin' life and I don't know what to do. Gram, you're the only person I can tell about this." He looked imploringly across the table: "Everybody in Hurstwood is a friend of Jen's, and everybody in the business is a friend of Steve's. I've got almost nowhere left to turn. Actually, it feels good just talking about it. You're the only person I've told. I need you to help me Gram. I know we've kind of grown apart over the years, but I still think of you as somebody that I can hopefully turn to when I need help. I really need help now."

Gram took in Matt's plaintive face while he considered the course of events. He hadn't been sure what had prompted Matt to ask him here, but had sensed that something had gone seriously wrong. And for him to be hinting that he needed Gram's help suggested that he was in deep trouble, and must have nowhere left to turn. Because, of all the people in the world, Gram would surely not be his first choice of saviour? He decided that for the time being, he'd enjoy witnessing Matt's misfortune. He'd been so impervious for the last seven years that it was somehow satisfying to see him brought low, and asking for his help. He played along. "The baby is definitely yours?"
Matt considered, and recalled the fraught conversation he had with Kate about the pregnancy.
Kate: "Matt, I need to tell you something. I'm pregnant. And you're the father."
Matt: "What! But surely you're on the pill?"
Kate: "No, I'm afraid I'm not."

Drive-By Shouting

Matt : "Well, how do you know it's mine?"

He had recoiled from the well-aimed slap across the face: "Because you're the only one I slept with, you bastard."

"What, I'm supposed to believe that in all of the months that we've been shagging, you haven't slept with Steve once?"

"Matt, you arsehole, I'm not some sort of slapper! I haven't slept with Steve in over two years. I think Steve is, I don't know, he's probably gay… He certainly has no interest in sleeping with me..."

"What? No he's not. But anyway, couldn't it be anybody else's?" The second slap had been, if anything, more of a stinger than the first.

"For fuck's sake Kate, I have to ask!!" He had moved back to avoid any further assaults. "Why didn't we take precautions then?"

"Because it was all spontaneous! And I suppose I was in denial. In the first year of our marriage, Steve and I tried, unsuccessfully, to have a baby, and I just came to the conclusion that I was, I don't know, infertile or something."

"Well that turned out to be a truly stupid assumption! And anyway, what do you mean Steve is gay? He adores you."

'What he adores is me on a pedestal, me looking pretty, and me being on his arm looking groomed and, critically for him, me looking rich. I'm an adored accessory, but he has no interest in me as a woman. The baby is 100% yours."

Matt returned to the present, to find Gram staring

Drive-By Shouting

expectantly at him: "It's yours, yeah?"
"Apparently, it's unquestionably mine."
"So why call me, what do you expect me to do?"
"Well, the big problem is that she wants to keep it. She's got all sort of religious about this possibly being her only chance at a child but, obviously, that rather fucks things because Steve will know it's not his, he hasn't been near her in years."
Gram shrugged impassively: "Oops."
"Yes, exactly. And worse still, she wants to leave him, and incredibly, has an idea that we might move in together and play happy families. This slightly ignores the fact that I already have a happy family."

For the first time in years, Gram felt himself relax in Matt's company. He realized that he felt almost happy and checked himself to halt the hangman's smile that was forming at the corners of his mouth. Seeing Matt's handsome face contorted with anxiety was soothing. Shameful to admit, but yes, it was soothing to see him squirm.

Matt gathered himself. He spoke slowly, as if his words were being spooled out of his brain, one at a time:
"Someone needs to talk to her. Someone needs to make her see sense."

There were no more words, the spool had snapped. Gram waited for more; maybe Matt had spoken so slowly that his words had sounded surreal even to himself. His face was expectant: "Well?"

"Well what, Matt?"

Drive-By Shouting

"Will you?"
"Me? Me! Are you off your head?" Gram could hear a note of hysteria in his own voice. The people at the end of the bar turned their heads momentarily before resuming their chatter. He tried to modulate his voice but could feel a molten core of anger rising within, he tried to smother its heat and replied with his own jagged spool; spitting out one crumpled word at a time. "Why the fuck. Why on earth would I do that?" He'd kept his voice low but the bar chatters were staring now.

Matt looked over and forced a smiled at them, then back at Gram:
"Because she likes you." He steeled himself. "What I hoped you'd do was, y'know, try to make friends with her? Like, engineer a meeting, and try to influence her against keeping the kid, or at the very least, keep my name completely out of it, when she tells Steve. I know where she hangs out and we can kind of stage an 'accidental' meeting. She really likes you and obviously, I'll make it very worth your while... like, financially... I could put you on a retainer, like a salary sort of thing...."

Gram became aware that his mouth had gaped open at the audacity of the request:
"Are you completely mad Matt? I've barely laid eyes on Kate Craw in over three years. When we did last meet, I poured a pint over her head. And, although I never actually told you this, I also posted a turd through her letterbox after that final vicious review..." Matt raised his eyebrows while continuing to listen intently to

Drive-By Shouting

Gram: "Why the hell would she want to be friends with me? And even if she did, isn't she going to find it a teeny bit suspicious, what with us having shared a flat and been in the same band for ten years?"

Matt was staring into the middle distance; "Er, OK, I admit I didn't know about the turd, but then, neither does she, or I am sure she would have mentioned it... It's not the sort of thing you'd forget. But, leaving that to one side, the thing is, it is plausible. She's moved back to Crouch End, so she lives near you, so bumping into you is explicable."
"But she knows I hate her, why would she even begin to entertain the idea?"
"Oh, she'll believe it! She really likes you, she says you had real integrity chucking the beer over her, she readily accepts that she deserved it, and the thing that gives it real credibility, it's that, erm; this is a little bit uncomfortable... She sort of has the idea that you…"
He paused awkwardly, knowing that this was a part of the conversation he needed to handle with sensitivity.

Whichever way he thought about phrasing it sounded wrong to Matt and so, despite his caution, he ended up just blurting it out: "Basically, she thinks that you hate me, and that we're not really speaking anymore." He paused again to grimace at Gram apologetically: "...so I think she'll be keen to forge a friendship, to hatch plans about the mutual enemy. Me." He ignored Gram's quizzical expression and ploughed on, like a train running out of control: "But, you can be the voice of reason. You know, even though you're not that keen on me, you still think she shouldn't tell Steve etcetera.

Drive-By Shouting

It'll actually have more credence that way."

Gram looked sternly at Matt, as he tried to process the information. After an unsettlingly long pause, he spoke: "And why does she think we hate each other?" Matt shifted uncomfortably under Gram's glare, aware that he needed to navigate carefully through the next couple of minutes. This was a can of worms that he'd prefer not to open, but he really had no choice: "Well, it was like this, er…, during our pillow talk, Kate and I talked about a lot of things, "Did I still see the band?" "How were things?" etcetera. And, I think I exaggerated things a bit.

Now I know that there is stuff between you and I that we probably should have dealt with before now, but I probably over egged it in my chats with Kate. I obviously gave the impression that you bore a… a bit of a grudge about the band's demise and the rather different career paths we've gone on – y'know, I was just blathering away, talking nonsense…. And, you know, obviously, it would seem that…" Matt swallowed and forced out the end of the sentence: "I kind of suggested that you held a grudge about songwriting."

Gram slowly raised his eyes to meet Matt's. The coming conversation was one he'd mentally rehearsed many times: "By which you mean a grudge about *I Like Your Style?* So, we're finally going to do this? After all these years of silence, we're going to discuss this?"

Drive-By Shouting

Matt held his gaze. "Obviously, the reason that I ended up having that sort of conversation with her, was because I'm aware that you have an opinion about that song, which, I have to add, I don't share, but I guess we need to get this out in the open, and y'know, I'm sorry that it's taken this crap to bring it into the open."

Ignoring the apparent anger brewing on Gram's face, he maintained as conciliatory a tone as he could muster: "Because you're right, it's a conversation we should have had quite a long time ago, and while I don't completely share your point of view, we do need to clear the air. So let's get that dealt with now and we can move on. Yeah?"

Gram's stare hardened and any thin vestige of friendship evaporated. "But you don't even know what my 'point of view' is Matt? You much prefer blissful ignorance.... But, ok, this *is* long overdue and I'll help you out. My opinion is this: you took *Walk the Mile*, a song that was half mine and, after a few cosmetic changes, re-registered it as yours, under a different title. That song has since earned you a fortune from sales and radio play. And since it became the theme song for *New York Diner*, it's been syndicated 'round the world endlessly, earning you more and more money." He took in the sight of Matt nodding sagely and felt a rage brewing within him: "So it's a total disgrace that it's taken you this long to look me in the eye and even discuss it. So there, that's my point of view."

Matt continued to hold his gaze, apparently confident of winning Gram back around: "Look Gram, let's not

Drive-By Shouting

fall out about this now, let's just talk it through, and put it to bed. I've obviously heard about what you think through the grapevine. Colin's muttered about it when I've bumped into him and you've alluded to it plenty of times, and I'm aware that it's been the great unspoken issue between us, and I *do* want to clear this up now. But, whatever you might think, the song isn't a copy of *Walk the Mile,* and in fact, it owes more to a whole host of other songs; how about *Wonderful World* or *Every Breath You Take*? They've both got the same chord sequence, but, funnily enough, neither Sting nor Sam Cooke has sued me! But because one song is based around the same chord sequence I wrote a song with in one band, you can't say that that gives you a lifelong copyright on anything I write in the future. That's not the way it works. That's just naïve. I mean, let's talk about it; I'm sure we can come to an arrangement, but let's not get it out of proportion."

He knew that Gram could be hot headed; he just needed to appeal to the sensible part of him, the level head that he knew lay behind the anger. He also knew that Gram needed money. Matt spread his hands in amelioration and tried to calmly appeal to Gram's better nature. "I accept that I've left this a bit late and that we should have talked so let's get it sorted and put it behind us. You're the only person I can ask for help with this, and I'm happy to come to some sort of sensible agreement on this, but y'know, I can't just accept what you think. Let's find some common ground and move on, because, yes, there *are* similarities, but lots of songs are similar? And, you know, let's just get this out of the way and then we can

Drive-By Shouting

sort something financially."

Suddenly impervious to the famous Mann charm and now feeling the sweat forming on his back, Gram maintained his icy stare: "Yes, lots of songs share similar chord patterns, but this one also shares the same tempo, the same drum beat, the same gaps and almost the same title, as a song written by you and me six years ago. As you well know, we always had the full understanding that if you and I were in the same room when the song was written, we jointly owned it even if one of us then decided to leave the room and tweak it a bit. You know that's true." Gram felt a rush of anger wash over him as he surveyed Matt, in his Italian suit and hand-made English shoes, confidently awaiting his meek acquiescence. His indignation began to boil over, "So, don't you sit and lecture me about what's out of proportion or not. Because, 'yes' I think you stole my song. 'Yes' I think you're a thieving bastard who stole the opportunities that a hit song would have given me. And 'yes' I should have sued you years ago. I just, foolishly, thought you'd do the decent thing eventually, because after all, we're mates, aren't we? The best mates in the fucking world!"
"Well, look Gram; I am trying to do the decent thing right now, so we can move on."

Gram laughed derisively at Matt, before gesticulating at him with a pointed finger: "No you're not. Instead of putting right what's clearly been wrong for years, you think you're now in a position where you can hire me for pin money, and buy me off as your lackey, to do your dirty deeds on the cheap. And that somehow,

Drive-By Shouting

throwing a few quid at me will also simultaneously clear up the whole song writing credit at the same time! As if that could repay all the chances you denied me. All the opportunities that I might have had." Gram got up abruptly and picked up his jacket: "So no, I won't help you with your self-created shitstorm, and I'm fucking amazed that you thought I would." He was delighted to see the panic register on Matt's face as he finally realized that the conversation had spiraled out of his control.

"Gram, please sit down and talk, you're not being rational!" Matt looked around Groucho's with embarrassment, as the few members present all looked up at the scene with alarm. "I didn't ask you here to talk about all this… I mean, I did, because it's relevant to the whole Kate thing. But this is a side issue. I know it's important that we talk about it; and we *can* sort it out, but we need to be rational. Let's just calm down a bit here and talk sensibly. You're right, you're right, we should have discussed this a long time ago. Let's talk about it now and really sort it out, so that we can move on. We're mates and we can get past this." Mustering as much sincerity as he could manage, he looked directly at Gram, "And I'm a mate who really needs your help right now."

"Mates? Mates?" Gram's fury was now in full flow and he stood over Matt glaring: "What sorts of mates have never even been to each other's houses in six years? But I'm sure you're keeping me at arm's length, just so I don't see how much of my fucking money you've nicked! Luckily though, I do get to leaf through old

Drive-By Shouting

copies of *Hello* when I go to the dentist, and there you are, with your big fat face and your smiling, smug wife, rolling around in your big fancy house and your swimming pool, or hanging out at your stables; all bought with, well, we both know what it was bought with…. "

"Gram, mate, sit back down. We *are* proper mates and I've always valued having you in my life, but that doesn't extend to giving away half the royalties to a song that I wrote.' He became indignant: "You need to drop this, and just see this for what it is; a chance to make some decent money, and, fuck me Gram, you look like you need it." Even as Matt spoke, he regretted his tone. He knew he'd blown it.

"Go fuck yourself Mann." Gram turned and headed noisily out of the door, leaving Matt to slide down on the leather sofa. He was acutely aware that he had badly miscalculated Gram's resentment. Ignoring the stares from around the room, he laid his head back and sighed, still cursing the way that he'd failed to steer the conversation. By failing to properly anticipate Gram's intransigence, he'd left himself without options, vulnerable to whatever was coming his way. Cathy, the waitress, appeared at the table: "Another Bloody Mary?"

Crouch End – Ninety minutes later.

Gram unlocked the flat door and walked through to the lounge. Colin diverted his attention from the TV to look over his shoulder and address him:

Drive-By Shouting

"Matt's phoned three times. He wants you to phone him urgently. You two had a row or something?" Gram scowled and ignored the question: "I know, he kept phoning my mobile, so I switched it off. He can fuck right off."
"Oh dear, handbags at dawn! What happened?"
"Well, we finally had the *I Like Your Style* conversation. Predictably, he denied everything. And at the same time, managed to insult me on every level."
Colin raised his eyebrows: "Well, you didn't think he would just roll over and offer you millions now, did you?"
"Actually, he brought it up, not me, but he's such a wanker. Thinks everyone is for sale. That he just has to shake a thin wad of cash in their face and they'll roll over and let him tickle their bellies."

Colin looked back in amusement. "Well, I'm more than happy to let him tickle my belly if he's paying..." He turned back and resumed watching the TV. "Put the kettle on will you?"

Gram picked up his bag and went through to the kitchen. He restarted his mobile phone while the kettle boiled. Once it fired up, he saw that Matt had tried to call him five times. As he stared at it, it started ringing again; the screen displaying 'Matt M.' He switched off the sound and let it vibrate on the table.

For the whole journey back out of the West End, Gram had fumed at the crassness of Matt's approach, thinking that he could sweep the enormous injustice

Drive-By Shouting

of the song to one side, while manipulating him into doing his dirty work. The issue around the song was belatedly coming to the boil, and finally, Gram was prepared to act, as the long-suppressed anger bubbled over.

He had long felt that the simple recognition of his songwriting credit on that song could have changed his life. The royalties alone would have lifted him out of the life he was currently condemned to, but far bigger than that, were the opportunities that a hit songwriting credit would have presented. He would have had the chance to build a career, to build on that initial success as it opened other doors; to write, to produce, to have the stamp of success.

Matt's stubborn and continuing unwillingness to even acknowledge that he had a just cause, had rolled around Gram's head for years, to the point that he had even started to half doubt that he *had* written the original song. After all, when Matt had so adamantly refused to be drawn on the matter, Gram had begun to wonder if perhaps he hadn't actually been there with him, picking out the chords and the melody all those years ago. He had, at times, felt that he was losing his mind in the face of such insouciance. But now, he knew. He'd looked into Matt's eyes and received all the acknowledgement he'd needed. Despite the bluster at Groucho's, he'd seen what he needed to see from Matt. It was evident that Matt knew he'd done a bad thing, but didn't know how to back out of it, now that he needed Gram's help. The intervening years of grinding failure couldn't be undone by a clumsy offer of cash. It was too late. And if Gram couldn't get justice, then he desperately hankered for a way to get revenge.

Drive-By Shouting

Chapter 4
1999: Three weeks earlier, Sussex. Matt Mann goes to London

At 5:30 am, the radio alarm came on and rudely awoke Matt Mann from his deep sleep. He killed the sound and instantly slid his feet to the floor (pausing was fatal; he'd be back asleep in seconds). He lunged upright and crept down the hall to the main bathroom (the en-suite was strictly out of bounds this early in the morning).

After showering, he went downstairs, pausing at the TV lounge to check that, yes, Sophia was already up, blanketed and propped up on the settee watching a video of Teletubbies. He bent behind the settee and kissed the top of her head, her eyes remaining fixed on the TV.

When he had begun working on *Live at 10!* ITV would send a chauffeur all the 70 miles down to Sussex to whisk him up to London. The key problem with this was that far from being 'whisked' to the set, he spent two hours on a tortuous journey, even with the early 5.45 start. He'd initially been flattered that he

Drive-By Shouting

warranted such star treatment as (barring the other presenters) everyone else on the production crushed themselves onto tubes and buses in order to get to the studio. He soon tired of the sequence of achingly slow journeys and so had agitated for the train instead. This had been strongly resisted by Shirley, the production manager. He soon learned that this was not because it was unbecoming for him to travel with the general public, but rather, because a chauffeur could be phoned, tracked and checked on, unlike a lost presenter on his own. It was simply too expensive to have a no show or a late arriving presenter on a live programme. He was slightly crestfallen to realise that he was viewed as simply a factor of production rather than a cherished public figure, but ploughed on in his determination to take the (far faster) train. Compromise was achieved, he'd take the train (in a first class compartment naturally) and then, rather ridiculously, be met at Waterloo East by a driver, taking him the 500 yards to the London Studios on Southbank.

As Matt stepped from the car park in Hurstwood, he was surrounded by the familiar throng of grey suited men homing in on the Victorian station building. It was unusual for anyone to speak at this hour, a protocol he took a while to absorb. He bought a coffee from the mobile coffee bar outside, collected his copy of The Guardian ("you're the only Trotskyite tax avoider I know Matt," one of the neighbours had quipped) and crossed the bridge to the London bound platform. The scene was magnificent in the cool

Drive-By Shouting

morning sunlight, the low sun breaking through the trees and dappling the train tracks.

Three minutes later he was in his familiar six berth, first class compartment. Unusually, the Hastings line still had the traditional slam door train carriages, with dark wood paneling throughout. Standard class was a tad spartan and draughty, but the first class compartments were, despite their age, luxurious and cosy. Disappointingly, they were due for replacement within a couple of years, but meanwhile, Matt was thrilled to ride in them. He was instantly in a period film of upper class, Home Counties privilege and felt gratified by it.

He'd been unaware of the politics of train travel when he had first taken a seat in his compartment a few years previously. The other occupants had smiled (he knew them from the village by sight), but there had been a slight frost in their acknowledgement of him. The reason for this soon became apparent when, ten minutes later, an agitated man had burst into the compartment at Tunbridge Wells and stood glaring at Matt. Once again, oblivious to the protocol, Matt had stared back and eventually asked "Got a problem mate?" The agitated man had considered a reply, but had quickly assessed Matt's 6' 4" bulk and thought better of it.

The man had reappeared at the same time for the next two days, but merely grunted (at one point actually saying the word "Harrumph") and melted away. After a few weeks, the rest of the compartment had eased into the new arrangement and confided that Mr.

Drive-By Shouting

Agitated of Tunbridge Wells had sat in that seat, in that compartment, for at least the last 15 years. Far from being embarrassed by his transgression, this made Matt feel thoroughly triumphant.

After fifty-four minutes of near silence (save for the soothing rhythm of the train tracks), he alighted at Waterloo East and found his driver standing at the bottom of the stairs, waiting to greet him. Three minutes later, he was striding jauntily into the reception at London Studios, the former home of Thames TV. The doorman, security and reception all greeted him cheerily and he took the lift up to the seventh floor and the production office. As he rode in the lift, he studied his chiseled reflection in the mirror. He looked good, and he looked rich. It still thrilled him that this was his life.

He exited the lift and walked along the corridor to the production office. Piles of fresh scripts sat alongside the croissants, orange juice and crap coffee. Jade, a researcher, looked up as he entered.

"Ah, you're here! You've got an early guest." She pointed to the office beyond. He turned to look, and upon seeing his female visitor's haunted look, Matt knew that the game had changed.

Drive-By Shouting

Chapter 5
The week after Groucho's – Wednesday

The following Wednesday, Gram woke to an early call from Rox Rentals telling him that, as things were quiet, he wasn't needed. Despite this meaning no money (and cash was already in short supply), he greeted it as good news, the sun was up and it was obviously going to be a great day. The previous few days had been dominated by his turmoil over the Groucho's meeting with Matt. It had re-enforced his belief that his life had taken a wrong turn, and that Matt had played an instrumental role in this. The morning sun cheered him 'though, and he felt positive for the first time since Groucho's. There was no tangible reason to feel better, but he felt happy, and, since seeing Matt, at least he no longer doubted the justness of his cause.

An hour later, he walked along Torrington Park and through the northern gate into Finsbury Park, heading straight to the Italian run cafe by the boating lake. He sat at the wooden tables outside and worked his way through a full English breakfast and a mug of tea,

Drive-By Shouting

watching a crane construct staging for the upcoming Fleadh Festival, which was held every summer in the park.

He finished breakfast and picked up the slices of bread that he'd saved for the ducks. Moving over to the railings he began to tear off small offerings, which he threw in a wide scatter across the lake. The ducks greedily snapped at the water-sodden bread, attempting to hoover up all of the pieces, before the swans and geese arrived and bullied them out of the way. He was tossing the last few bits into the oily water, when he noticed that he had been joined at the railings. He turned to see who it was.

"Oh, for fuck's sake! This is fucking unbelievable."
His companion recoiled: "Whoa! Okay, my mistake. I'll leave you alone." Kate Craw turned to leave.
"Yeah, fuck off."
She turned back to face him indignantly: "What *is* your problem? Seriously, what's *wrong* with you?"
"Yeah, forgive me for not wanting a chat with somebody who stabbed me in the back!"
"Oh for Christ's sake Gram. It was a long time ago. No one even remembers."
"Precisely. Nobody *does* remember. You wrote us off completely."

She sighed and held up her palms in partial submission: "Okay, Okay, I get it. And I am sorry for sticking the knife in, but you know how it works. The whole of the NME was dripping in vitriol and we all dipped our pens in it. Shouldn't have done it, but I can't undo it now. Anyway, I'll leave you alone..." Once again, she turned to leave.

Gram called after her angrily:
"Has *he* put you up to this? What's the game now... eh?"
"What? Who?" She looked genuinely confused: "Listen, I don't know what you're on about, and I'm really sorry I disturbed you, my mistake. I just saw you as I was walking by; realised it was you and thought I'd say hello. She backed further away, almost as if he was too unpredictable to turn her back on.
"Well that's a bit of a fucking coincidence, don't you think? You just happening to show up now, after all this time? Do you think I'm an idiot?"

Kate was turning a deep shade of red: "I... I don't know what you mean? Let's just forget it eh?" Gram suddenly realised that she might be on the point of tears. He studied Kate's face and, seeing her utter confusion, sensed that she may be telling the truth, and that she genuinely had no idea what he was talking about. They stood for a moment and Gram felt a vacuum replace all thoughts and words in his mind. The only idea left was that his temper had boiled so close to the surface of late, that he could almost taste the bile. An acrid bitterness that sat like a film on his tongue.

He called after her as she made her exit:
"Wait! Wait a minute." He swiftly marched to her side: "Sorry... I just thought... you know? Bit of a coincidence. Apologies, I was obviously being paranoid... I didn't mean to get so angry with you.

Drive-By Shouting

Well, not on this occasion anyway..." He forced a weak smile in an attempt to counter her discomfort. Her eyes were red and he felt instantly ashamed for being so aggressive. As he turned to leave, she reached forward and touched his sleeve.

"Actually Gram, I *do* know that it's me who should apologise. We'd always got on pretty well before I wrote those pieces." She shrugged awkwardly before looking directly at him, "It was a different me back then, and I know it was shitty for you, y'know? The kicking that everybody gave you."

"Yes, it was," he looked sternly at the ground.

"Well, I'm not asking for forgiveness. I didn't really have a choice at the time, it was the only way to get ahead. But still, I know it was probably hard to be on the receiving end of all the stuff we wrote." She corrected herself: "The stuff *I* wrote. So, for what it's worth, I'm y'know? Sorry. I actually always thought that you were a really nice guy, and a really good guitarist, but I guess I just got caught up in the mob mentality when it came to reviewing you." She shrugged awkwardly again.

"But I realise I've intruded and you don't care about me wanting to say hello, so I'll leave you in peace with the ducks." She smiled shyly before turning and starting to walk away. After prevaricating for a moment, Gram softened his tone and called after her: "Listen, I'm sorry I got so angry. It's been a funny week and I'm probably over reacting to things. The *Cymbal* days have been on my mind a bit lately, and I think you just caught me at the wrong time. Sorry I overreacted."

Drive-By Shouting

He felt his anger melt away as she stared directly at him, evaluating his trustworthiness, which Gram found disconcerting. Eventually she answered: "Ok. Let's agree that we're both sorry, eh?"

Gram shifted uncomfortably under her gaze. The redness had gone from her face and her familiar proud bearing was once more evident. In the vacuum, he felt compelled to speak: "So, this isn't where I'd expect to bump into you."

She looked back up at him, intrigued by the shift in gear: "I actually come quite often. They do the best Spag Bol in the café, and I'm a northern girl, so I like a decent plate of food." She smiled and turned once more to carry on walking. Gram also turned and faced the idiot ducks, swirling in circles through the shiny film that covered the water's surface. After a moment's reflection he set off after her.
"Wait... I'll walk with you a bit..." Kate turned, surprised but pleased: "Okay, if you're sure...?"

After the strange intimacy of their brief argument (and his display of anger), Gram walked awkwardly alongside her, unsure of what to say. Eventually he managed to blurt out a question: "So, I wouldn't have really imagined that this would be somewhere that you'd hang out, certainly not since you ... er... moved up in the world?"
"What? Since I married into money?" She laughed ironically.
"Well, yes, that, but I was mainly meaning you're on the telly quite a bit these days? I wouldn't have thought

Drive-By Shouting

that Finsbury Park would be somewhere you'd hang out. Don't you get people bugging you for autographs?"

"Hardly at all actually. I think I look quite different without all the slap on, so I tend to slip by un-noticed. But, I think it's also a lot to do with whether you walk around demanding attention or not. I don't demand it, so I tend not to get any."

Gram looked at her doubtfully: "What, you can switch it on or off depending on what mood you're in?"

"Sort of..., I mean, like I said, it's not like I'm mega famous or anything, but I find I can sort of choose to be invisible, if I want to. I saw it done really well once, you know, the invisibility trick, by David Bowie." She stamped her foot and grimaced comically. "Sorry, that was a bad visual joke about the sound of a name dropping!"

"Pretty good name to drop, mind you..."

"Yes it's forgivable then..." She smiled at him shyly, still unsure of his mood.

"I went to interview him at the Town & Country Club a few years ago, when he was sound checking with Tin Machine. This was about 4pm in the afternoon, but already there were hundreds of people outside the venue. He insisted on having the band present for the whole interview, but part way through, we went for a walk around to stretch our legs and ended up at the front doors, and I saw him 'switch on' the whole David Bowie persona, and walk outside. Obviously, the crowd went nuts and the security guys had a massive issue holding them back. He just instantly *became* the role, y'know? A proper rock star, just like you'd expect him to be.

Drive-By Shouting

But, funnily enough, I went back later that evening for the gig and was upstairs in the circle bar, when somebody grabbed my arm. I turned 'round and it was him, in a roomful of his fans, and nobody had noticed him! He grabbed me by the hand and led me out so we could chat, but still nobody noticed him. It was really weird!"
"Perhaps he really is an alien after all!" Gram immediately winced inwardly at the naivety of his own comment.

Kate raised her eyebrows and looked at him kindly: "Possibly. Anyway, that made a big impression on me and I thought about how having that ability to melt into the crowd, or to turn on the star thing, it gives him the choice of being at work or not. It's a neat trick."
Gram tried to remain cool, despite his secret thrill at discussing David Bowie, with somebody who had actually met him: "He can't do anything wrong in my book - he's a genius."
"Well, only somebody who didn't go to any of the Tin Machine gigs would say that!" She grinned mischievously at him.
Gram's smile vanished: "Oh, there it is, the inner bitch again."
Kate's face fell: "I was joking Gram - being ironic. And anyway, nothing I say would ever diminish David Bowie, he's above all that."
"Lucky him... wish we all were..."

The awkwardness had returned to the conversation and they walked in silence for a few moments before Gram spoke again: "Listen, maybe this wasn't such a good

Drive-By Shouting

idea, let's leave it there shall we? Before I get all bitter and twisted again. See you around, I'm glad I bumped into you, and I do appreciate you saying what you did. It's just that I'm in a funny place right now. So, see you." He awkwardly patted Kate's arm twice in quick succession and walked away, ashamed that he'd once more lapsed into bitterness and recrimination. She turned and watched him go: "Me too Gram... maybe bump into you again....?" She watched as he walked behind the bushes surrounding the lake and disappeared from view.

Drive-By Shouting

Part 2

Bridge

Drive-By Shouting

Chapter 6
1983 - Northampton

Simon Kane had been in Northampton for three hours, but already knew he had made a crap choice. Following a dismal set of 'A' level results, he had desperately scoured The Times University Clearing Pages, before reluctantly lifting the phone to call Northampton Polytechnic.

He'd been accepted onto a Joint Honours; Bachelor of Arts in Social Science, although he had struggled to see where the honour lay, if its intake was comprised entirely of low-grade students scraping the bottom of the last barrel in town.

Since he'd arrived he'd established that, no, there was no accommodation available and that, yes, following a walk around the place, Northampton was the world's ugliest town centre. Effectively homeless, he'd been billeted on to a camp bed in a seminar room, in the company of over 30 other male freshers. The randomly assembled group was now climbing the steps into the

Drive-By Shouting

student union, looking for the bar. Once in there, he fought his way through the throng, bought a discounted pint of Directors Bitter and looked around for somewhere to stand, without appearing lost and friendless. Given that 90% of the people in the bar were doing the same thing, he soon fell into a series of dismal circular conversations about 'What course are you doing?' 'What A-levels did you do?' 'Which halls of residence are you in?'

He drifted through a series of near identical conversations, always with one eye on the better option. In the corner of the bar, he noticed three guys humping a small PA system onto a couple of mini risers, where a neat little stage had been erected in the corner. He moved towards it, magnetically drawn to anything that may have a tenuous link to guitars, his obsession.

As he got nearer, he noticed a group of four apparently pretty girls hunched behind the stage, smoking. One of them abruptly sprang up, and turned. Simon was surprised to see that the girl was a) 6ft 4' and b) most definitely male. The guy ostentatiously swept his long hair back and surveyed the room, looking like a prettier Jim Morrison. Simon noticed that all three of the smokers kept their eyes fixed on his back. The androgynous guy, satisfied with his survey of the room, reached to pick up an acoustic guitar (which appeared to have a picture of Albert Einstein painted on to it) and sat back down.

Drive-By Shouting

The bar was too noisy for Simon to hear, but the girls sat in rapt attention as the guy strummed and, apparently, sang. One of the roadies was now thumping the microphone. Eventually, as his colleague located the correct channel, each thump produced a deep boom and he launched into a long soliloquy of the "one, two, one, two" variety. Even at Simon's tender age, he doubted that this had any purpose, other than getting the roadie to be noticed. Although, dressed as this guy was, Simon thought that was probably the last thing he needed.

The first one having kicked in nicely, Simon wrestled his way back to the bar for another pint of Directors. As he was taking his first sip, the roadie, empowered by the glory of amplification, addressed the room:

"Alright..., welcome to Northampton! I'm JP, your Ent's secretary! It's Fresher's night!" There was an unenthusiastic cheer from near the front, "We've got loads going on tonight. In the main hall at 8 o'clock *Gene loves Jezebel* and *Spear of Destiny*. Then at 10 o'clock the 'downstairs bar alternative disco', with live music from *Cairo,* supported by *Dead or Alive*! All beer, 50p a pint!! And, to get us started now, we've got some great acoustic stuff for you, from a bunch of second years, local heroes that they are, big Matt Mann & The Bohemian Kills..." At which, the androgynous guy stepped up to the mic, followed by the three girls...

Drive-By Shouting

Northampton 1983 - Day two

Simon awoke from a highly disturbed night, in the company of the thirty other homeless freshers. He sat up on the camp bed, which immediately buckled, folded and tipped him onto the floor. He extrapolated himself and stood up, instantly recalling the 7 pints of Director's bitter that he had worked his way through the previous evening. His dormitory mates all appeared comatose, so he wormed his feet into his boots, grabbed his leather jacket and shuffled through the maze of beds and sleeping bodies.

Outside the building (the home of 'Modern Studies,' although Simon was unsure of what that meant), he felt the cool autumnal air on his skin and magically felt better. It was after 10am, so he wandered through the campus towards the twin cathedrals; one, a bombed out husk, preserved as a heritage site and, across a wide passageway, what Simon viewed as its rather ugly replacement. He climbed the steps to walk between the two monoliths and simultaneously saw and heard a busker playing, somewhat implausibly, an acoustic version of *Tainted Love*. He instantly recognised the Einstein guitar and its owner.

As he drew nearer, a couple of tourists threw some coins into the open guitar case. Matt Mann nodded in appreciation and continued the song. Simon hovered, before finding a metal fence to lean against and perched there to listen. Matt finished the song, took a derisory look into the case and rested his guitar against

Drive-By Shouting

a wooden bench. While he fished in his pocket for a packet of fags, Simon wandered over:

"Saw you in the union bar last night. Good stuff..."
Matt looked up, a fag hanging on his lower lip: "Why, thank you. You a fresher then?"
"Yes. A homeless one!"
"Oh, I heard about that, another glorious fuck up from the housing office! Managed to miscount the academic intake by suxty-three people... Genius! So, where are you sleeping?"
"A seminar room in the Modern Studies building, on a camp bed. Not really the start I had planned..."
Matt laughed: "Luxury, welcome to Northampton!"
"Yeah, it's Christmas and my birthday all rolled into one. Well, not really. My birthday is actually June the 12th." Gram had no idea why he'd volunteered this, but was feeling slightly intimidated in Matt's presence.
Matt looked at him doubtfully: "You're kidding?"
Simon was confused: "About what?"
"Your birthday. June 12th, that's the same as mine!" Matt drew on his fag and exhaled exaggeratedly, 'Wow, spooky! Separated at birth!"
"Yeah, that is a bit of a weird co-incidence." Simon looked over at the Einstein guitar and gestured, "So, is that your band that you were with last night - you and the three girls?"
"Oh no, not really." Matt feigned nonchalance. "We had a good band, *Bohemian Kills,* last year, and the girls did some backing vocals towards the end. But the bass player just graduated and the guitarist managed to fail his first year and is now working in his dad's greengrocers in Essex. Silly fucker! You don't have to

Drive-By Shouting

do much to get a pass in Communication Studies, but he, genius that he is, managed to screw it up. So, for the time being, I'm bandless."

"Well, actually, I play lead guitar."

Matt looked at him impassively and thumbed a gesture towards the Einstein guitar: "Feel free Mr. Hendrix..."

Simon screwed up his face: "It's a bit tricky to play lead on a twelve string..., but, what the hell." He moved across and sat on the bench, pulling the guitar across him. After twelve bars of Simon tapping and hammering at a rather unique version of Van Halen's *Eruption*, Matt squealed: "Whoa, that's brilliant! I've never seen anyone actually play that before, especially on 12 string acoustic! What's your name?"

"Er, Simon."

"Well, you can play, and you look good. Want to join a band? We'll have to change the name of course."

"What, the band?"

"No, yours. Simon isn't the name of a modern rock god."

"A modern rock god?"

"Yeah, that's got to be the plan..."

Matt ignored Simon's confusion while he paced around, distractedly dragging on his fag: "Yeah, we need something that makes you sound a bit fucked up, a bit druggie. Sort of Jimi Hendrix, Iggy Pop. What's your full name?"

"Er, Simon Graham Kane."

"Ooo that might work. Not Graham, obviously, that's as bad as Simon. But maybe Gram. Like Gram Parsons, that sort of thing. Actually, that might work... What's your surname again?"

"Kane."

Drive-By Shouting

"Well that's it then! 'Gram Kane' – that sounds good actually. Gram Kane... It suits you! So, we're sorted. Welcome to the band Gram..."

Although the religious connotations made Simon shudder, the sense that somebody else could instantly sense his life's misalignment, felt like a balm spreading over him, healing all of the tiny cuts that life had already inflicted.

Simon realised that he'd just been born again.

Northampton - Three weeks later

Matt rested his acoustic against the filing cabinet and lit a fag:
"Come on, it's eight o'clock, let's go to the bar. And, there's a house party up the Billing Road later." They (Matt, the re-christened Gram and the enthusiastic, if indifferent, drummer Kevin) swiftly downed 2 pints in the bar, before joining a ragged procession of students through the town centre, buying two cans each of Special Brew on the way.

After stashing their cans behind a neighbour's bin, they entered the non-descript terraced house, pushing through the mass of bodies. The party seemed to have no epicentre, so they instinctively found themselves drawn into the kitchen and fell into conversation with some girls from Matt's halls of residence. Kevin drifted off to find someone who might want to talk about

Drive-By Shouting

drums, leaving Gram and Matt leaning against the cooker, Matt holding forth about the inevitable and imminent success of the band.

"We're totally brilliant; me and Gram here have written five definite hits in the last three weeks. We're like Lennon and McCartney or Page and Plant..." The three girls looked nonplussed at the second reference, one of them cocking her head and looking doubtfully at Matt.

Gram tried to match Matt's nonchalance with the girls and with the pretty head-cocker in particular. He had seen her going in and out of various places on campus. She had a cropped postpunk cut and wore paint splattered indigo dungarees most days. Her clothes, hair and make-up seemed designed to do anything other than make her attractive to men. He'd overheard Matt saying "Yeah, the cool thing about her, is that she's dressing completely to please herself, rather than appeal to guys, which is sort of sexy." Gram had looked at her anew after this. She was so unlike the girls from home, with their cheap perms and Grattan catalogue clothes, they were preened and presentable, perfect for taking home to Mum (not that Gram would ever have done so). This girl wasn't like that. Still only eighteen, she exhibited confidence and, strangely for an eighteen year old, a real sense of integrity.

Gram looked back at the green eyes bearing into his:
"And what do you do in the World's Best Band?"
Gram tried not to sound apologetic: "Lead guitar."
"You're not one of those boring twats who twiddle around with a solo for ten minutes in every song? We

Drive-By Shouting

had one of those on my foundation course, and he was complete ear ache."

Gram's eyes widened, he'd never met a girl that actively analysed individual musicians in a band.
"No I'm not like that. I mean, yes, I can do all that stuff, but when you've heard Eddie Van Halen, what's the point?"
"Fazakerley!"
"What?"
She smiled: "Sorry, something I picked up from my cousin. He's a Scouser, and every time he should say '*exactly*,' he says 'Fazakerley' instead. It's a place in Liverpool, I think."
"I know. I grew up near there..."
"Well, you don't sound scouse."
"It's my dark secret."
"Apparently..." She smiled sweetly at him, making Gram blush. "Anyway if you're not noodling around playing Van Halen solos, what are you playing like?"
"You've heard *U2* yeah? I like The Edge, very simple, it gives their sound lots of power."
"Yeah, saw them play when I lived at home last year. Bass player wore a white lab coat and Clark Kent glasses on stage. Very cool. Went backstage and partied. Well, I partied, they're all Christian, so it wasn't exactly jumping...!"
"You met them? Wow, what's The Edge like?"
"He was the nicest one, along with the bass player. The drummer was pretty moody, and the singer was a bit opinionated, to say the least."
"Well, that's singers for you, just look at Matt here!" he said, gesturing with his thumb towards Matt.

Drive-By Shouting

"Oooo, scratch your eyes out! The battling egos are already out!" Matt, having heard his name, was looking at Gram and grinning. He nodded at the back of the girl's head in a lascivious manner, his tongue repeatedly poking the inside of his cheek. Ignoring Matt's lewdness, Gram looked at the girl once more, realising that he had never met anyone quite like her before:
"What's your name?"
"Jen."
"Good to meet you Jen. Don't meet many girls who can talk knowledgeably about bands, especially about bass players, guitarist's etcetera..." He summoned his courage, "You're pretty cool."
"Well thank you. But actually, I'm not a girl, I'm a woman." She stared directly into his eyes.

Unable to cope with her directness, he looked away and half stumbled through a sentence: "Yeah, er, by the way, I'm Simon. Although, everyone seems to call me Gram, since Matt decided to change my name! Er, listen, do you want a drink or something, I stashed a couple of Special Brews outside?"

She grimaced: "Christ, that stuff's like tar, I'd rather drink this." She reached into her dungaree pocket and retrieved a quarter sized bottle of clear liquid. "I'll stick to the vodka thanks, stops me needing to pee all the time." He took this as his cue, having been aware of the growing pressure on his bladder, from the pints he'd had in the union:

Drive-By Shouting

"Actually, I really do need to pee, so I'll nip out and I can grab a can while I'm there. Won't be long. You sticking around?"
"We'll see... I deffo wouldn't hang around for a Simon, but, who knows, a Gram might see me later..." She gave a coquettish flash of her eyes and turned away.

He pushed and shoved through the hall to the front door and out into the cool air. Having checked the street, he quickly peed into a bush and retrieved one of his cans. Re-approaching the house, he found Kevin, the indifferent drummer, talking to a slightly nerdy looking guy just outside the front door. Gram, eager to return to the kitchen, attempted to breeze past. Kevin however, blocked his path.

"Gram the Man, brilliant...! You need to meet Colin." Gram looked doubtfully at Colin, before reluctantly extending his hand. Kevin continued, "You're gonna love this. Colin's joining the band!" Colin shifted uncomfortably as Gram glared. Maneuvering Kevin away from the reddening Colin, Gram half whispered: "Bloody hell Kevin! Aren't you being a bit premature? That's something that we'll all need to decide. What do you think you're doing?"
"No, listen!" Kevin interrupted sotto voce, "Colin's a brilliant bass player. He's got an Aria bass, and a Trace Elliot stack! And, get this... a car!" He resumed normal volume. "So really, we should at least have a jam to give it a go. What do you think?" Kevin beamed expectantly, but Gram's thoughts were fixed on getting back to the kitchen and the delightful Jen. But then again, a bass player with gear and a car? That was

Drive-By Shouting

exactly what they needed, so maybe this was a worthwhile diversion.

"How long have you been playing bass Colin?"
"Since I was twelve. Started on double bass."
"So, you can play fretless?"
"Yes, that's what I've got, an Aria Pro Two fretless, just like John Taylor's, but without the frets obviously." A look of panic spread across his face, "I don't know why I said that, I don't even like *Duran Duran*, Mick Kahn from *Japan* is who I really like." Gram surveyed the diminutive Colin with his oversized rugby shirt and bowl haircut and doubtfully tried to picture him on the same stage as *Japan*.

"You'll have to do something about your image Colin. You don't exactly look like a rock star"
"Well, that's the thing. I think that it should be about the level of musicianship, not about your haircut. That's what people should look for. All this image stuff, it's just bollocks really isn't it?"
"Er, no actually, it's not. Image is really, really important." Gram's demeanor remained unfriendly and his primary impulse was to wrap this conversation up as soon as possible. "I suppose there's no harm in us having a jam, and we can worry about all that later. But just to be clear, we'll have to talk about the hair if all goes well? We're having a rehearsal in the Union on Tuesday night, the singer's somehow occupied an office there. Why don't you bring your stuff along then and we can have a go?"
Colin nodded enthusiastically as Gram continued. "But Kevin can fill you in with all the details. I need to

Drive-By Shouting

get back inside, there's a really nice girl I was chatting up, and obviously that's far more important than this right now!" He smiled and re-entered the house, barging onwards into the hall and rejoining the scrum required to get through to the kitchen.

Finally squeezing between two large rugby club guys, who were insisting on standing in the kitchen doorway, Gram found himself once more by the cooker, but also found that the room was half empty. The back door was open and he heard laughter and what sounded like empty milk bottles being knocked over. He followed the sound and went outside. The backyard was filled with people smoking and drinking, but there was no sign of Jen. He turned on his heel to go back down the side alley to the back door and past the bathroom window on the way. He half sensed, half saw a large figure beyond the privacy glass and, despite the distortion, worked out that the red shirt identified the figure as Matt. Gram stopped and stared. He appeared to be embracing someone.

Gram stepped through the outer kitchen door, just as the bolt on the bathroom clanked back and out of the bathroom came Matt, closely followed by Jen. One of her bib and brace buttons was undone and there was a smear of lipstick at the corner of her mouth. She glanced at Gram, before quickly walking away. Matt turned to face Gram and grinned widely "Gram the Man!! Hiya mate! Good party eh?" He turned and continued in the direction that Jen had gone.

Drive-By Shouting

Gram backed out of the door into the side alley and lent against the wall. He reached into his pocket, opened his can and guzzled the entire contents in one go.

Monday 1983 - Two days later

After making himself very conspicuous during his frequent visits over the past few weeks, Gram breezed past the Reception at the halls of residence, most of the security guards now being of the opinion that he lived there. He headed to J Block and trudged up the stairs to the first floor. After traversing the maze of corridors, he came to Matt's door, which was, as usual, ajar. Matt was shirtless, sprawled across his unmade bed, studying the ceiling. He sat up enthusiastically upon seeing Gram.

"Gram! How're you doing? Where were you yesterday? I thought you'd baled on us! I hear Kevin's been inviting half of Northampton to join the band, but that you said it was okay?"
"No, that's Kevin talking crap again. He presented some nerdy guy to me at that party. I said we could give him a try-out tomorrow night. But I'm a bit worried about him, he looks a bit shit."
"So I heard. But he does have good gear – and a car would be a god-send. Don't worry; we can always dress him in a crash helmet or something if he looks too awful. And, if he's just too bad, we can give him the bum's rush, or keep him on as a roadie." Matt busied himself lighting a cigarette while he discussed Colin's

Drive-By Shouting

imaginary future. "Anyway, what happened to you on Saturday, you disappeared?"
"Well, it was a bit rubbish and then, to cap it all, you copped off with the girl I fancied. The one I was in the middle of chatting up."
Matt either didn't detect the hint of resentment in Gram's voice or chose to ignore it. "What? Jen? Should've made your move faster mate, because all's fair in love and war.' And anyway, I saved you from a night of utter frustration; she's a total prick-tease!"
"What, she was immune to the Mann charm? Turned you down?" Gram couldn't hide his delight.
"Worse than that. Came back and stayed here and then led me on for the whole night! Let me touch her up and all that. But wouldn't let me in, if you know what I mean." Matt grimaced wryly.

Gram smiled broadly on hearing the news. Having spent Sunday nursing a hangover and regretting not being more overt with Jen, he was delighted to hear of Matt's frustration: "You've obviously lost your touch Matt."
"Not really Grammy. I'm just going to have to play the long game, now that she's become a bit of a challenge. She'll give in eventually. They all do."

Gram's smile faded. He stared out of Matt's window at the buses negotiating their way around the Bus Station, across the road. "Poor Jen," he thought, "just a bit of throwaway action for Matt."
Suddenly animated, Matt jumped up off the bed, swept back his hair and picked a crumpled shirt off the floor.

Drive-By Shouting

"Right, let's get over to the Art Fac Refectory... I missed breakfast and I'm starving."

Drive-By Shouting

Part 3

Verse

Drive-By Shouting

Chapter 7
1999 – Saturday June 10th – Finsbury Park

At 8:23am Gram parked the truck at the back of the main stage. The gates to the main auditorium didn't open until 10am, but access (for anybody except artistes) was nigh on impossible after 9am, so he was glad to be in the venue and parked in plenty of time.

He wouldn't be needed for at least two hours and so, having found the inevitable tea urn and helped himself to a cup, he opened the vehicle's rear door to give himself a seat in the morning sunshine. Through chinks in the backstage security fencing, he could see (and hear) the hi-viz vested security staff being given their instructions for the day ahead.

He climbed into the back of the truck and retrieved one of the guitar cases within. He opened it to take another look at the Gibson Les Paul Custom with the tiger maple top, marveling at the beauty and complexity of the polished book-matched grain. It was immaculate, like gazing into a swirling golden universe, making even his own beloved Les Paul look rather ordinary. He picked it up out of the case and plucked a few chords, his fingers mechanically going to shapes and patterns,

Drive-By Shouting

like an experienced driver who no longer needs to think about gears or clutches. He quickly lost himself in playing, losing all sense of time and place as his fingers felt their way around the guitar's neck. It was almost a form of meditation for Gram to play like this. Not mechanically ploughing through cover versions, but exploring where one chord or phrase led, without ever really seeming to steer the direction that the music took. He'd heard other songwriters talk about tunes simply 'falling from the sky' and that they had simply been stood in the right place, waiting to catch them. At times like this, he truly understood the feeling. Phrases and melodies seemingly emerged from nowhere in his hands, as if this unfamiliar instrument was instructing him on what to play, and he never failed to be awestruck by the process. He wasn't creating melodies, they were simply choosing him. It was the time that Gram felt most alive and connected with the world. He happily whiled away twenty minutes in the surprisingly tranquil morning sun, before he saw another tech guy he knew and, enervated by his time playing, joined him for more tea.

By midday, backstage was throbbing with activity and with the bass from the thundering PA which, while projecting most of the sound forward, still gave the backstage area a consistent sub-bass throb, like a prolonged nearby earthquake. Gram had been scheduled to meet the American spoof rock band, *The Undertakers*, at 10.30am, as they were borrowing all of the backline, drums and guitars that were in Gram's truck. At 12.15pm, they finally sauntered through the gate, all teaseled hair (wigs, he wondered?), spandex

Drive-By Shouting

and *Ray Bans*. They high-fived a group of guys and hugged various people. Gram saw who he assumed to be the manager (he was bald and fat) and approached him:

"Michael? Michael DiMarco?"
"Nope, not me buddy. I'm Tony, the drummer." He turned and pointed to the most overtly rock god figure in the entourage, "He's Michael, that's your rock god manager, buddy. As you can see, he's enjoying the role-play!"

Gram fought hard to keep his eyebrows level and approached Michael, who could have passed for a very convincing Keith Richards impersonator: "Mike, er, Michael. I'm Gram from Gibson and I've got all of your gear."
"Yo. Excellent. Where is it?"
Gram gestured over his shoulder, "it's all in the truck, back there."

In an appalling impression of a cockney accent, he replied: "Well, it's no friggin' use in there, is it mate? You'd better get humping. Hah!" Michael slapped Gram on the shoulder and turned his back to him, and with that, Gram was dismissed. He felt the familiar heat rising. Being discounted as nothing more than a nameless roadie was something he should be used to by now. However, it always rankled and infuriated him and it was somehow worse, to be discounted by people who were merely play acting the role of rock stars.

Drive-By Shouting

He set about unloading and shifting the backline amps & drums and the treasured guitars, all so they could be used by an unfunny, comedy rock group. He was growing to hate music, he thought. More specifically, he hated the music industry and its random selection of those deemed worthy of success. It followed waves of fashion, a glut of misery bands, a glut of Manchester ravers, succeeded by a wave of exuberant poseurs. Now, the arbiters in the sky had deemed that irony was 'in,' hence, the rise of the spandex clad and deeply crap *The Undertakers*.

Once the drums and the backline were in place, all queued and ready to be placed on stage, he sought out the guitarist and bassist in their Portakabin dressing room to hand them their instruments. The bassist was indifferent; not even opening the flight case, but the guitarist threw his case onto a daybed and snatched at the clasps.

"Man, that's cool..." He grabbed the Les Paul and turned it around to admire it. Gram joined in the appreciation: "She's really beautiful, isn't she?"
"Fucking yeah!!" And then in another shockingly bad 'mockney' accent, "Spot on, mate!!!" Gram rolled his eyes behind his dark glasses and turned to leave. "Look after her..."

He exited the dressing room and was stepping down into the communal area, when he heard a shout:
"Gram, Gram. Over here!" It was Kate. She moved swiftly over to him, wafting long yards of chiffon behind her and he reluctantly admitted to himself that

Drive-By Shouting

she really was something to behold. She arrived beaming her radiant smile. "God, how funny is this? I don't see you for years and then twice in a couple of weeks! If this was a film, no one would believe it!"

She laughed and, despite himself, Gram noticed her beautiful lips and smiled back. He had regretted his anger and tetchiness at their last meeting, because, while he felt that his historical ire was entirely justified, continuing to feel so bitter and resentful simply made him feel worse. He had decided that, in the unlikely event that they met again, he would give her the benefit of the doubt and here it was, the unlikely event had arrived. He sought to put her at ease:

"Yes, more than a little coincidental! And, in Finsbury Park again? You obviously never leave here. You just have a little den in the bushes that you go to at night," She grinned warmly at him, pleased to find him receptive: "Probably not, I understand that it's pretty active in the bushes here at night, and I'm not talking Wombles!"

Gram found himself smiling broadly again. "I'm sure it is. Very shocking for a convent girl like you."

Kate continued to beam up at him. "But seriously Gram, I'm really pleased to see you again, and let's put all the shit behind us eh? We always got on well before that."

He smiled in acknowledgement. It felt good to let go of the resentment: "Yeah, let's. Life's too short. Anyway, what are you doing here?"

"BMG invited me, but this place is full of boring shits! What are you doing? You working?"

Drive-By Shouting

"Not really. I brought all of the gear for The Undertakers and now I'm just hanging around until they do their set at 4pm when they hand it all back."
"*The Undertakers*? Oh Christ, they're dreadful! Still, if you're free. And you don't mind being seen with me. Do you want to go and get some lunch in the VIP area? If that's OK? Now that we've moved on."

Once again, Gram found his ambivalent feelings about Kate completely overridden by a strong desire to spend time with her, and the idea of a free lunch also chimed nicely. With a hint of regret in his voice, he said, "I can't. I've only got a technical area pass."

Kate grabbed the pass on Gram's lanyard and studied it. "Hmmm... Shouldn't be a problem. Wait here." She walked away, turning after ten yards and pointing bossily at him; "*Don't* go away!"

Again, Gram found himself smiling at Kate. He continued to ponder this odd set of developments. First, his refusal to meet Kate at Matt's behest and then bumping into her twice. More extraordinary than that of course, was the fact that, against all of his better judgement, he was finding it impossible to continue disliking her.

After a couple of minutes, she skipped down the steps from the Portakabin that she had invaded, gesturing triumphantly. As she got nearer she announced loudly: "Told you. I'm the queen of the liggers. One 'All Areas Pass' for you, sir!"
"Impressive! How did you manage that?"

Drive-By Shouting

"Easy. I'm very persuasive..." She beamed up at him eagerly.
"I'll give you that Kate. Very persuasive!" He gave a reassuring smile and saw her register it.

She led him towards the security checkpoint and, passes checked, they went through the black draped barriers and into a large grassy area with a small stage and PA in one corner and a large Bedouin tent occupying the whole of one perimeter wall. On the small stage, a duo of young guys with acoustic guitars, were doing battle (unsuccessfully) with the ambient noise from the main stage. Gram gave them a pitying look, before following Kate into the tent. Half empty, it was decked out with carpets, sofas and drapes and felt strangely calm and insulated from the noise outside. A waiter took their order for food.
"Any drinks?" he enquired.

Gram jumped in: "Er, just fizzy water for me. I'm driving. And I guess you'd better have the same in the circumstances?" He turned to find Kate looking at him quizzically, "What circumstances?"
Gram flushed, as he instantly realized his mistake: "Sorry, I just assumed it was a bit early for cocktails."
"Well, I'm minded to suggest that it's never too early for cocktails, but as it happens, I'm on a bit of a health kick, so yes, and sparkling water for me too, please."

Gram's panic abated and they settled into an easy flow of music chat. Kate was enthusing about the acts on the bill, "I really can't wait for Neil Young, I totally love him...!"

Drive-By Shouting

"That really depends on which one turns up. If it's *Heart of Gold* and *Harvest* Neil Young, it's the best thing in the world. But if he's in the mood for playing endless crap guitar solos, then it'll be a long night!"
"Really? You don't rate him as a guitarist?"
"Are you kidding? He's a world-class songwriter and a great acoustic player, but a strictly fourth division lead guitar player. You music hacks really don't know anything, do you?" He smiled broadly to ensure she knew he was being light-hearted.
"Oh well, that's me told. I'll bow to your superior knowledge!"

They continued to talk for the next hour, Gram barely noticing the food, unlike Kate, who greedily tore into her plate of Moroccan food, before helping herself (without invitation) to uneaten tidbits from Gram's plate.

He was finding Kate's company captivating. Since breaking up with Lucy, his last 'proper' girlfriend, over a year ago, he'd fallen into a pattern of one-night stands and brief affairs, where sex had been the main driver of the relationship. It felt immensely good to be in the company of somebody as funny and gregarious as Kate and the ease of their conversation felt wonderfully affirming to Gram. Now that he'd finally cast off the past and his ancient resentment, he felt tremendously at ease with her, with none of the anxiety that he often felt when talking to women. It was an added bonus that she was undoubtedly beautiful to look at, as she raced through one inappropriate celebrity story after another, relishing his amusement

Drive-By Shouting

at the punchline. After a while, she suggested that they go to the VIP viewing area to watch a couple of bands from the side of the stage. They left the catering area and were approaching the checkpoint, when Kate suddenly froze.

Stumbling, rather unsteadily through the security point, was Matt Mann. He looked up and drunkenly took in the sight of Kate, arm linked through Gram's. A look of terror spread across his face as, behind him, a clearly angry Jen passed through the checkpoint, shepherding their two children.

Matt stood mute, trying to assess the situation through an alcoholic haze. Jen looked up and a surprised expression replaced the anger on her face. She forced a smile: "Well, hello you two. What a surprise!" She air-kissed both Kate and Gram, while Matt maintained his horrorstruck glare.

Jen, keen to disguise her husband's drunken state, continued talking, "Wow, it's been ages Kate. And even longer since seeing you Gram. I didn't know you two hung out together?" And, with a lascivious wink, "Anything I should know?"

Sensing that Kate was almost as dumbstruck as Matt, Gram stepped in. "It's all perfectly above board and platonic Jen. Kate's a married woman, don't you know?" He glanced at Matt.

Jen instantly looked flustered, "Of course. I didn't mean anything by that. I was just joshing with the two

Drive-By Shouting

of you! I just hadn't expected to see the two of you together."
"And neither had I." Matt had finally found his voice, "Last I heard you two were at war. And yet here you are... just like the best of friends." He pronounced his words pedantically, apparently afraid of slurring. Gram looked him in the eye.
"We're mates, Matt. Very good mates." He grabbed Kate's hand and squeezed it.

The terror returned to Matt's eyes and he blustered: "Well, don't want to keep either of you. And the kids are getting bored. So we'll get off and say hello to... to... Shane McGowan. He was on my show yesterday... Yeah, lovely guy."

He turned to Jen, "Come on, let's go and see him and the band." He moved off, pulling hard at Jen's arm.
"Matt, what are you doing?" She snapped at him angrily. "Why the fuck are you dragging me?" She half-turned and gave an apologetic look to Gram and Kate, manufacturing a laugh as she said, "I'm sorry, my husband's a drunken brute!"

As they departed, Gram turned to look at a very pale Kate: "Are you okay Kate? You've gone rather silent." She looked up at him, glassy eyed: "I'm so sorry Gram... I don't know what's come over me. I'm just not feeling so good all of a sudden." A tremendous urge came over Gram to tell Kate that he knew about the affair, the pregnancy and of Jen's total ignorance of it all. Before he could speak, she jumped in, "Listen Gram, I do feel a little weird all of a sudden. I wish

Drive-By Shouting

there was somewhere quiet to go. There are too many people here... Perhaps I should just go."

Gram considered for a moment: "No, stay a while. I've got the perfect place."

With the rear doors opened towards the sun, Gram and Kate sat at the back of the truck with their legs dangling out:
"Thank you Gram. I'm sorry about the funny turn. It must be a woman's thing."
Gram put his hand over hers and patted it:
"Just take your time, and anyway, it's quite nice being that extra hundred yards further back from the stage, you can actually hear yourself think for a change."
"So speaks the high decibel rock guitarist!"
"Yes, I know, ironic isn't it? I spend half my time making a right racket and the rest craving a bit of peace!"

The sun cast a dappled light through the trees and a light breeze caressed them. Gram levered himself down and lay back contentedly on the rag packing blankets that he'd spread across the metal floor:
"This is the life Kate. None of your VIP backstage bullshit here!"
He sensed her chuckling and squinted at the silhouette of her back as she continued sitting and swinging her feet off the end of the van:
"Thanks for looking after me Gram. You're a very nice person."

Drive-By Shouting

"Hmmmm... I haven't been accused of that lately!"
She twisted round and looked at him stretched out, "So, what's the deal with you and Matt? You seem fairly spiky with him?"
"Well, you've worked with him, what do you think?" He tried to read her face, but the sun continued to place her in silhouette as she considered his question.

Finally she spoke: "I'm not sure who Matt is. He's very good at moulding himself into what people want. Obviously I knew all of you a bit from when you were in the band together, but after that … I only knew him socially from a few weekends and dinners with Steve when he'd invited the two of them over and he seemed okay. Nice enough. Then, when I started co-presenting with him, I thought I saw something a bit deeper, that he actually had a bit of substance to him. Now, I think he's a bit of a shape shifter. He kind of senses what people want and sort of bends himself to that shape. But you've known him a lot longer than me. What's your take? I don't sense there's much love lost, or have I misread it?"

Gram pushed himself up and turned to sit cross-legged facing Kate across the wheel arches at the back of the truck. "It's complicated. When I met Matt, I was a little bit, and I mean this in a totally heterosexual way you understand? But I was definitely a little bit 'smitten' with him. He's very impressive in lots of ways. He looks great, he can certainly sing and he's quite a charmer. So, I think I felt a little bit blessed when I formed the band with him. He was cool and laid-back, while I was a bit more retiring, and prepared to do the

Drive-By Shouting

legwork musically, so it kind of worked. I mean, you sort of captured the essence of Matt in one of your 'nice' reviews. That bit where you wrote something like: 'charismatic and good-looking in a vacant Byronic sort of way.'"

"Yes, I remember that. When Steve and I first met, he insisted that Matt and I get to know each. Meet up and patch up our differences. I thought that the 'Byronic' thing would be one of the lines that I'd really have to apologise for. But I think Matt simply took it as a compliment; ignoring the vacant bit and simply feeling flattered by the 'good looking' and 'Byron' references!"

Gram smiled wryly: "Yes, you can always rely on Matt's vanity to triumph over adversity! But, going back to what I was saying, while I had a brief period of being smitten with him, he soon showed his true nature. Funnily enough, it was me who was initially pretty keen on Jen. Difficult to believe now that she's a stuck up cow, but when we were all eighteen and nineteen-ish, I did fancy her. She was on the same floor as Matt in Halls when we were all at Northampton and I thought she was really nice. Funnily enough Matt hadn't given her a second look, until, of course, he found out that I was interested in her. So, he moved in on her, just to prove that he could."

"Really?! Bloody hell, that's not what mates are meant to do."
"Well, to be fair, we were all young and I hadn't known him that long when it happened. But it sort of alerted

Drive-By Shouting

me to his true nature, he can be ruthless when he wants to, and he does like to win."

Kate winced. "Still, I'm not sure I would have remained friends with a girlfriend of mine if they'd copped off with a guy I had declared a real interest in. It pretty much breaks the rules!"

"Yeah, it does, but I just kind of moved past it. I wanted to push ahead with the band and being totally honest, thought I'd get further ahead *with* Matt than without him. So I forgave, but I didn't forget. And of course, knowing Jen as I do now, he probably did me a favour! She's changed into a snobby, hardheaded bitch, not at all the airy art student she was at 18. All she seems to care about now is money."

Kate looked at her hands awkwardly: "I don't know her that well. She's probably got her hands full, being married to him. Maybe money is the trade-off to being married to someone like Matt?"

"Possibly. Anyway, I'd still rather him than me ending up married to her! But, despite the years of humiliations, the shagging around, the indifference, she hung in there. I guess, under the dreamy artist exterior, lay a rather steely core. And once she'd set her mind to it, he wasn't getting away."

An injured look briefly crossed Kate's face: "So he's had lots of affairs?"

Gram realised that he'd twisted the knife, but thought that Kate deserved to at least know who she was dealing with: "Yeah, He was the biggest shagger in Northampton. And when we all moved to London, he

Drive-By Shouting

was forever copping off with girls after gigs. But always going home to 'mummy' afterwards."

Kate looked at him squarely. "Wow, you really hate him!" It wasn't an accusation, but Gram felt a little stung by the truth, which he'd barely allowed himself to see for years. He nodded.

She continued to process the information and asked unsmilingly, "So, she knew about all this?"
"She may not have known all the sordid details, but she knew enough. She definitely knew about other girls in Northampton. Matt told me that one time she stayed over at his house and in the morning he fished amongst all the crap next to his bed and said 'Here you go Madame, your knickers.' And handed them to her. Except, they weren't hers!"
She laughed, despite herself: "Christ, how awful. How did he manage to wriggle out of that?"
"He told me he just shrugged and made up some story on the spot, 'somebody else must have stayed when he wasn't there', that kind of crap. But, you'd have to be daft to believe that. And whatever else she is, Jen isn't daft. So, yeah, she knows."
"God, what a way to live."

Gram once more felt a desire to blurt out the details of Matt's Groucho's plan, but checked himself. Why hadn't he mentioned it straightaway? Despite everything that Matt had done, he still couldn't bring himself to completely betray his confidence. There was something in the way that Matt had said that there was nobody but him that he could talk to about it, that had

Drive-By Shouting

touched Gram, and flattered him. Despite the more overwhelming feeling of anger, this made him pause. So he once more suppressed the urge to speak about the Groucho's meeting. Nonetheless, he saw no reason why he shouldn't paint Matt in his true light. So far as Kate was concerned, she may as well know the facts of what she'd got herself into. She needed to know that Matt was a shagger, but he decided to hold back on quite how scheming and Machiavellian he could also be. Gram also realized that he cared about not hurting her.

They sat, soaking up the sun and talking for the next forty minutes, until Gram checked the time: "Kate, I need to go back and be there when *The Undertakers* come off stage, so I can retrieve the gear. So, I need to go really. What about you, what are you doing now?"

"I don't want to go back with all the VIP wankers. I might just go out front with the real punters. There's more atmosphere. And, I'd prefer not to end up stuck with Matt and Jen; they're far too pissed for my liking." She jumped down from the truck and stood on the grass. "Once again Gram, you've been lovely company. If we don't find each other later, because I'm not sure how long I'll stay, how's about I buy you breakfast at the cafe by the lake, one day next week?" She looked at him hopefully.

Gram found it remarkably easy to concur. "You're on. I'd never say no to that!" Reluctant to break the spell of their time together, he sadly locked the van and they made their way up to the technical area, Kate

Drive-By Shouting

immediately turning left, intending to access the area around the front of the stage. Before she parted from him, she stretched up on her toes and kissed Gram's cheek, "Well, this was unexpected. But I really enjoyed hanging out. Ta ra, lovely man. I'll call you." She flashed a movie star smile and turned to leave. Gram watched as she went through the security checkpoint and melted into the crowd.

Entering the technical area, he arrived just in time to see *The Undertakers* coming down the steps from the rear of the stage, their performance complete. They moved in a huddle across the square of grass towards Gram, the bass player passing his instrument into Gram's outstretched hand. Gram followed him into the dressing room and replaced the EB bass in its case, before snapping shut the clasps.

He turned to find the outstretched hand of the guitarist holding the tiger maple Les Paul towards him. Gram could immediately see the damage, with gouges ripped out of the upper side of the bodywork. He was aghast; "What the fuck have you done?"

"Yeah, got a little chewed up by the studs on my wristband." He shrugged nonchalantly, "You know shit happens man?" Gram turned the guitar over silently and inspected the rear, which had been equally chewed up by the guy's belt buckle. A rage grew inside him, as he recalled playing the guitar that morning; he turned to address the guitarist. "You're a total fucking wanker! You've got no respect. This was a beautiful

Drive-By Shouting

instrument and you've totally fucked it up, you Yankee twat!"

The guitarist looked at him in amusement: "Hey, take a chill pill man! It's not a problem, the record company will pay. And anyway, what's it got to do with you? You need to remember that you're just a fucking roadie, so jack off, mate!" The guitarist turned and joined the group outside the dressing room.

Still furious, Gram replaced the damaged guitar in its case and carried it and the bass back to the truck, shaking his head as he went. What had just happened seemed to be a microcosm of Gram's entire experience of music, his personal love of the essence and beauty in playing a wonderful instrument pitched against the coarse commercial reality. Everything beautiful seemed to end up in the wrong hands. He found he was shaking with emotion.

Returning to collect the backline amps, he entered the technical area to find *The Undertaker's* guitarist facing the opposite way and talking to, of all people, a clearly inebriated Matt Mann. Matt saw him approaching and, sensing the fury radiating from Gram, apprehensively took a step backwards.

"Don't worry Mann; this isn't about you, although I reckon it won't be long 'til it's your turn."

Matt looked truly terrified.

Drive-By Shouting

The Undertaker's guitarist turned to see who he was addressing: "Oh, I see, it's Mr. fucking high and mi..." He crumpled under the force of Gram's fist connecting with his face and rolled on the ground.
"You fucking maniac! Jesus, what the fuck?!"
Gram looked at Matt; "Unless *you* want some too?"

Matt held up his palms defensively, while *The Undertaker's* guitarist squirmed on the floor holding his face and groaning, his nose pumping blood across his cheek. All eyes in the enclosure were on Gram, Matt and the stricken guitarist, although nobody, even the backstage security guys, chose to intervene. There was something about the force emanating from Gram that held everybody at bay.

Gram continued to snarl at Matt, who was frozen into in-action: "Didn't think so, you fucking coward." He turned and strode back towards the truck. By the time he reached the vehicle, he was aware of someone behind him. He turned to find Matt following apprehensively six feet behind him. He was excessively drunk and slurred as he spoke.

"Gram, have you, like, y'know, lost it? This is sooo fucked up. What are you, like…, doing with Kate?"
"Fuck off and mind your own business…"
"But Gram man…" He stumbled and managed to correct himself in time to remain upright. "…it *is* my business…. I mean, what's she said? what have you said..? I know I shouldn't a asked you…" Even through his alcoholic haze, Matt was clearly frightened by the day's turn of events. He looked imploringly at Gram as

Drive-By Shouting

he swayed, grabbing the side of the vehicle to steady himself.

"You're pissed, Matt."
"I am. I totally fucking am. I'm fucking terrified of what's happening here. And then... that guy.... what the fuck? It's all too... too weird."
"Just go home Matt. You're too far gone to make any sense, so just go home."
"But Gram..." He was too drunk to forage for any more words and the logic of his sentence seemed to abandon him. "... I mean Gram... mate?"

Gram stared at him impassively, his anger abating: "Nothing is going on. Nothing that's any of your business anyway." He climbed into the truck and started the engine. Through the open window he addressed Matt, "Get out of the way. I'm right in the mood to run you over."

Matt moved uneasily away, taking refuge between two other vehicles: "Gram... we need to just... y'know, talk...?"
Moving the vehicle forward, Gram looked sideways at him through the window: "No Matt. *You* need to talk. But *I'm* not interested in your bullshit..." He revved the van and drove towards the exit gate.

Drive-By Shouting

Chapter 8
The following morning - Crouch End

The next morning Gram woke up on his settee and allowed his gaze to settle on the crushed Stella Artois cans and roach butts which littered the coffee table. The TV and table lights were on, although the sun was sufficiently strong through the lounge curtains to suggest that it was mid-morning at least. He heard a clattering from the kitchen before Colin appeared in the doorway:

"Christ Gram, what a whiff, it bloody ronks in here. What a state!" He moved over to the windows and swept back the curtains, the sun flooding into the room. As Colin opened the sash window for fresh air, Gram allowed his eyes to readjust and assessed his condition, still fully dressed, he felt sweaty and uncomfortable as a queasy ball moved around in his stomach. His throat felt raw.

With a husky croak, he implored Colin: "Make us a cuppa, would you Col?"

"Already have, it's just brewing. What happened to you last night? I got in around eleven, but you were already

Drive-By Shouting

comatose. Looks like you smoked most of Jamaica last night."

Gram scanned the coffee table once more: "Yes, I may have overdone it a little. I was a bit upset." He was about to recount the tale of Matt Mann, the arsehole guitarist from *The Undertakers* and how he had meted out retributive justice to him for the guitar vandalism, when his horrific omission flooded back to him:
"Oh shit Colin. I've really fucked up." He sat upright, immediately regretting it, as a wave of nausea hit him. Despite his tenderness, he quickly rose to his feet.
Colin stared at him querulously: "What've you done?"
Gram could barely bring himself to say the words: "I've... I've left all of the back line at The Fleadh! I meant to go back later!" He groaned and closed his eyes, "Shit! Shit! shit! I've been really stupid. I'll have to go!" He stumbled through to the bathroom and splashed water onto his face and hair, before retrieving his jacket and opening the front door. He shouted behind him, "Sorry Col, I've been a total wanker and I need to try to rescue this!"

Colin heard the door slam.

Driving once more through Finsbury Park's North gate, Gram clung to a faint hope, although in his heart, he already knew it was a lost cause. Coming over the brow of the hill down towards the main stage, he could see riggers dismantling the stage structure. Within five minutes he had established that the drum kit and

Drive-By Shouting

amplifiers had gone, and he knew with certainty that this meant they had gone for good.

His head pounding, he re-parked the van away from the stage and ordered coffee from the Italian cafe at the lake. After two coffees and some toast, he was able to properly evaluate the situation and the prospects were not good.

He stared across at a family pushing buggies around the lake and decided to make a phone call. Kate answered almost immediately:
"Kate, it's Gram."
"Gram! I hadn't expected to hear from you so soon."
"Well, that makes two of us; I hadn't expected to need to call so soon. Listen Kate, I've had a bit of a fuck up and I'm really at a loss about what to do. Don't know why, but you were the first person I thought of calling."
Even in the blur of his hangover, he knew why. His only other option these days was Colin and he rarely had anything sage to offer.
She sounded concerned: "What's happened? Are you ok? Where are you now? I can come straight over."
"No, no, I'll come to you if that's okay. I need to get away from the scene of my stupidity. What's your address?"
"Okay, but come straight over, yeah?"

He jotted down the information and, armed with her location, tentatively drove the van out of the park towards Crouch End.

Drive-By Shouting

Twenty minutes later

They sat at the garden table. Kate was drinking tea, while Gram was on his second pint of cold water:
"So what can you do? Can you retrieve the situation?" Gram massaged his forehead: "Simply put, no. I've really buggered it all up. The gear is done for. Someone will have loaded all of it into a van. Probably sold it already." Gram smiled wryly, "They'll fire me, no question about that. Abandoning the gear is a cardinal sin; there is simply no excuse for it. Even without me doing that I think that punching the client in the face is also frowned upon." He managed a wry smile. "So, in one fell swoop, I'll definitely lose my income and my van." He continued to massage his forehead.

"Without overstating it, this is a bit of a crisis point for me Kate. Yesterday has to be the end of all the craziness, because I'm just wrecking everything at the moment. I've kind of gone off my head for the past few years; ever since Cymbal got dropped really, and I really want to break the pattern. I go through phases of being productive, of thinking that I can make things happen, and I beaver away at music and get really enthusiastic. Then I hit the inevitable wall of silence, where whatever I do just gets ignored, just kind of goes into a vacuum. And then I fall back on smoking too much and drinking too much, and you get results like yesterday's cock-up.
"So why don't you stop it?"
"You think it's that simple?"
"Yes, I do. Just stop it."

Drive-By Shouting

He looked at her doubtfully "The bigger problem is my rage. I've got myself so wrapped up in bitterness and anger. Anger that everybody else seems to have got ahead in their careers, while I've just repeatedly banged my head against the wall. And now, I can go from zero to full on-rage at the flip of a switch."

"I know. I still haven't forgotten the duck-pond!" She smiled fondly to let him know she was being light-hearted.

"Well, like I said, I'm sorry about what happened then. It was pathetic, me going off at you like that. But really, that was nothing compared to what happens when I really get confronted with the injustice of it all. The thing that really triggers it is when I'm face-to-face with the Music Biz bullshit, how it hands success to all the wrong people."

She looked at him doubtfully: "Really, do you think that? Because, there are plenty of brilliant artists out there who fully deserve to be there."

"No, I don't mean everybody. I'm not talking about the Bowie's or McCartney's or Prince. But I do go mad at the Matt Mann's, and *The Undertakers,* those people are just too much of a slap in the face. And it's my inability to be rational in the face of those people getting success that leads me into crazy situations like yesterday. It's like I turn into The Hulk or something. And the whole thing was triggered by the guitar. It just seemed to symbolize the whole stinking, warped set-up. I just blew my top. And I find it scary that I've become like that, because I didn't used to be that sort of guy."

"I know that. I wouldn't have bothered saying hello to you if I had thought that that was who you were. And,

Drive-By Shouting

I may as well tell you, I was pretty surprised by your anger at the duck pond, because, other than when you drunkenly decided to tip beer over me." Again, she smiled re-assuringly, "I'd always really enjoyed your company. You were always by far the funniest guy out of all the bands when you were in the mood to be. And I think that guy is still in there, he's just getting a bit edged out by The Hulk at the moment!" She beamed warmly at him.

"Thank you. That's good to hear... I do want to get back to being that guy 'cos he was a lot happier. But, what now? I've only ever been in bands, making records, touring, and other than that I've lumped heavy gear around the place. So, I've just screwed myself for any of the other music service companies, because this cock up will follow me everywhere I go. Trouble is, I'm unemployable for anything else, and it's not what you'd call a conventional CV."

"So, what are you going to do?"

"That's just it. I haven't got a clue which way to turn. Sorry to bring this to your door Kate, but I just don't know what to do. And I don't know why, but you were the person I wanted to talk to."

She rested her chin on her hand and mulled for a while. Eventually she spoke: "Gram... I think this may be a good thing that's happened."

"You are kidding! Why?"

"Hear me out." She looked intently at him. "Can I be blunt with you Gram?"

He looked at her uneasily; "Okay... Go on."

Drive-By Shouting

"I've only just got back on to friendly terms with you. But I'm going to just risk all that and tell you what I really think. If that's ok?"
He considered this and nodded: "That's fine. I need some straight talking." Even as he said it, he doubted that he actually wanted to hear whatever was coming.
"Okay. When I look at you, I see a really bright talented guy. I see a guy with real potential, who's funny and kind, and is lovely to talk to. But, from everything you tell me, I suspect that that's not what you see when you look in the mirror?"

Gram shrugged in acknowledgement of the truth. She continued:
"But for a few twists of fate, and a few less bitches in the press," she gave a wry smile, "you could have been a really successful artist. But the fates didn't conspire to give you that and, while I may have had a role in denying you that, it was probably a minor role in the greater scheme of things." She looked at Gram sincerely. "But, leaving that aside, you need to put all that behind you and look forward. I really think you can do better than this. And this is not just my slight guilty conscience talking!"
Gram rubbed his chin:" I know. I think I probably blew your role out of all proportion, I think I just needed someone to blame, because it all seemed so unfair."

"I get that. But just because that particular rock star scenario didn't pan out, you're still this lovely, intelligent, creative guy and to be frank, I can't believe that you're stuck doing all this roadie shit."
"Me neither…"

Drive-By Shouting

"You probably don't remember this, but when I first met you, it was in a pub in Camden when I'd been sent to interview you all."

"I do remember, I thought you looked far too good-looking to be a journalist. I figured you'd got the job on looks, so you'd be crap!"

"Hmmm, well let's leave that to one side for another day! Anyway, I'm glad you remember, because I came away thinking that you were this amazing guy. You just seemed so sussed, like you'd got the world figured out. And you were bloody funny that day too. And so, to see that we're here, ten years down the line and you're driving a van. It breaks my heart Gram, honestly!

It's almost like you've been punishing yourself for the lack of success, doing the shittiest job available, because you were denied the top prize. You'll have to forgive my bluntness but that's real *victim* behaviour, hobbling yourself with the worst outcome, just to prove how wronged you were. Because, if you believe that you've had a mortal blow struck against you, that's forever condemned you to this shit fate, then you certainly won't prove yourself wrong. It becomes self-perpetuating. It's impossible to succeed without acknowledging that your core belief is wrong. It really is time to move on Gram, you're not completely thick! You must be able to do something better than this."

Gram shrugged. "But what? Who's going to hire me? I wouldn't know where to start with getting a job. And it's not as if my skills are transferable. All I've ever done is writing, play and produce music. I can't do anything else."

"Produce? I didn't know you did that?"

Drive-By Shouting

"Well yeah, I sort of unofficially produced a lot of the Cymbal stuff and then, a couple of years ago, during one of my dope-free phases, I started developing a girl band and we released a few indie singles for them last year. They looked really promising, but after a few radio plays on evening shows, it all just faded away."
"I had no idea you'd done that. Who was it?"
"Oh, you won't have heard of them. They were called *Blue Dolls*."

She looked at him with sudden intense interest: "You produced *Blue Dolls*? I loved them! They had that brilliant single *Manifesto*. Now, *that* should have been a hit! And it was a great production too. Wow, I'm impressed. And aside from the production, what a great song!"
"Thank you, I wrote it." He smiled proudly.

Kate's eyes widened in appreciation: "Wow, you really do hide yourself under a bushel, don't you? If I'd written and produced that, I'd wear a big badge saying so. All of the time!"
"Yeah, but it failed and I can't brag about something that, other than you, nobody's heard of. I think it sold less than a thousand copies, so not exactly a smash hit."
"But Gram, that's not what's important and it's not the way to measure what you do. I mean, what does the general public know? Millions of people buy burgers every day, but that doesn't mean it's good food?
You've produced loads of work that you can be proud of, irrespective of whether it sold. Because, as you've already seen, that's random, down to a hundred

Drive-By Shouting

arbitrary decisions from radio schedulers, critics, and, of course plain dumb luck. Release it at the right time, you get a hit, release it at the wrong time and you get nothing. But for you, as an artist, *you* make really great work and that really is the important bit."

Gram gave an ironic smile: "And like all of the artists through history, I get to starve into the bargain. Or, do menial work."
"Okay, we've already established that you're wasted doing all this roadie shit, so even if they don't fire you tomorrow I really think you should jack it all in."
"And do what?"
"Produce! Because you're certainly good enough. But you'll never believe that you are while you're doing all this menial crap."
"And what do I live on? I mean, I'm signing on as well, but it's really not enough to live on."
Kate's eyebrows shot upwards. "Really? You're signing on? Well, that needs to stop too, because if anything is going to rob you of your self-worth, it's being on the dole. Anyway, you don't need to worry about money. I've got money, and frankly, I do owe you one."

Gram shifted uncomfortably in his chair: "I'm not taking charity Kate."
"So, you're uncomfortable taking my money, but you'll happily sign on illegally? Interesting moral dilemma!" She grinned conspiratorially at him.
"That's different. I can't just take money from you for nothing. And anyway, you've enough big problems of your own, without taking on mine."

Drive-By Shouting

Kate momentarily looked alarmed: "What do you mean by that? What big problems have I got?"

Gram had instantly realised his mistake, but still railed against having to reveal everything that he knew, although the compulsion to tell all was becoming overwhelming, as the closer he got to Kate, the worse he felt about covering it up. "I mean... I know that you're in a difficult position right now and that you don't need my employment or career issues piled on top of that."

She spoke slowly and deliberately: "And what are my precise problems Gram?"

The fog in Gram's head's swirled and the queasy ball in his stomach rotated as he sought to steer away from the tricky waters, but the pull of the deep was too great. He couldn't bring himself to lie to her and realised that the only option he had was to fully explain himself. Kate continued to stare at him expectantly.
"The thing is Kate... I know you're having issues with Steve and your marriage... And... I also know about Matt and the affair."
Kate visibly recoiled.

"And I know about the baby."
She closed her eyes and slumped in her chair.
"Kate. I should have told you earlier that I knew, and I nearly did on a couple of occasions. But I really hadn't planned on bumping into you and then, when I was still unsure about how I felt about you and all the shit from the past, there was just never the right time to

Drive-By Shouting

broach the subject. Are you okay about me saying this?"

He looked up at her, but her eyes were still closed and tears were rolling down her cheeks: "Oh Kate, I'm so sorry; I really didn't mean to upset you."
She wiped her eyes with the back of her hand and sniffed: "Don't be sorry. It's sort of a relief. I haven't told anyone else about it, apart from my sister and of course, Matt, who was a total arsehole about it all." She sniffed again and rubbed her nose, "I presume it was him that told you? Well, it must have been; nobody else knows."
"Yes, he did."
She looked confused: "But why? He told me that the two of you weren't friends, and if the atmosphere between the two of you yesterday is anything to go by, I'd say that you're anything but friends. I thought you were going to punch him, and that was *before* you went completely tonto with the guitar guy."
"I should have done."
"So why, of all people, did he tell you?"

Gram rubbed his chin thoughtfully: "I'm not sure I can tell you this Kate."
She looked up imploringly at him: "Well, you have to now. Because this sounds like something I should know."
He breathed deeply to quell his rising nausea: "Okay. I don't see why I should protect him anymore. But I'm worried that you may be a bit… upset by what I'm about to say. Don't shoot the messenger."

Drive-By Shouting

Gram felt his throat tighten, he didn't feel any loyalty to Matt anymore, but his default position had always been not to snitch. He felt his tongue press against his teeth like he had to stop it wagging. He longed to tell Kate how he'd waged war on Matt but knew that he'd done so to avenge his own slights, not Kate's.

She wiped her eyes again and looked at him intently. "Go on..."
Gram rubbed his face with his hands until he could delay no longer. "Well, like you've just done, Matt also spotted that I'm a bit down on my luck. The difference is, where you've tried to help me, Matt only ever sees opportunities for himself in other people's misfortune. And I think he saw me as somebody who was open to being manipulated. He asked me to meet him in Groucho's because, obviously, Matt likes to show his life off to me. I'm his yardstick to measure his achievements against, so he can really see how far he's risen by comparison with me.

I usually only see him once a year for an awkward birthday pint, but this year he was mad keen for us to meet about six weeks earlier than usual, so I knew he was up to something. Anyway, he told me about the, frankly ludicrous, situation he's got himself into, and all the ramifications for him with Steve. How his whole career could go down the chute. And then, he made a rather improper suggestion, which, before we go any further, I want to emphasise, I refused to have any part of. It's important that you know that.'

She sat frozen in anticipation. "Go on."

Drive-By Shouting

"After he'd told me about the two of you and outlined all of the dangers and inconveniences to him, without really making much reference to what this might be doing to your life, he suggested that..." He looked warily at her, "Basically…, he wanted to employ me, to engineer a meeting with you. To become your friend. And to steer you away from telling Steve." Fearful of losing his nerve, he raced on. "And, if possible, to persuade you to have an abortion." He forced himself to meet Kate's eye again. She was horrorstruck.
"The bastard!"
"Yes, isn't he just? I had a massive row with him. Told him to fuck right off and stormed out. And then, against all the odds, I just randomly bumped into you the following week."

She sat stunned: "God, you must have loved that, given how much you hated me?"
He shrugged: "Honestly? I was too full of my own bile to spare any in your direction!"

There was a long pause, before Kate fixed her eyes on him: "So, just to be clear Gram. How random was it? Are you, or are you not, being paid by Matt to make friends with me?"
"No! I thought I'd explained that very clearly. God, how low do you think I'll go? I promise you, I told him where to stick it! And it was then a ridiculous coincidence that we met in the park. And, actually, it was you who approached me, if you remember, not the other way around?"
She mulled it over: "Yes, I do remember."

Drive-By Shouting

"Kate, I would never have anything to do with his sleazy scheme, and obviously, when he suggested it all, I didn't even refuse out of any loyalty to you, because we hadn't 'made up' yet. It was simply that I refused to be some pawn that he could move around the chessboard. But I did think it was a shitty thing to try to manipulate someone in your situation, even if at the time, you weren't amongst my favourite people. But, I promise you Kate, I'm a hundred per cent on your side now and a hundred per cent committed to somehow poking Matt Mann in his fat face." He looked up to find Kate's wet eyes locked on him.

"Okay Gram, I believe you. But I'm just stunned that he would try to manoeuver me in this way. He must be fucking desperate."

"He's petrified, because he knows that his whole world might implode at any minute." Silence hung in the air between them for a few seconds before he reached over and placed his hand lightly on Kate's. He was aware that their roles had entirely switched during the previous few minutes.
"I know this is a lot to take in Kate. But, aside from Matt Mann being a manipulative bastard, what are you going to do?"
She looked distraught as she considered this: "I really don't know, it's such a fucking mess, and it's all my own fault."

"I still don't understand how somebody like you could end up in this mess, with of all people, Matt! I mean, from the outside it would appear that you've got

Drive-By Shouting

everything: money, success, and, you're pretty gorgeous."
"Thank you, that's sweet of you to say." She flashed him a forced smile. "I guess he just caught me at a weak point. My marriage to Steve's been... less of a marriage, more of a public profile for over two years. We don't live as 'man and wife,' if you follow my meaning?"
"I think I do."
"But, despite the end of any marital relations, Steve's still basically continued to be kind and generous, to me at least. He still represents me professionally and puts me up for all the good jobs, which is how I ended up doing the maternity cover on *Live at 10!*

I'd got to know Matt a bit better since being with Steve, obviously, although I'd always thought he was a bit of an empty vessel. Like we said yesterday, 'vacantly Byronic.' Anyway, working together every day, you talk endlessly. Co-presenting is a bit like an arranged marriage, where you're thrown together and forced to 'get along.' But, through all of the talk, I thought I saw another side to him. Although, I now think that it was just me seeing what I wanted to see. It was also probably a bit of me sort of projecting an image onto a blank canvas. Maybe I was as much to blame as he was, with his ability to look like whatever you want. Anyway, I was lonely, and one thing led to another; and this is the result." She unconsciously rested her hands on her abdomen.

Gram's eyes followed her hands to her lap: "And how far gone are you?"

Drive-By Shouting

"Three months. And I still haven't got a clue what to do."
"Well, there's a high price to keeping the baby isn't there? It'd surely mean a permanent split from Steve. It sounds like he'll definitely know it's not his, but maybe that's a good thing. Your marriage doesn't sound like a bed of roses."

"Oh, on the surface it is. He's rich, successful and knows everyone who's anyone. So we've lived a real social whirl. But, you're right – I've seen a side of Steve that I'm... uncomfortable with, which has made me withdraw into myself around him, which is very isolating. And it's pathetic to be lonely in your own marriage. Surely that's the antithesis of what it's supposed to be about? Whatever I decide to do with the baby, the marriage is over.

My choices are do I keep my baby or not? At the moment, I can't even contemplate the idea of getting rid of it. It's my baby after all, and I may not get another chance. And if I do keep it, do I reveal that Matt is the father? And, by doing that, find myself in the middle of a particularly messy shit-storm? Obviously, what you've just told me makes me want to wipe the smile off Matt's manipulative gob, but that's not a good enough reason on its own."

"How will you be financially? I have to ask." he grinned in an attempt to lighten the mood. "Especially as you're going around town offering money to every wannabe record producer you meet!"

Drive-By Shouting

A reluctant smile flickered across Kate's face, as she attempted to join in with the levity: "Financially darling, I'm tickety boo." The sadness quickly returned to her face. "I still own this flat, which I bought before meeting Steve. It's been rented out for the last few years, but the tenant moved out six months ago and I decided to keep it available for me. I kind of figured that I might need it. But, I've also got money, Steve is very generous and he'll be fair when we split. I've also made quite a lot from the books, and presenting has been pretty good. So, money isn't an issue."

"How nice for you!" Gram immediately regretted his tone. "Sorry, that sounded bitter. I have to remember that I've, we've, moved beyond all that resentment stuff. What I mean is, I'm glad. At least you don't have to worry on that front. But you've still got some big decisions to make."

Kate sat in silence as she thought, before smiling defiantly at Gram: "And so have you Gram, so let's be decisive together." Her mood lifted as she stood up. "Christ, this has been like the heaviest group therapy session on record! We've managed to completely deconstruct each other in half and hour! Are you hungry?"

"Starving, but I think that's the hangover talking!"

She picked up her purse and house keys: "C'mon then, let's go and get brunch at *Banners*. We can make some plans."

Drive-By Shouting

Drive-By Shouting

Part 4

Bridge Two

Drive-By Shouting

Chapter 9
Marlow, Buckinghamshire - 1985

From the M40, Matt steered the lumbering mass of his Vauxhall Viva estate towards town, the car labouring under the weight of its seven occupants. Sitting alongside him, Gram took in the quaint charm of Marlow, its timeless picture postcard high street, distinctly unlike the windblown concrete satellite towns outside Liverpool, where he had grown up.

Matt provided a running commentary. "So, this is the old town, but we live down the hill nearer to the train station. Not as quaint, but it's where all the fuck-off mansions are! And did I ever tell you that one of the Bee Gees lives in our road?"
Gram smirked: "Yes, but only a million times!"

Matt cornered at a roundabout, eliciting complaints from the occupants of the boot space (their bandmates, Colin & Kevin), as they rolled chaotically into each other and the sidewalls. The second row of seats cooed amiably. It comprised Jen, along with

Drive-By Shouting

Jackie & Sarah, Gram and Kevin's current girlfriends respectively. Despite his deep longing, Colin still didn't have a girlfriend.

After a few more turns of the groaning car, they came to a road lined with elaborate gates, so high that they obscured everything bar the vast expense of ornate finials that topped the distant gables. Gram's sense of foreboding intensified. After about five hundred yards, they turned through a set of impressive pillars, the change in the cars acoustics signaling that they were driving over gravel onto the circular driveway of a large opulent house. To Gram's eyes, it looked like a manor, with the front door set into a tower which rose up the front of the house, with numerous windows suggesting a staircase rising up its three stories. Matt shrugged it off with nonchalant irony: "Yeah, it's a shithole, but it's home!"

Carrying his rucksack into the house, Gram felt the familiar mix, the drag of unworthiness, mixed with indignation that this style of living was available to some people, at the expense of others. The unworthiness always won out and he fought to bolster himself to be, at least to observer's eyes, uncowed by the ostentatious wealth.

Having established that the house was empty, Matt herded the party into the kitchen and immediately raided the fridge, although it appeared relatively bare: "Don't worry, mother must be down at Waitrose. I told her to get a total car load." Gram wondered why he emphasised the word 'Waitrose'. It was a Southern

Drive-By Shouting

supermarket brand, not seen in the North. It was Tesco or nothing at home, but a supermarket was a supermarket, surely?

He found himself being escorted on a tour of the property, Matt relishing the opportunity to show off the house. It was indeed the biggest house Gram had ever been in. Having traversed the other two levels, they descended the stairs in time to witness the arrival of Matt's mother, who leaned up to kiss him on the cheek once he had skipped across the parquet hallway, like an eager puppy.

"Matthew, darling! What on earth have you done to your hair? You look an awful fright!"

He feigned indignation at the comment, for the amusement of his guests: "Oh mum, don't embarrass me!" while fanning himself melodramatically with his hands.

They were introduced in turn, each receiving a limp handshake from Mrs. Mann. Gram thought it might have been the coldest handshake he had ever received. After the car had been relieved of its full load of shopping, Matt shepherded the visiting party into the garden, where they began drinking the beers that had arrived with Mrs. Mann. As the afternoon wore on into evening, they were joined by a succession of Matt's old school friends, each seeming to Gram to be even posher than the last. He couldn't help but reflect on the vast chasm that existed between the free flow of friends and alcohol in Matt's home and the rigid authoritarian

Drive-By Shouting

rule of his own parental home. He couldn't recall more than four or five friends ever having visited him at home and they had been made so unwelcome by his father that they had soon left. The idea that he could host a similar gathering to this in his parent's small overly neat back garden was simply preposterous. People simply didn't do that in Maghull. If you wanted a party there, you bought beers at the off-licence and drank them in the park, taking care to pick a space not frequented by the hard nuts, who were always available for a fight on a summer's evening.

As he drank his third beer, Gram continued to consider the contrast between the welcome afforded to Matt and whomever he wished to invite and the cloying atmosphere of his own home. Yes, Matt's mother clearly disapproved of his new polytechnic friends (the coldness of her greeting still lingered with him), but she was happy to allow him free reign over her house and garden and to feed and water whoever he invited. On the upside, he mulled, there was plenty to drink.

As dusk started to gather, a group of three pretty local girls arrived, hugging Matt like he was their collective long lost love. He supplied drinks to all three of them before sitting in a private group of four chairs a few feet from everybody else. Jen, already inebriated, helped herself to another drink and pretended to ignore the proceedings, with only the occasional sad glance in Matt's direction revealing her true feelings.

By about 10pm, Jen could barely speak and was helped into bed by Jackie and Sarah. The gathering gradually

Drive-By Shouting

thinned, as the locals drifted home, leaving the four band members and a few others in the garden. Matt and one of the three pretty girls had now joined the main group and in the dim light that bled out from the house, Gram could see his left arm nonchalantly draped round the girl's shoulder, fingers languorously caressing her clavicle and occasionally slipping under the fabric of her blouse. The group was animatedly discussing the highs and lows of David Bowie's career, a subject the band members never tired of debating. While Colin was in mid-flow, controversially proposing that *Loving the Alien* was up there with Bowie's best work (on account of its bass line), Gram sensed movement to his left and turned to see Matt rising from his seat, in tandem with the girl. They turned and, hands lightly held, walked into the darkness of the garden, in the direction, Gram recalled, of a summerhouse at the far end.

The girl's two friends nudged each other.
"See, told you! Nothing changes! Girlfriend or not, a leopard doesn't change its spots!" They giggled drunkenly and Gram turned once more, just in time to see the ghostly image of Matt and his accomplice disappearing completely into the darkness.

The next morning, Gram awoke early and ventured downstairs in search of food. Mrs. Mann was busily bustling around the kitchen.
"Oh, good morning, it's you. I'm sorry, too many names, which one are you again?"

Drive-By Shouting

"Gram."
"Well, Gram, good to see another early riser; very commendable. I'm just making some tea and toast for another one of your lot, who's out in the garden. Why don't you go out and join her and I'll bring you some too?"

She turned and, having been dismissed, Gram walked through the French doors, where he found Jen staring disconsolately at the table.

"Hi, didn't think anybody else would be up yet."
She looked up blearily: "Yes, it's bloody annoying. I really want to sleep in, but I can't. I think I might still be a little bit drunk. No hangover yet, so I'm guessing that it's on its way soon." She rubbed her swollen eyes and rocked on the chair. Matt's mother delivered the promised tea and toast with unsmiling cold efficiency. "So, you two, here you go." She turned and quickly retreated into the kitchen.

Jen greedily bit into the toast and was midway through a second bite when, over her shoulder, Gram saw Matt emerging from the summerhouse, some two hundred yards away. His companion closely followed him. Seeing Gram and Jen on the terrace, Matt stopped and contemplated for a moment, before appearing to come to a decision. He then continued up the garden towards them, friend in tow.

With her back still to the garden, and unaware of the impending arrival, Jen had continued to ram toast into her already overloaded mouth and, cheeks bulging,

Drive-By Shouting

was unable to answer when surprised by Matt's cheery greeting.

"Morning both! Beautiful eh?" Jen turned to see Matt and his accomplice as they ambled towards the patio. Even from his oblique angle, Gram could sense Jen's shock. She quickly spun around and gulped down the contents of her mouth. She turned again and spoke as the pair arrived at the table: "Where have you been?"

He was nonchalant: "Oh, just crashed out in the summerhouse. There's a bed and a settee in there. We were catching up. You met Deborah last night, yeah?" He thumbed a reference to the girl. "Yes, we did sixth form together and were just chatting. Must have just fallen asleep. How about you two, did you sleep okay?"

Even though he had now known Matt for some time, Gram was still astonished by his brazen performance and apparent indifference to the barely concealed distress etched on Jen's face. She sat, dumbstruck, as Matt breezily extolled the joys of his parent's garden and last night's boozy gathering. Eventually, Deborah, who had at least the good grace to look uncomfortable with the situation, butted in on Matt's monologue.
"Listen everyone, I should go, my mum will be worried, I didn't mean to, you know, fall asleep?" She bid some awkward farewells and Matt followed her towards the kitchen, addressing them over his shoulder as he left: "I'll just say cheerio to Debs, see you in a minute."

Drive-By Shouting

They disappeared from view and Gram once more looked at Jen's sadness and distress. Before his eyes, the expression melted into one of resigned acceptance, as her mental turmoil seemed to have reached some sort of conclusion.

"Are you okay Jen? Are you okay with all that?" He gestured towards the kitchen. She steeled herself to speak,
"Of course, she's just an old friend. You heard him, they just fell asleep." She looked at him defiantly. For her, the matter was settled. Gram held her gaze for a moment, before raising an eyebrow and reaching for his tea. They sat in an uncomfortable silence, before Matt once more emerged from the kitchen and walked around to stand behind Jen's chair, resting his hands on her neck and gently massaging her shoulders.

"So, my cherub, how are you feeling? You sank a few last night. Had to be put to bed!" She closed her eyes as he rubbed her neck and shoulders, before reaching a hand up to rest on his, allowing him to interlace his fingers with hers.
"Oh, I'm okay so far, might have to lie down for a bit though."
"Well, I might lie down with you, in that case." Matt looked at Gram, grinned and winked. Gram found that he had involuntarily returned the grin and immediately felt ashamed. He got up, gathered his plate and cup and retreated into the house, leaving Matt to caress his girlfriend.

Drive-By Shouting

Part 5

Chorus

Drive-By Shouting

Chapter 10
East Sussex 1999 - The day after the Fleadh

Matt pressed the 'End Call' button as (yet again) Gram's voicemail kicked in: "For fuck's sake. Answer, you bastard!" He muttered to himself. He heard Jen calling from downstairs and shouted in reply. "What? I can't hear you!"

After a moment, she appeared in the bedroom doorway: "I've been calling you for five minutes. Breakfast's ready and on the table." She eyed the phone in his hand, "Who have you been calling?"
"Oh, it was just Gram. Didn't really get to talk to him much yesterday. I just wanted to catch up."

Jen looked to him doubtfully: "I don't know why you bother. He's a loser. And anyway, he didn't look too pleased to see you yesterday, barely said a word. And, at the risk of repeating myself, Kate Craw gets to be more of an awkward bitch every time I see her. Did you see the weird way she was looking at us?"
Matt stared at her impatiently: "Didn't we discuss all this last night?"
"Yes. But you weren't exactly making much sense!"
He sighed: "Well, anyway, it's nothing personal. I think she and Steve are struggling a bit, that's all."

Drive-By Shouting

"Well, that's hardly surprising if she's hanging out with other guys. I mean, even scraping the barrel with someone like Gram. She must be desperate."

Matt turned and looked at her quizzically: "What, you think there's something going on between the two of them?"
"Dunno, but they're both weird and they certainly seemed to be as thick as thieves yesterday. And anyway, how do you know things are difficult with her and Steve? I thought you'd barely spoken to him since he's been in the States?"

Matt feigned nonchalance: "Oh, he mentioned something briefly. Said it was hard being apart for so long. And Kate did mention something when we did the co-presenting together."

Jen looked askance at him: "I thought you said it was all a bit strained between you two when you worked together, that you didn't really get on?"
"Oh it was...You know, it was nothing. She just mentioned something in passing, that's all."
"Hmmm, really? I reckon you're not telling me the full story, as usual Matt. But anyway, the kids are at the table and the food is getting cold, so let's just get down there, eh?"

Later that afternoon, Matt awoke in a garden recliner, feeling parched. He walked unsteadily through the pool house and got a cold Coke from the fridge,

Drive-By Shouting

draining it in one go. His head still throbbed from yesterday's excesses, which had continued once they had returned home to Sussex, but that was nothing compared with the turmoil in his mind.

Just what the hell was going on? First of all, Gram refused to have anything to do with the idea of befriending Kate and the next thing he's arm in arm with her, backstage at The Fleadh, looking for all the world like they were 'together?' And both of them had been so weird. Matt felt doubly queasy at the thought that everything he held dear, his house, the rolling acres beyond, his status as a star of TV and music, all of this could be destroyed. That Kate and Gram held the key to it was terrifying.

So much of what he had was borne of his relationship with Steve Coombes. And if that relationship was destroyed, it would spell disaster. Steve had the Producer of *Live at 10!* in his pocket and one word from him would see Matt dropped like a stone. Yes, he would still have royalties from the songwriting publishing if he lost everything else, but those royalties had markedly declined lately and revelation of the affair might also wreck his own marriage, meaning he would have to split everything with Jen. She was proving far less compliant these days.

Historically, Jen had always taken the stance of 'preferring not to know,' but he had noticed a shift in her attitude in the last couple of years, and could no longer be quite sure that she would look the other way about his indiscretions, especially those so close to

Drive-By Shouting

home, and so destructive to their lives. Above all though, it was the thought of losing the house that horrified him most.

He mulled on the idea of simply getting in the car and driving to Crouch End. He could confront Gram and Kate and find out what plan they were hatching and do everything he could to prevent it. However, Jen was already keeping a watchful eye on him and she would definitely get suspicious if he disappeared for hours on a Sunday afternoon.

In many respects, Matt reflected, Jen had been the perfect wife for him. When they first started going out together in Northampton, Matt soon discovered she was very forgiving when it came to his off-piste activities. She had furious outbursts when his numerous dalliances inevitably came to light, but somehow, always seemed able to put it behind her.

After Northampton, they had remained a loose couple, both moving to London, although still maintaining separate flat shares, Matt had been very careful to avoid ever over committing and co-habiting with her. Over the next few years, he had pretty much done whatever he pleased (with whomever he pleased) and, so long as he was discreet and didn't openly humiliate her, Jen had still proved willing to turn a blind eye, providing him with the security of a long term girlfriend without the compromises that were usually demanded. This arrangement was never explicitly stated, but so long as his activities remained undisclosed, it remained in force.

Drive-By Shouting

He'd come to appreciate the huge benefits of this. When he wanted fun, he could have it. And when he wanted comfort and genuine affection she was always there. And so it was that they had eventually drifted into living together when *Cymbal* were signed to RGA Records. Matt was frequently travelling, or recording away from home, which gave him the necessary outlet he needed, and he consequently never felt stifled by living with her. Jen had morphed from the free arty spirit that he had been drawn to in Northampton, but still retained the essential hippy outlook, although, to Matt's knowledge, she had never strayed elsewhere. So, on every level, Matt was happy to let the relationship role on.

Throughout it all, he had never imagined that he would end up married to her. Then, when she had got pregnant with Callum, it had forced a decision on him. Eight years later, he was still rather bemused that he had been quietly ushered into this role, but compared to most husbands; he had seemed to have a fair amount of leeway. At least until the last couple of years.

It was once Matt had become a public figure that Jen's appetite for 'looking the other way' had evaporated and he had consequently had to be far more circumspect in conducting his affairs. Since coming off the last *Kensal Rise* tour and starting on *Live at 10!* Matt had, without Jen's knowledge, quietly purchased a small terraced house in Waterloo, just two minutes from the TV studios. He never stayed overnight, but it was a very useful base in the afternoons, his absence

Drive-By Shouting

from home explained to Jen as 'long production meetings' for the following day's show. It was here that he had taken Kate and where the affair had been conducted.

He pictured Kate, her golden hair spread on the pillow in the Waterloo house. He had liked her a lot. Despite all of his better judgment, he found himself incredibly drawn to her and this had overridden any loyalty to Steve Coombes. Anyway, by then, Kate had also confided that things were rocky with Steve and so he convinced himself that he wasn't doing anything untoward in seducing her. It wasn't like she and Steve had a happy marriage anyway, was it?

He once more pulled his mobile phone out of his pocket and selected Kate's number. It went straight to voicemail.

Drive-By Shouting

Chapter 11
A few days later - The London Studios

"Coming to titles... And... In thirty..." The vision mixer's voice counted down the clock in Matt's earpiece, as he mechanically read the goodbye script off the autocue. As the voice counted down from ten, Matt forced a cheery smile, playfully slapped Faith Lerner on the leg and gave his trademark mock military salute to the camera, by way of farewell to the audience. The camera pulled back to give a wide shot and he animatedly engaged in an (apparently) hilarious tale with Faith as the credits rolled.

As the theme tune came to its conclusion, the voice in his ear said "And... We're clear!" At which, Matt's 'professional' face evaporated, replaced briefly by the one worn by frightened men the world over. Faith, in her usual Mother Earth persona, picked up on it as they rose to their feet.
"Matt, you've been looking a bit *off* this week, is everything okay?"
"Got a few things going on, that's all. Let's speak in a second." He gestured to the radio mics that were being removed by two of the sound guys. Faith knew the code, never discuss anything important while wearing

Drive-By Shouting

a radio mic, as your voice was invariably still booming out of the speakers in the studio gallery, for the entertainment of all of the production staff.

Once the mics were removed, they walked towards the dressing rooms, Matt rather reluctantly high-fiving Gordon, the over-friendly floor manager, on the way out of the studio.

Although Faith was a highly experienced old hand in journalism and TV presenting, she'd taken the time to bring Matt under her wing when he had first stood in for Simon Wood, after Simon had had his first bout of 'illness.' Matt, lacking any presenting experience (save for a hastily arranged Sunday spent practicing autocue scripts in an empty MTV studio, a favour pulled by Steve), had been unusually nervous to be pitched into co-presenting a ninety minute live show, with a two million audience. Faith, however, had been wonderful, gently guiding him on how to look natural on camera and quickly training him in tempering his gauche urge to jump in and talk over interviewee's answers.

He was retrospectively grateful for her patience and nurturing, but had other, and more calculated, motives for having sought to become close friends with Faith. He did genuinely like her, but at Steve's urging, Matt had determinedly set out to befriend Faith, even if he had to fake it. It was in Faith's 'gift' to decree whether he lasted one week or the whole three weeks as stand-in host. As she had said to him on their first, rather forced meeting: "This is like an arranged marriage, isn't

Drive-By Shouting

it? Although, of course, I do have an exit clause if you don't turn out to be my ideal husband!" She'd laughed, but he'd received the underlying message: "your fate is in my hands young man, so don't forget it." She regularly pulled rank, ensuring that it was she who single-handedly conducted the 'big-star' interviews, but Matt knew the score and very deliberately chose not to rock the boat.

The time invested in Faith had paid off when, two months after Simon Wood returned to the show, he'd been *outed* on the front page of the sleaziest Sunday newspaper, as a seasoned cocaine user. By Tuesday, it was all over for Simon and Steve had swiftly shoehorned Matt in as a temporary stand-in. Three years later, he was still here, with his annual contract set for renewal in the next month.

He followed Faith into her dressing room and slumped onto her couch as she sat at the illuminated mirror and began automatically wiping the make-up off her face. She viewed him in the mirror through one eye as she wiped away the thick foundation: "So, what's going on? You've been distracted all week, missing cues, losing your way with interviewees. Not really present." Matt blew out his cheeks: "I've got a few problems at home. You know, marriages, they have their ups and downs."
"Really? I thought you and Jen seemed like a good team. Anything you want to talk about? You've not been playing away, have you?" She winked at him in the mirror.

Drive-By Shouting

"No, no, just the usual pressures. Kids getting older, that sort of thing."
She looked at him impassively: "Hmmm, not very convincing Matthew, my dear. Remember, you can't kid a kidder. After three marriages, I can spot a man in trouble!"

Matt looked away, unwilling to give visual confirmation to Faith's hypothesis. He stood up: "Faith, I'm really sorry I've been so distracted. I'll sort it out, I promise. I'll just and go take my slap off. See you upstairs in ten?"
"Fair enough." She returned to removing her make-up.

He exited her room and ten yards along the corridor swung open the door to his own dressing room. He jumped back, startled to find his sofa occupied by the burly frame of Steve Coombes, talking quietly into a mobile phone. Steve looked at Matt, silently gesturing apology for being caught up on his phone call. He continued talking into the phone.
"... Anyway, look, I've got to go... Just going into a meeting... Yes, yes..., great, speak later."

He pressed the call end button, rose and approached Matt, still standing apprehensively at the open door. After a second of awkwardness, Steve nodded at Matt: "Good to see you," he half whispered, "shut the door. I don't want Faith seeing me! She's been badgering me about the bloody contract endlessly, and I could do without a repeat of the conversation. That's why I asked them to billet me in your dressing room discreetly." Steve's tone made his mood almost impossible to read.

Drive-By Shouting

"Yeah… good idea…." Matt fought to sound calm. "I thought you were in New York?"
Steve smiled "I was. Got into Heathrow this morning and then straight to the office, but I can't concentrate, so I thought I'd come over here to see you. I want to have a chat and it's not something I could talk about over the phone."
A chill went through Matt as Steve continued, "So, let's go over the road for some early lunch and we can talk." It wasn't phrased as a question.

Matt concentrated hard on keeping a neutral facial expression: "Well, obviously I'd love to, but the after-show debrief starts upstairs in the production office in ten minutes time, so I'm a bit..." Steve held up his hand to stop him, "Not a problem. I fixed it with Shula in Production; she's fine about you ducking the meeting. So, see you over the road at Mario's, the little Italian place, yeah? Now, pop your head out of the door and see if the coast is clear. I need to get down the corridor without bloody Faith seeing me."

Matt did as requested and watched as Steve swept past him, walking briskly towards the double doors at the end of the corridor. Matt turned, closed the door and sat at the table, looking at his made-up face in the mirror. A muscle underneath his left eye twitched vigorously.

Drive-By Shouting

Mario's Café - Waterloo – Twenty minutes later

By the time Matt entered the cafe, Steve was already working his way through a plate of food.
"Apologies, I couldn't wait. Sit down." He gestured to the chair opposite.
Matt ordered coffee and faced Steve: "I was pretty surprised to see you Steve; I thought you were staying in the States a bit longer?"
"I am." He took a pause from his food and rested his fork, "But I needed to come home for a couple of days to sort a few things."
"I thought that Vanessa in the office was looking after things ok? She's been very efficient with me."
"Oh, it's not that. Vanessa's great, and work on the whole is good, but I need to deal with Kate."
"Deal with Kate? That sounds ominous." Matt felt his pulse quicken.

"It's nothing sinister. Well, not really..." Steve paused and wiped his mouth with a napkin. "You know I told you a while ago that things were a bit strained at home? Well, it's a bit more serious than that. We've sort of drifted over the last year or so, what with me travelling so much and Kate spending her time writing. As you know, she'd always enjoyed going down to the coast on her own for a few days. But then she started spending more and more time at her old flat in Crouch End when the tenant left, says it gives her space to think. Which is ironic, given that the house in Hampstead is, as you know, huge? And most of the time, she's got the place to herself. Anyway, for

Drive-By Shouting

whatever reason, she's chosen to start living there, in Crouch End, pretty much full time."
Matt felt compelled to fill the silence. "Oh, I'm sorry, I didn't know."

Steve looked at him impassively: "Well, anyway, I've got friends who see her around town. And I've been hearing reports about her and I think she may be seeing somebody else." He looked directly again at Matt, "And I need to ask you a straight question and I need an honest answer." He held his gaze as Matt sat, not blinking and bracing himself. "Tell me honestly Matt. Is there anything going on between Kate and your mate from *Cymbal?*"

Matt gasped inwardly and reeled, trying to comprehend the question: "You think it's Gram?"
"Yeah, that's him. Stupid name, if you ask me..."

Having convinced himself in the previous forty seconds, that Steve might, in fact, have known the truth of his relationship with Kate, Matt now struggled to catch up with this new state of affairs. He tried to remain present as his mind whirred with the possibilities and dangers that the new situation presented.
"Steve, I just don't know anything about this. I haven't seen much of Kate since we finished the co-presenting stint, and I'm not really on speaking terms with Gram."

Steve looked at him archly. "But, you saw the two of them at The Fleadh? I heard they were there, together,

Drive-By Shouting

and that you and Jen were wandering around backstage too, and you were seen chatting to them?"
"Who said that?"
Steve leaned in: "Walls have ears, Matt."
The panic rose once more in Matt's chest: "I literally bumped into the two of them as we moved between backstage areas. We didn't really say much. And I was pretty much *plastered* anyway."

"Very professional Matt." Matt felt like a naughty child, squirming in the Headmasters office. "Anyway, I'd already been told it was frosty. But I also heard that you had a bit of an altercation with this Gram guy, down by his truck, after he'd decked some American idiot in a wig? I wondered if that was you asking him what the hell he was doing with my wife?"
"Who told you all this Steve? I feel a bit spied on?"
"I've got friends in low places Matt. But did you, or didn't you, have a row with him?"
"I did, but that was part of my ongoing ruck with him about the fucking song. He's still going on about how I 'stole' it from him."

Steve looked disappointed: "Really? So it wasn't about Kate?" He looked away in confusion. "Okay, I got the wrong end of the stick. I thought you'd seen them together and gone mad at him. On my behalf." His eyes once more returned to Matt. "I mean, didn't you think it odd? Your mate hanging around with my wife?"

Matt fought to hide his discomfort under Steve's gaze: "I just thought they'd bumped into each other, that's

Drive-By Shouting

all. I didn't read anything more into it than that. I've never seen them together before. And anyway, Gram's certainly not my mate any more so I was more focused on that, but I wouldn't jump to conclusions Steve. I can't imagine that Kate would stoop so low. I mean, the guy's a fucking roadie, sitting in a sweaty vehicle all day, delivering gear. And, all the while, signing on the dole. Can't really see Kate going for someone like that. I'm sure you're worrying unnecessarily."

Steve considered for a moment: "Signing on, is he? That might be useful... Why did he hit that bloke anyway?"
"No idea... he was acting pretty crazy."
"Thinks he's a hard-nut this guy, yeah?" He tore a chunk of bread with his teeth, even managing, to Matt's eyes, to look menacing during the simple act of eating. "Well, he's out of his league now. Because, whatever the truth of what's going on, Kate is hanging out with this guy loads. She's seen him quite a few times this week alone. And I'm not having' that!"
Matt's eyes narrowed: "Has she?" Matt wondered what this meant for him. "How'd you know all this Steve? Are you having Kate followed or something?"
Coombes ruminated while he chewed his bread, before quietly answering. "Between you and me, yes. Not all the time, but I've got a guy checking her out pretty regularly."
"Bloody hell Steve, that's pretty over the top. How long has he been tailing her?' Matt felt the sweat sticking his shirt to his back.
"For a couple of weeks..."

Drive-By Shouting

Matt inwardly unclenched at this news: "But not before that?"

Steve gave him a searching look: "That's a strange question, Matt. Why are you asking that?"

"Oh, you know, just wondering how long things have been bad Steve, that's all."

Steve held his gaze for an uncomfortable moment, before pushing his half-eaten food to one side: "Knowing what's going on is what I do. It's why I am what I am; which is the most connected agent in the fucking country. There's hardly a tea party at Buckingham Palace or 10 Downing Street that I'm not invited to... And remember, I come from the wrong side of the East End, the nasty grubby side. So, having some eyes and ears over here, is all part of my usual operation. And let's not forget, she *is* my wife?" She sounded like his possession, as if he'd invented her. "So, yeah, we've been having a bit of a rough patch, but that doesn't mean I'm going to leave her out there for other guys. It's just a difficult phase and we'll get over it."

Matt attempted to steer the conversation: "Why has that happened, do you think? I mean maybe you could talk to someone about it?"

"That's what I'm doing. I'm talking to you."

"I was meaning someone professional, y'know, a therapist?"

Coombes looked aghast at the suggestion: "You must be joking! Me? Seeing a therapist?"

Matt looked at the red face opposite him and re-considered: "Yeah, maybe not... But, on the other

Drive-By Shouting

hand, you might, y'know, get some insight into what went wrong?"
"Oh, I already know what went wrong. It's me, not her. She's amazing, she's like some kind of goddess to me, and always has been. But I think I've put her on such a high pedestal that now I can't bring myself to, you know, *get it on* with her.

I, frankly, like my sex filthy and dirty. I'm a guy who likes the stench of the street, that's where I'm the happiest. When I met her, I thought that she could pull me out of the gutter and up to her level, but that's proved rather difficult. So, it's my fault, not hers. I already know that." His face fell and he briefly looked vulnerable, something that Matt had never witnessed before. Almost instantly, the vulnerability vanished, to be replaced by the customary belligerence. "But I still don't want some other guy moving in on her. I may only take my Ferrari out a few times a year, but it's still *my* fucking Ferrari!"

Matt looked down partly to hide his shame and partly because the word on the tip of his tongue was 'Neanderthal.' "I get it Steve. So, what are you going to do?"
"Well, I need to speak to her. Ask her directly what's going on. She's not a dishonest person. I think she cares enough about me to tell me straight."
Matt consciously fought to keep any note of desperation from his voice: "Maybe you shouldn't Steve? Maybe it'll all go away if you just let it slide for a bit?"

Drive-By Shouting

Steve smiled wryly, and with his customary menace. "Do I strike you as the kind of guy to let things slide? No, I have to know, even if it's shit news, I'd rather know the truth. I'll go over this afternoon. Surprise her. I'll know more after that."
"She doesn't know you're back?"
"No, she still thinks I'm in New York."
"What time are you going over there?"
"I dunno, soon. Why? Why does that matter?"
"Sorry Steve, it doesn't. I don't know why I asked. Listen, I really do need to get back to the studio. I've got some stuff to do for tomorrow's show; you going to be okay?"
"Yeah, I'll be fine… You set off Matt. I'll settle up here."
"You're sure you're okay?"
Steve nodded mutely in assent.

Matt stood up, relieved that he was getting away from Steve's relentless eyes. "Listen Steve; call me when you've seen her. We can have a chat, yeah?" He turned and walked out of the cafe. He made his way up the road towards the studios, under the high railway arches carrying trains into Waterloo East Station. Just before The White Hart pub he turned and, after checking that he was unobserved, veered off to the right along the row of Victorian terraced houses. He glanced around him nervously again, before stopping and putting a key in the door of number thirty-one.

Once inside, he urgently keyed Kate's number, which instantly went to voicemail. He laboriously scrolled through letter menus and frantically composed a text message; 'STeve in LondOn. Call mE!' He pressed send

Drive-By Shouting

and sat down in an armchair, rubbing his temples and staring at the phone, willing it to ring. After a minute, it did so. He snatched it up and pressed the green button.
"Kate! Thank Christ!"
A curt, angry voice replied: "How do you know he's in London?"
"Because I just sat and watched him eat lunch! He came to the studios and was waiting in my dressing room, that's how!"
"So, I guess I'll see him when I see him." She sounded casual, which alarmed Matt.
"But Kate, he's coming to see you. He knows something's wrong; and I know that he's going to be asking you some awkward questions, because he's just bloody done that to me." He was aware that Kate might curtail the call at any time, so he cut to the chase; "He's had someone keeping an eye on you Kate. He knows about you and Gram, he thinks you're having it off with him. Are you, by the way?"

She ignored the taunt: "He's having me followed? He told you this?"
"Yes, but obviously you can't tell him I told you. Otherwise, he'll suspect me. This way, it's sort of ideal. Like I said, he thinks it's Gram that you're seeing and it does sort of look like you are, by the way."
"Mind your own fucking business!"

He sighed audibly: "Kate it sort of *is* my business. I'm really fucking freaking out here. I'm begging you not to mention me. I've got, you know, my kids, my marriage, everything, on the line. And if Steve already thinks that

Drive-By Shouting

it's Gram you're involved with, well then, what's the point of ruining my life? Jen's life? My kid's lives? And, completely destroying Steve into the bargain?"

"You're such a manipulative bastard aren't you? Gram is absolutely right about you. You honestly think you can remote control me into repeating your script and sacrificing your oldest friend into the bargain. Gram told me about the offer you made to him; how you wanted to put him on a wage to manipulate and control me? You worthless piece of shit! And I wouldn't be surprised if this situation now, was your plan all along, to put Gram in the frame, so that there was an alternative candidate for the father of my child! That's it, isn't it? That was your plan all along!"

"Kate, listen, I don't know what Gram's been saying, but that's simply not true..." Matt flailed, desperately trying to think of something convincing to say, "I never offered him money, I just..."
"You're a liar!"
"No, no, you've got to believe me! He's all fucked up about songs and royalties and shit and he's trying to get back at me. I did meet him and ask him to maybe put in a good word for me, but..," He paused, desperately trying to compose himself, "but it was then that he turned on me and got all bitter and twisted. He's a fucking nutter!"
"You're a liar!"
"No, it's true Kate, you have to believe me..."
"I don't have to believe you. You're a liar."
"Please Kate, just talk to me. Let's talk this through before you see Steve."

Drive-By Shouting

"No chance."
"But what are you going to say to him?" Matt was desperate and making no attempt to hide it.
"You'll see..." The line went dead.

Matt frantically redialed, in the full knowledge of the futility of the action. Predictably, the call went to voicemail. Placing the phone on the coffee table, he held his head in his hands and rocked back and forth, the sweat dripping down his temples and the back of his neck.

Crouch End - One minute later

Kate put down the phone and walked outside and into the garden. She silently picked up a glass of water from the garden table and drank from it.

Gram spoke first: "I really was trying not to eavesdrop, but you got quite loud at points. Do you want to talk about it?"

She considered for a moment, attempted to speak and then thought better of it, while she processed all of the information. Eyes moist, she eventually formed words: "I feel disgusted with myself. I'm genuinely ashamed of having got even slightly involved with that slimy, lying, manipulative bastard, who is still only thinking about himself. He's completely and utterly self-centered. I really must have blinkered myself to not see

Drive-By Shouting

it." She angrily wiped her eyes with the back of her hand.
"He's a very accomplished liar, Kate. You really can't blame yourself."
"Can't I? I'm really wondering what kind of state my life was in, to have been involved with a husband who, apparently, has had me followed. And to have had an underhand relationship with one of his best friends, who is a complete bastard. I must have a big neon sign above my head saying 'bastards welcome.'

Gram was alarmed: "Steve has had you followed? Who by?"
"'Oh, who knows? Steve has contacts in all the seedy walks of life. He's always loved swinging between royalty and lowlife, so if dirty deeds need doing, he would always know people who could do it. Apparently, he's back in London and has had someone tailing me for weeks. How could he do that?"
Gram looked up at her: "Well, I don't know the guy, but to be fair to him, he does have some justification to wonder if something was going on?"

"So he should just ask me! Not have me followed! And by Christ knows who? Probably some East End psychopath, one of his *'associates.'* That's his problem; he'd rather do the underhand thing than simply talk directly to me. If he'd have asked me why I was moving back here, why I needed to live separately, we could have talked about the state of our marriage and maybe got somewhere. But instead, he prefers to just assume that I'll have a bit of time on my own, do some writing, and then happily walk back into being his trophy wife.

Drive-By Shouting

I'm utterly ashamed of what I've done and where I've ended up. Maybe the reason I attract bastards is that I'm not a very nice person? From the current evidence, I think that might very well be true." She steeled herself and suppressed a sob.

Gram sat listening mutely, aware that he was woefully ill-equipped to offer relationship advice. Kate wiped her damp eyes again, holding real tears at bay: "Anyway, it's my mess and I need to sort it out. Listen Gram, Steve's on his way here soon."
"Oh Christ!"
"Yes, exactly. You should probably make yourself scarce."
Gram stood, an alarmed look on his face.
"You may have gathered from my phone call... Steve thinks that I'm involved with you, because we've apparently been seen together by his spies."
"But, nothing *has* been going on between us."
"No, but we've been seeing a lot of each other over the last few weeks, so, somebody watching could get the wrong idea. And the worst of it is, I deeply, deeply suspect that this was that bastard Matt's plan all along. To put you in the frame as my love interest."

Gram looked doubtful: "I wouldn't jump to that conclusion Kate; Matt's not exactly a chess player. He's manipulative and he's a liar, but he presumably didn't know you were being followed, because he could just as easily have been seen with you?"
"But maybe he did? Maybe he's known about it since he found out about the baby? And saw an opportunity to have somebody else take the blame?"

Drive-By Shouting

"Well, if that's true, then he's even worse than I thought."

She reached and touched his arm: "Gram, you'd better go. I don't know when Steve will turn up, but you don't want to be here. It's going to be a difficult enough conversation anyway."

"I know you're right; I should get going. Are you going to be okay though Kate? Is he the sort of guy to get physical or nasty?"

"No, never, not with me. Whatever else Steve is, he's not personally a violent guy to women, so far as I know. Although he undoubtedly knows other people who are. But, no, he wouldn't hurt me. I may have low standards Gram, but not that low." She forced a weak smile.

Gram returned the smile: "Call me later if you want. I can come back."

She squeezed his hand. "Thank Christ I've got one decent, lovely man in my life. Go on, make yourself scarce."

Gram closed the communal door to Kate's house, still thinking about her rather dire situation. His instinct was to phone Matt and call him every name he could think of, but, on reflection, felt that silence was probably the best punishment for him. As he closed the front gate and turned down the street, he noticed a parked car across the street about fifty yards away. It was occupied by a large man, who was making no secret of observing him. He stopped walking and stared at the driver, who continued to stare back in his direction. Just as Gram was deciding whether to confront the man, a woman carrying a baby came out

Drive-By Shouting

of an adjacent house and opened the passenger door to the car. The driver got out, walked around and began assisting the woman with a child car seat. Gram felt his heart rate reduce and continued walking down the street, feeling relieved and a little foolish for having jumped to conclusions.

A hundred yards behind Gram, the driver of a dark VW Passat placed his camera and telephoto lens onto the passenger seat and picked up his notebook.

Crouch End – About ninety minutes later

Opening the front door, Kate managed to feign surprise at Steve's appearance.
"Hello stranger. You might have let me know you were in the country?" She smiled weakly, nervously anticipating the exchange to come.
"You look lovely Kate, as always." His tone was cold and matter-of-fact. He mechanically pecked her on the cheek and walked through to the lounge where the doors were wide open onto the garden.

"Do you want to sit in the garden Steve?"
"No, Kate, we need to have a talk. It's a bit more private in here."
She gripped the back of a chair for support, before moving around it and lowering herself nervously onto the seat: "I know. We've needed to talk for a long time." She held his gaze until a spasm of shame made her avert her eyes.

Drive-By Shouting

Steve remained standing, his arms folded. Eventually, he joined her, sitting in the seat opposite: "Kate, let's not beat about the bush. I know you're seeing another guy."
Despite her knowledge that the question was inevitable, Kate was shocked by its early arrival and fumbled for a reply: "Steve... We've been drifting for a long time..."
"Bullshit!" He suddenly flushed with anger, "I've given you everything a wife could want!"
"But it's not about 'things' Steve. It's about talking to each other, sharing things, sharing a bed even."

"Well it seems you found someone else to do that with anyway. I hear you're hanging around with that loser guy who used to play with Matt? So he's your boyfriend?"
"No, he's not."
"Oh don't bullshit me Kate! I've heard all about it. You've been seen by loads of people."
"Loads of people, or..." She trailed off, aware that revealing her knowledge of Steve having had her followed would lead, without fail, to the full disclosure of the affair with Matt, the child, the whole horrible situation. She diverted.

"Gram is his name. The guy you're referring to."
He glared back at her: "Yes, I fucking know that!"
"But I promise you Steve, there's nothing going on there. He's simply a friend. He's been really nice to me and yes, I have hung out with him a lot lately. But it's strictly platonic."
"I don't believe you."

Drive-By Shouting

"Well that's your prerogative. But I'm telling you; hand on heart that nothing has gone on with Gram. So I don't want you doing anything to him? He's blameless. Okay?" She remained silent as Steve's eyes bore into hers. Summoning her courage, she ploughed on. "But you're partly right; there *was* someone a few months ago." She eyed him nervously. "And, I'm ashamed to say," she closed her eyes to avoid the reptilian stare, "that yes, I had a fling with him."

Steve grimaced angrily, as if he'd been kicked. He punched the coffee table, sending cups flying: "You bitch! After all I've given you…" He got up and walked to the open doorway. After a few seconds, he turned, his face red with fury. "So if it wasn't this dickhead guy, who was it?"
"Steve, it's all over, so it just doesn't matter." Her mind raced with the consequences or not of her next words. "It's no one you know. Just some guy and it was because I was lonely. And you and I both know the reasons. We've been living separate lives, and I was basically profoundly lonely."

Steve walked back and sat down in the armchair again, before staring at the floor.
"Steve, I'm truly sorry that this happened… But it was sort of inevitable that one of us would do this, given the state our marriage has been in."
"Oh, so it's my fault now!" His eyes flashed angrily at her.
"It's both of our faults Steve. But how do you hold a marriage together when we don't talk for weeks, we seem to literally exist in different time zones, even

Drive-By Shouting

when you're in the UK and, we don't even sleep together. And let's be honest, that side of our marriage evaporated a long time ago."

Steve sat, staring unhappily at his hands. His brief flash of anger had subsided. "I know you're right about the marriage. And yes, I've been an absent husband. But I still love you Kate. Is it truly over with this other guy? Because, we can put this behind us. I want us to be happy, so let's start again?"
"It's more complicated than that Steve."
"It's not! I adore you. I know I don't always show it and I'm a bit of crap husband sometimes, but I think, if we change the way I am, we can really make this work?"
Kate felt nausea rising within her, her mouth was dry and her stomach was churning. "Steve. We can't start again..." She closed her eyes before delivering the hammer blow. "I'm pregnant."

Kate opened her eyes to see Steve frozen, the shock registered on his face. "I'm so sorry Steve. It obviously wasn't planned this way. But it just happened." She struggled to look at Steve, sitting stunned and silent.
"Please say something Steve." An unchecked tear rolled down her cheek, as he sat, stunned and silent.

Eventually, he answered her in quiet, measured tones. "Well Kate, you've always had the power to surprise me..."
"I'm sorry Steve. I'm really so sorry..." She wiped her face with the back of her hand and sat in silence. Steve shifted in his seat, knotting his fingers, with his eyes clamped shut. After over a minute of oppressive

silence, he half rose from the chair before collapsing to kneel at her feet. She opened her eyes as he clasped her hands and looked up at her. "Kate, we can make this work. I'll take this child on. Who knows, this may be a blessing."
"But Steve, this is imp..."

He shushed her: "No, listen to me. I'd always thought that there was a chance I was firing blanks. Like you already know, I had chickenpox when I was 19 and then, when you didn't get pregnant a few years ago, I may as will tell you now, I got myself checked out. The doctor said it was really unlikely that I'd get to be a dad. I know I should have told you, but I was ashamed. I knew you wanted children and I guess I just chickened out and pretended it wasn't true. I think this affected me in the bedroom department too. I felt, y'know, not fully a man? But this could be our chance. This way, we can be a family." He looked up and smiled hopefully.

"Steve, it's not going to work."
"But it is! If, like you say, this was just a fling with some anonymous guy, well maybe he's done me a favour? We can be really happy Kate. With a baby, we can be a family." He looked imploringly at her.

Kate felt more tears roll down her face: "Steve... You're a good man and the fact that you are even willing to contemplate taking on me and this child... is... amazing. It proves that you've got a big heart underneath all the tough stuff, but..."
"So, let's do it!"

Drive-By Shouting

She shook her head: "But, we can't. We were unhappy and isolated before and the baby won't fix that. Especially a baby that's come about like this... from a... sordid fling..."
"I don't care about that. I want you and I want the baby."
"Steve, no! We need to read this sign for what it really is. This isn't a new beginning. It's the end. Surely you can see that?"

His eyes were filled with tears: "No Kate, it's not!"
"Yes, it is! We were unhappy before and we'll continue along the same path. Only now, I'd have to live with you raising another man's child. Knowing that, deep down, you'll resent him or her and resent what I've done. I can't do that. Not to you, to me, or to the child. I can't have him or her growing up in that environment."

Tears were now rolling down Steve's cheeks: "Kate, this is unbelievable. Please? I'm offering to take on you and the child and give you a wonderful home and a wonderful life. To give the kid everything he could ever want and be its dad!"
Kate's suppressed anguish poured out and she sobbed: "I can't do it! We need to talk about a divorce." Steve slumped backwards and sat quietly on the floor, poleaxed by this development, trying to get it to register.

Kate, still weeping, rose from her chair and walked past him and into the garden, hoping to curtail the conversation. After a few minutes of cathartic sobbing,

Drive-By Shouting

she began to feel strangely calm and, almost happy, now that she had finally unburdened herself; at least partly.

Steve called from inside the flat: "Please Kate, come back. Talk to me." He was sobbing between phrases. She walked to the far end of the garden and sat on the grass with her eyes closed, willing the meeting to end. From within the lounge, she heard Steve moving about on the wooden floor. A further few minutes later, she heard the faint but unmistakable sound of the latch on the front door closing, and Steve, presumably, leaving.

When she was as certain as she could be that Steve had gone, she walked, with some trepidation, back into the flat. It appeared that he had indeed left, the impression cemented by the folded note on the table, held in place against the breeze by a glass.

She picked it up and read it.

"Kate. This is <u>not</u> the end. We'll talk later - I'll give you time to think. Despite everything, I still love you. S x"

She re-read the words *'despite everything'* which re-affirmed that she'd done the right thing and had to remain firm in her commitment. Still, she cried. Partly because the end had finally come; a marriage that, at the outset, had seemed so brimming with possibility had finally ended. But partly, she cried because she simply felt sorry for herself and it felt comforting to allow herself to wallow in this.

Part 6

Middle Eight

Drive-By Shouting

Chapter 12
BBC Elstree Studios - Borehamwood 1992

Matt stood and surveyed the main area of the BBC bar. Although he knew that this was a temporary situation (and even though the bar was dark and dingy), he finally felt that he was where he belonged. Around him were most of the acts that had just completed the recording of that week's *Top of the Pops*.

He turned back to the bar and gladly took a beer from Annabel's outstretched hand.
"Thanks missus. And thanks again for getting me the gig. I really appreciate it."
"I always look after the good guys Matt!" She winked and turned back to retrieve more drinks from the bar.

Matt looked across the throng of pop stars, backing musicians and TV crew. His gaze settled on tonight's guest host, Simon Wood, the BBC Radio One DJ. He was standing chatting with the thick set and rather intimidating looking Steve Coombes, the well-known (and somewhat notorious), show business agent and manager. As if sensing that he was being viewed, Coombes momentarily turned and locked eyes with

Drive-By Shouting

Matt, before smiling and nodding in acknowledgement. Initially doubting the gesture was intended for him, Matt paused for a second before smiling back, raising his beer in a mimed toast and looking once more at Annabel.

"That's bizarre, Steve Coombes is smiling and nodding at me, although I'm certain I've never met him?"
"Ah, the same problem as me, that's what Steve has, can't resist a handsome guy!"
"What? Steve Coombes is gay?"
"I don't think he knows what he is. Our Steve? Let's just say, he doesn't limit his options!"

Matt raised his eyebrows and fell into conversation with Tom, the keyboard player. Over Tom's shoulder, he spotted that Jasminder and the backing vocalists had occupied a corner settee and he was about to move over and join them, when he felt a hand lightly grip his arm.

"It's Matt, isn't it?" He turned, to find Steve Coombes looking at him keenly, with his hand now outstretched in greeting. Matt took his hand and shook it vigorously.
"Wow, er, yes it is, and you're Steve. Well, obviously."

"Nice to meet you Matt. I saw you backing up Jasminder earlier and then finally realised where I knew you from. Took me a while and then I thought; of course, it's the guy from *Cymbal!*"

Drive-By Shouting

Matt couldn't hide his surprise: "Bloody hell, you're about the only person in Britain that could pick me out of a lineup! How do you know about *Cymbal?*"

Steve smiled: "You're very humble. I actually thought you had a good band there, and you in particular are very good.' He looked meaningfully at Matt, who managed to mutter a thrilled "Thank you – I'm flattered."

"I saw you play at Subterranea ages ago. A friend dragged me along and I even got your album afterwards."

"You bought our album? Bloody hell!"

Steve smiled broadly: "Well, obviously I didn't *pay* for it! Got a copy off Annabel! But I *did* like it. Good writing and you've got a great voice."

Matt, unused to such positive praise from within the entertainment industry, flushed with pleasure: "Thank you. I really appreciate you saying that. Especially *you* saying that."

"No problem, just saying what I think is true. So, anyway, I obviously hadn't expected to see you here tonight, but this might turn out to be a happy accident."

Matt felt the heat rising under his collar: "Might it? How so?"

Coombes bowed his bullet head and rubbed the back of his neck: "I heard that you got dropped a few months ago, which I was very sorry to hear about, but y'know, that's entertainment! But, as it happens, maybe, as my granddad used to say: 'when one door closes, another one opens'" He looked meaningfully at Matt and gestured towards the corner, "Can we head over there where it's a bit quieter and have a chat?"

Drive-By Shouting

Matt felt a thrill running through him. He had no idea what Coombes had in mind but, providing that he wasn't simply being chatted up, it felt as though something significant was about to happen. They made their way to the far corner of the room and sat in a couple of tub chairs opposite each other. Steve eyed him sincerely, "Sorry to be mysterious, but I'd rather keep things private for the time being. I have a proposal, and I want you to hear me out, because you'll probably initially think that it's not the right thing for you. But honestly, since I saw you on stage tonight, I think this could be great. Really great..."

Matt eyed him earnestly, listening with keen interest: "Fire away... I'm all ears."
Steve nodded: "OK. Basically, I'm putting together a vocal group, four guys, it's sort of a boy band, but more mature. And way, way cooler than anything that's gone before. It's kind of 'tough guys with leather jackets and tattoos', a sort of updated Rolling Stones thing, but still nice enough for grannies to buy the album for Christmas presents – yeah? I've lined up two really good guys, although, in all honesty, neither of them is a real front man. But, and I really think this could work, I think that it *could* be you. You really understand stagecraft. I think you could be a bit of a star."

Matt blinked and widened his eyes: "You want me to join a kind of older boy band? Really?" Matt's mind whirred as he tried to process the information. Boy bands represented everything that he (and Gram, now

Drive-By Shouting

he thought about it) had detested in the music business. Manufactured groups singing bubblegum pop. Puppets, usually having the strings pulled by a Svengali figure, who almost always emerged with all of the cash anyway. Matt composed himself, "Right, right... Okay, that's a lot to process Steve. I must confess I've never seen myself as that kind of... of... y'know, artist? I really need to think how something like that would look."

Steve continued to look at him keenly: "It would look great. Listen Matt, I hadn't even considered this myself until half an hour ago, but after seeing you play, and remembering what a great front man you are, I thought 'yes,' this could really work! The two guys I've already got on board, who are good writers and great singers by the way, they approached me a few months ago asking if I knew any good music managers. But really, I don't know anyone who could do a better job than I can, so I thought 'why not?' However, they're not the finished article. They're great, but they lack that 'star quality' element. They need a bit of raunch in them. And that's what you've got. You look great. You've got star quality. You're very charismatic, and the long hair really works, it gives a different take on the whole thing."

Matt wrestled with the proposition: "But... and I'm not saying *no*... but I'm not that comfortable with the idea of being like a puppet, singing crap songs."
"Oh, the songs won't be crap. The two guys, Paul & David, have got some good self-written stuff and it's that which got me hooked in, by the way. Having said

Drive-By Shouting

that, we could do with a couple more singles, but the stuff's good. And of course, if you've got any unreleased stuff, I'd welcome the chance to hear it. It's all potentially up for grabs, a new record deal, writing credits, everything. So, what do you think?"

Matt considered the situation quickly. In six days he would be back at Rox Rentals, picking up the van keys and *Top of the Pops*, *Wogan* and all of the rest would soon become a very distant memory. And then what? He'd clocked the fact that half the guys driving the vans had once had record contracts, but were still there, doing the 'temporary' job, smoking endless joints to get them through the boredom whilst their hair grew thin and their teeth turned yellow. It wasn't as if his attempts to get a proper job were getting anywhere. The baggage of being an ex-rocker with no real work history was proving insurmountable. And Jen's plan, that he cut his hair and work for her father was simply horrific. He recalled some advice he'd overheard, 'always say yes to everything until you have to say no. At least you'll leave the door open. At least the decision is still yours.'

"Okay, I'm definitely interested. What's the score? Is this an indie project or are you looking for a major deal for this?"
Steve smiled and warmed to his theme: "Oh, it's definitely a major label project. I'm very good friends with Dougie Bowley at Oxy Records, he's already ninety per cent of the way there, based on the concept and the guys that I've already got. I reckon a couple more hit songs and the right guys on board and we'll

be an absolute shoe in. And, he'll back me, and the band, to the hilt too."

"And money? If that's not being too mercenary?"

Steve nodded and smiled: "No, that's not mercenary, this is business, not pissing about. Yeah, there'll be a small salary, maybe eighty quid a week to get it going? We want to keep costs low at the outset. But we'll get good 'points' on the deal and if you do have some hits up your sleeve, maybe some tasty publishing too? And I know you've only just met me Matt,' Steve looked sincerely into Matt's eyes, "but I know a winning horse when I see one. This really could be massive. There's nobody really doing the bad boy thing at the moment. Everything else is all a bit squeaky clean pop, so we need to move fast before someone else does it. Because, if one person's thinking it, you can bet your arse, another thousand people are too! No such thing as an original idea, y'know?"

Matt's doubts began to melt fast as the warm feeling of possibility flooded through him. He found himself grinning widely: "Okay Steve. I admit I was really unsure when you started talking about this, but the more I think about it, the more I like the idea. And I'm really flattered, and surprised that you've singled me out to have this conversation."

Steve laughed: "I'm probably just as surprised as you, but I'm feeling really excited by the prospects. First things first, you need to meet Paul and David, but I'm certain they'll like you."

Drive-By Shouting

Annabel had wandered over and was now loitering behind Steve, "So what's going on here you two? Planning a military coup?"
"Something like that, darlin'." Steve stood and accepted a kiss from Annabel on the cheek, before turning back to Matt.
"Here's my card Matt. Call me tomorrow and we can talk a bit more." He patted Annabel's arm as he walked by and made his way back over to the presenter, Simon Wood, who was evidently suffering a dull conversation with one of the Top of the Pops researchers. Matt watched him go, before turning to address Annabel.

"Is he okay, d'you think? I mean, you know him. Do you trust him?"
"Depends on what he's proposing. Was it business or, ahem, personal?" Annabel grinned lewdly.
"Nothing like that. Strictly business."
"Then you'd be in good hands."
But what about the rumours? He's supposed to be a bit, you know, a bit of a gangster?
"Oh don't believe all that crap! He just likes to let people believe all that, so that nobody crosses him. He's a pussycat really. And he's good, he knows how to develop people, and he knows absolutely everyone! He can open doors for you. Ooo, look at you, Matt Mann, getting noticed by all the right people. You little star! You'd better remember who gave you the leg up when you're rich and famous!"

Long after Steve Coombes departed the BBC bar, Matt was still taking advantage of the seemingly never ending drinks tab, which Annabel was only too happy

Drive-By Shouting

to run up. The bar was still full with what appeared to be almost all of the performers from *TOTP*, with only the American megastars having departed (they were all far more serious about their 'job' than their British counterparts; even US heavy metal bands seemed to go easy on the booze and ensured that they got plenty of sleep. Matt wanted to say something withering about their long termism, but grudgingly, he realized that he couldn't help but admire their professionalism).

He fell into conversation with a group of musicians from other bands, before Annabel signaled that the car was outside to take him home.

Pleasantly drunk, he watched the lights blur as the car sped around the North Circular, before weaving through North London. He asked the driver to stop about a mile from home, relishing the idea of a late-night walk. He felt like he was walking on air. He had really thought that this series of shows with Jasminder would be his last hurrah, his swansong, so far as music was concerned and that the big compromise of his life was looming and inevitable. It was simply a matter of working out the least worst option: working for Jen's father or taking the first lowly telesales job that he could find, both of which filled him with utter horror. His pride precluded him asking his own parent's for help, and his father was such a distant figure, that he couldn't imagine initiating such a conversation anyway.

As he walked, he replayed the conversation repeatedly in his head, thrilled that he'd been noticed and thought

Drive-By Shouting

to be charismatic. Especially when the opinion holder was Steve Coombes. All of his previous doubts had now receded completely. Once the alternatives were put on the scales, the opportunity to be part of this was a heavyweight godsend, firing all of the other options out of the water, and into oblivion.

His thoughts turned to Jen and the inevitable resistance when she heard that, once more, the conventional life had been put on hold. Sadness suddenly enveloped him when he thought about the Jen he had met in Northampton with paint splattered clothes and her laid-back hippy stance on everything. He knew that the corollary of his creative life was that Jen would continue to have hers trampled beneath the dirty boots of childcare, monotony and loneliness. The endless carefree time of her youth had passed. The days and days they had spent aimlessly pleasing themselves in Northampton, had been supplanted by drudge and resentment. He wanted Jen to be thrilled by his news, to be filled with hope, to be able to dream. He doubted that would be the case.

He turned into Mount Pleasant and paused outside the flat. He noticed, with pleasure that the lounge lights were switched off. Jen would be asleep, so he could reminisce and enjoy tonight's sparkling developments in isolation until the morning.

Drive-By Shouting

Chapter 13
Five weeks later – North London 1992

From the tube station, Gram walked down Caledonian Road until he was almost opposite Pentonville Prison, where he took a right-hand turn into Brewery Road, going past John Henry Studios where *Cymbal* had spent so many months rehearsing over the previous few years. He entered the vehicle yard for Rox Rentals, picked up his van keys from the hook and looked at the docket for his morning deliveries. He winced as he spotted the third item and marched in to see Tony, the genial transport manager.

"Tone, you are kidding aren't you? A forty-eight track machine out of Angel Studios? That's four flights of stairs!"
Tony smiled benignly: "Sorry Gram, someone's got to do it and today that *someone* is you! But there'll be four of you doing the lifting, so you'll be fine. You're picking up young Dave from his flat, you know, on the

Drive-By Shouting

estate behind the Cally pool? And then Tom and Pete will meet you there at eleven, to help you out with it."
"But it's insanely heavy! Even with four of us, it's a nightmare to lift. Especially down all of those stairs."
Tony smiled patiently: "There's twenty-five quid extra for each of you."
"And what's that, danger money?"
Tony smiled at him again: "It's only dangerous if you drop it. So just don't drop it!"

Gram, turned away, still dreading the job to come and wondering how he'd got to the stage where a mere £25 would tempt him to carry something that weighed the same as a car, down four flights of stairs. The story amongst the drivers was that they'd dropped a forty-eight track machine once, while taking it down a flight of stairs; and that the guy at the bottom had only avoided death because his head had gone through the partition wall. If the wall had been solid, he'd have popped like a melon. He'd initially assumed that the story was apocryphal, but after hearing it repeated so many times (and so graphically) he was no longer reassured by this. What he was certain of, however, was that moving these machines felt dangerous and frightening. He went into the warehouse and assembled the rest of the morning deliveries into the back of the van. He jumped in, turned on the engine and drove out of the yard and onto the road.

After negotiating his way around the maze of streets behind the Caledonian pool, he was annoyed to find no sign of Dave when he arrived at the complex of council flats, with the inevitable jacked up cars and

Drive-By Shouting

loitering youths. He phoned upstairs and established that Dave was, as usual, running late. Gram turned off the engine and leaned back on the headrest surveying the dismal scene outside. It reminded him of the worst parts of Liverpool, specifically, parts of Kirkby came to mind and his thoughts returned to his recent, and awful, visit to his parent's house in Maghull.

Since experiencing the delight of leaving home for Northampton a decade earlier, return visits to his childhood home had always been rare and fraught. His father, Joe, was a bluff Yorkshireman. He was a Printer by trade and an enthusiastic amateur trad-jazz saxophonist, during the numerous evenings he spent at the local British Legion. He patently disapproved of his son's life choices but, while Gram was doing his degree and while *Cymbal* had the legitimacy of a record deal, his disapproval had been relatively mute. This last visit had been very different.

In the suffocating atmosphere that existed whenever his domineering father was in the house, Gram had kept a low profile (much as he had in his teens) and chosen to avoid, rather than confront his father. On his last night there however, as he sat at dinner with Joe, his mother Pauline and sister Deborah, his father had struck; eyeing him sharply, before moving in for the kill.

"So then Simon, have you finally learned your lesson and got over all your nonsense?"
Gram stared back at his father in alarm. Having made it unscathed until the last evening, he thought he'd got

Drive-By Shouting

away without having to have this conversation. Reluctantly, he answered: "What do you mean by *nonsense*?"

"This bloody popstar crap! All this pissing about with guitars and all that rubbish? It's fantasy, never going to happen, just like I told you. People like you don't get to be stars. But that's you all over. Getting above yourself, as usual."

Gram bristled under his father's gaze as his mother and sister squirmed in their seats: "Actually Dad, it wasn't a fantasy. It was a record contract. And I made two albums that I'm really proud of."

"And what a waste of bloody time that was. I mean, what've you got to show for it lad? Nothing, nothing at all. No money, no job."

Gram felt his anger rising: "You might perhaps show some respect for what I achieved. I mean, I…"

"Respect? Respect! What for? You thinking you're a big shot? Being a clever dick? Thinking you're better than everyone else? And now here we are, back where we started, just like I told you when you left school. You're too old for all this nonsense now. You're nearly in your 30's! You need to cut your stupid hair, dress properly, settle down and get yourself a job."

"Well, I am. I am getting myself a job." Even as Gram spoke, he knew that he was simply walking further into the quicksand.

"Oh yes? This'll be interesting. And what job is that exactly?"

Gram steeled himself: "Well, I'm going to do a bit of van driving for one of the music companies, one of the

Drive-By Shouting

ones that we used to use when *Cymbal* were signed, but that's just while I try to get some work as a record producer."

His father looked at him with disdain: "And you call that a job? Bloody hell lad, you're in cloud cuckoo land and you always have been. I lined up a perfectly good job with Bill when you were sixteen, and printing *is* a proper job, and a job for life. But you were too high and mighty, you wanted a degree. Oooh, look at me, I've got a degree!" He laughed a mocking, mirthless laugh, "And where's it all got you? Nowhere!

So, instead of you taking the job, Bill hired Betty's boy Michael, from down the road and now he's got a house and a car and a lovely family. Fat lot of good a degree and a broken record contract have been, because now you're going to be a bloody van driver! You're a bloody useless fantasist." His father held him in an angry stare.

Completely unexpectedly, his sister Deborah rallied stutteringly to his defence: "Actually Dad, it's not just a fantasy. I mean, Simon's friend Matt was on *Top of the Pops* a few weeks ago, so it's not just…" she ran out of words under the pressure of the icy stare emanating from her father.

"Of course he was. He was only ever looking out for himself, that Matt bloke. But he," Joe jabbed a contemptuous finger in Gram's direction, "*he* wasn't on it was he? No, Simon, sorry, 'Gram,' was too busy being Gram, who drives the bloody van!"

Drive-By Shouting

Fighting his overwhelming desire to simply leave the house, Gram managed to speak: "Actually, I was offered the *Top of the Pop's* thing too; they offered it to both Matt and me. Except, I turned it down."
"Bollocks you did!"
"No, it's true. I turned it down. It's not what I got into music for and…" Gram realised he was simply flailing around, unable to fully explain, even to himself, why he had said 'no' to Matt.
"Then you're a bloody fool. At least you'd have something to show for all the wasted years. At least your mother would have something to tell her friends when they ask her what you're up to. As it is, she's too embarrassed to even mention you."

Pauline meekly piped up: "Oh that's not true Joe!"
"Yes it bloody is! What are you supposed to say? That our Simon, the one who changed his name to the bloody stupid 'Gram,' is now driving a van, but it's okay, we're really happy about it all because his friend was on *Top of the Pops!* He's an embarrassment Pauline. And if he isn't to you, then he is to me."

Gram's fury peaked as he stared back at his father's puce mocking face and took in the sight of his mother and sister avoiding his father's eye and staring mutely at their plates. He tried to respond, but felt, with horror, something rising within him. It prevented him from speaking.

Joe's baiting continued. "Well, don't you have anything to say, Mr. 'I'm-too-good–to-be-a-printer'? Eh?" His father continued to stare with contempt,

Drive-By Shouting

until his expression turned to triumph, as Gram lost the battle with himself and, with mortification, felt a tear roll down his cheek. He wiped it away, but the merest touch from his mother's outstretched hand induced an involuntary sob and fresh tears rolled unchecked down his face again.

His father's disgust grew: "Oh, for Christ's sake Pauline, look at him! Don't bloody comfort him! You've been too bloody soft on him all along. It's all his own doing and it serves him right for thinking he's better than everyone else. Well, you've made a right hash of it. And look at you now. Flat broke and crying your eyes out. Pathetic!"

His father gave a final look of contempt, before levering himself up out of the chair and marching out of the room. Pauline and Deborah had moved around to hug Gram, trying to ease the pain of this latest humiliation.

Back in North London, the memory haunted and tormented Gram, just as it had done for the few weeks since his visit. He was abruptly shaken out of his reminiscence by the passenger door being violently wrenched open and Dave's lumbering frame stepping up into the cab.

"Sorry mate, my bird's kids were being a pain in the arse and I just couldn't get out of the flat any quicker." Dave was twenty-one years old and had recently

Drive-By Shouting

moved in with an unmarried mother of two, in preference to continuing to live with his own mother and five siblings. Gram suspected he would never leave. Dave turned to look at him: "You all right Gram? You don't look too clever. You look like someone's given you a slap."

Gram gathered himself quickly: "No, I'm fine, just a bit knackered." He feigned a smile and turned the key in the ignition, "We've got a lovely day today Dave, a forty-eight track machine down the stairs at Angel."
"Oh, for fuck's sake!" Dave threw his hands up in amused despair. "It's glamour all the way with this music lark, innit!" He cackled and Gram managed to join in with a manufactured chortle. He drove towards Islington, but his head was still in Maghull, weeping at his parent's kitchen table.

By mid-afternoon, Gram had been so busy driving around London's recording and rehearsal studios and avoiding injury with the forty-eight track recorder that his spirit had partially lifted. It was further improved as he climbed into the cab after delivering a keyboard to Soho's Berwick Street Studios.

Dave was rolling up on the dashboard. He glanced at Gram and filled him in, "Got a nice little one to get us home. Tony just called, wants us to drop into Wessex on the way back to collect an effects rack."
Gram visibly brightened at the news: "Really? Wessex? Excellent. It'll be good to go back." He turned to look

Drive-By Shouting

at Dave, "You know we did our second album there, yeah?"

Dave looked singularly unimpressed as he licked the Rizla glue strip. "Yeah, you've told me that. It was when you was in a band with that guy who did a bit of driving for us, the poncey one."
"That'll be Matt. He's not actually poncey once you get to know him. Well, maybe a bit. Anyway, we were the songwriting team in the band and with a bit more luck we would have been really big."
"Yeah, you told me that too." Dave spoke distractedly while he concentrated on shoving the roach into the flimsy end of his creation. "That Matt bloke was on *Top of the Pops* last month wasn't he? Kept standing in front of the singer all the way through. He's definitely a ponce."
Undeterred by Dave's lack of enthusiasm, Gram continued whimsically: "But anyway, it'll be great to go back in. We were at Wessex for a few months, off and on. It was like a second home, they're brilliant people there. Gerry, the owner, Stella, the studio manager. It'll be great; we can stop for a cuppa there. Catch up a bit."
He pulled the vehicle away from the curb and continued to enthuse about Wessex, while Dave lit up the joint.

After a hazy twenty-minute drive, they turned off Highbury New Park onto Wessex's long driveway, before pulling up at the front of the converted church building. Gram turned to Dave: "You've been here before, right?"

Drive-By Shouting

He looked doubtfully at the edifice: "Nah. I dunno. Maybe. But they're all the same anyway. One studio is the same as another to me, mate." He sniffed dismissively.

"No, they're really not. This one is special! This is where *Queen, The Pretenders, The Pistols,* loads of people, y'know, *Motorhead* and *The Clash...* this is where they recorded all their best albums!"

Dave continued to look uninterested, managing only a shrug, before retrieving his stash from his jeans jacket and peeling off three new Rizlas. "I'll roll us a nice big doozy, while you pick up the gear, yeah?"

Gram rolled his eyes, not quite able to comprehend Dave's complete lack of interest. He stepped down from the vehicle, gathering his clip-board of delivery and collection notes. A broad smile spread across his face as he strode through Wessex's main doors into the corridor between studios one and two, happily anticipating the chance to reacquainting himself with Stella, the lovely studio manager. It had been over a year since he'd been a client, but he knew they'd be pleased to see him. Especially Stella, following their drunken kiss on that last night at the pub, once their final recording session had wound up. Now that he was single again, maybe...

Gram stopped abruptly, finding his path blocked by a large fat bearded man, staring indignantly at him: "What you doing just walking in here like you own the place? Who let you in?" He eyed the clipboard in Gram's hand.

Drive-By Shouting

Gram ignored the man's aggressive tone, confident as he was of a warm welcome behind one of the doors: "Er, no-one, the door was wedged open. But anyway, I'm Gram from Rox Rentals. I've come to get the effects rack, but, I'm also a former client too. Where's Stella, by the way? She can explain."
"Gone."
"What do you mean gone?"
"I mean gone. Not here. Doesn't work here anymore."
Gram was crestfallen, but soldiered on: "What? Well, where's Gerry then?"
"He's gone too. Sold up. Not that it's any of your business. If you're the delivery boy from Rox, what the fuck are you doing coming through the front door? The deliveries and collections are all round the side. You should know that."
"Yeah, but I'm a client too. I did my second album here about a year ago."
The man looked at him dubiously: "Oh yeah, but you're also a roadie?"
"I'm… I'm not a roadie. I'm just doing a bit of this while I get a new contract."
The fat man smirked at him. "Yeah, you and everyone else who's driving for a music company. Now, go round the side, like a good boy, eh? This is for artists and staff only."
"But, we're almost at the side door here. That doesn't really make any sense."
The man snarled as he spoke: "Go back out and around the fuckin' side, like I told you!" He stared aggressively at Gram, who, after bristling and searching fruitlessly for a retort, turned in futility and walked back out of the building.

Drive-By Shouting

Back out on the driveway, he dearly wanted to simply get in the van and drive away, but the equipment was needed back at base and so, under Dave's curious eye, he reluctantly trudged around the building to the side door, to find the fat man already glowering and waiting for him. He held out a flight case before putting it roughly onto the ground. "Here it is. And don't let me see you at the other entrance again or I'll be making a phone call and you'll find yourself out of work." He turned abruptly and slammed the door behind him. Gram bent to pick up the case and turned to find Dave standing a few feet behind him, the lit joint in his hand.

"Just came to see what was going on. Didn't look too friendly after all!"

Gram nodded silently in assent, as Dave nonchalantly took a drag on the joint, turned and walked back towards the vehicle.

The next morning, Gram walked out of the flat early. The Rox van was parked over the road, Gram having been allowed to take it home overnight, as he had an early departure to a residential studio in the Buckingham/Berkshire borders that morning. He was still feeling bruised from the previous day's humiliation and, coming as it did, so soon after the Maghull debacle, it had left Gram feeling angry and depressed, feelings accentuated by him having overdone the beer and dope the previous evening.

Drive-By Shouting

He drove fitfully down from Crouch End to Holloway, before joining the stuttering traffic on Camden Road. He crawled tortuously along as it narrowed firstly to two lanes and then, after the Camden Park Road junction, into a bus lane and a single lane for other traffic. He found himself moving in tandem with a white Ford Sierra and, as the traffic ahead was joining the single lane in turn, he sought to make visual contact with the driver, who studiously ignored him and kept inching forward. As the two vehicles moved forward together, Gram found his indignation growing at the other driver's refusal to acknowledge him, and his apparent intention to jump the queue. As Gram drew closer to the bus lane and found his path blocked, he found a familiar rage building inside him and violently accelerated a few feet ahead onto the bus lane, before swerving at an angle in front of the white Ford, which had also accelerated in an attempt to block him. Before he was quite aware that he was planning to do so, he found himself standing on the Ford's bonnet, pointing at the terrified driver and screaming, "Do you fucking want some?" Even as he felt the veins bulge in his neck and saw the driver raise his hands in compliant and petrified acceptance, he knew that he was turning into somebody he'd never planned to be. He also knew what he looked like to the startled pedestrians and the other drivers in the queue. An embittered angry failure.

He self-consciously turned and crunched off the newly dented bonnet of the Ford and directly through the open door, back into the cab of his van. The traffic ahead had moved forward and he took his 'rightful'

Drive-By Shouting

place in the queue, feeling increasingly small as he inched forward, one place in front of the Ford. A cold wave washed through him, as he imagined anyone that he knew, or cared about, witnessing what had just happened.

By the time he reached the bottom of the Camden Road, he was shaking with emotion, but whereas he'd lost the battle in Maghull, he was damned if he was going to shed a tear in NW1, behind the wheel of a battered Transit van. The rollercoaster of negativity over last few weeks had taken its toll on him and he felt himself in the midst of a crisis. He wasn't sure how much more of this he could take. He didn't know it then, but the answer was, about six years.

As the traffic turned south onto the A400 and began to pick up speed, he opened the window and began to scream 'Fuuuuuuuck!' It was an endless primal sound of horror. He was oblivious to pedestrians stopping and staring in alarm as he accelerated down the one-way street. As the road curved into Oakley Square he fought to corner the speeding vehicle, clipping the curb, but somehow avoiding going fully out of control. He pulled the vehicle to a halt just after the Eversholt Street intersection, having scared himself sufficiently to induce an instinctive self-preservation. He had stopped screaming.

He got out of the van and walked over to the grass verge to sit, trying to make sense of the tsunami of emotions that were hitting him. Ten minutes later, after briefly considering the pros & cons of simply feigning illness

Drive-By Shouting

and returning home, he got back in the van, wiped his sleeve across his face, moved into gear and rejoined the traffic heading towards the Euston Road.

Within thirty minutes, he was leaving Greater London and heading off the M40 into rural Buckinghamshire. The sun was out and the green fields lay on each side of him. He felt unburdened after his emotional outburst and a sense of calm had enveloped him. He had considered all his options in the previous half hour, but really, he had no choice other than to carry on doing what he was doing. He was a musician, writer and a creative producer, and if he had to be a roadie to keep his options open, then so be it. It was only a matter of time before his opportunity came and he would prove his father wrong. He would prove them all wrong.

Drive-By Shouting

Chapter 14
Five months later - 1993

Matt crossed over the Archway 'Suicide Bridge' and moved down a gear, before trying to coax the reluctant Peugeot 205 up Highgate Hill. He preferred to take the scenic route to Steve's office in Swiss Cottage, sweeping over the top of Hampstead Heath, past The Spaniard's Inn, towards Hampstead Village and then weaving down the west side of the Heath and up past the Royal Free Hospital. It was a crisp, cold and sunny day and Matt felt the, by now familiar, nervous buzz of possibility ahead. Steve Coombes had been true to his word. He'd introduced Matt to Paul and David, and to Matt's pleasant surprise, they had all got on famously. Steve had then 'discovered' Clive, an athletic (and according to Jen, "utterly beautiful"), male model. He could sing a bit, although the tuning did tend to be on the flat side. However, he brought good looks and "ethnic cool" (Steve's words) to the project and they could keep him low in the mix if his pitching issue proved insurmountable. Clive was happy to go with the flow and had no real interest in the creative process. Matt, on the other hand, had been determined to shape

Drive-By Shouting

the group into something that he could be proud of. Today would be instrumental in that.

Despite his optimism, Matt still felt the sting of Jen's words this morning as (five months pregnant) she had lifted Callum out of his high chair.

"Okay, off you go to play popstars again with your new best friend, Stevie. I'll clean up the flat and then see what joy I can extract from another mums and toddlers group. If I'm lucky, I might get to sing *'The Wheels on the Bus'* until I'm physically sick. But the main thing Matt, is that you're feeling fulfilled and, after all, that's what counts when you're 30 and about to have a second child." Rather than be drawn into this endless cyclical argument, Matt had taken it as an opportunity to exit, sweeping up the Peugeot keys as he left (a gift from Jen's father to help her in getting around with the baby buggy while pregnant).

He felt slightly guilty about taking the car, but Jen could easily walk to the playgroup and onto the park, whereas taking the bus and tubes to Swiss Cottage was a real pain in the arse journey. It made perfect sense to Matt that he should have priority over the car, and anyway, he really loved this scenic route.

He skirted the bottom end of the Heath before turning off South End Road and up Pond Street, past the incongruous Royal Free, an ugly concrete sprawl that appeared to have been randomly dropped on the edge of London's most desirable 'village.' Hampstead had always loomed large in Matt's fantasies. It was where the highly successful celebrity rock star would choose

Drive-By Shouting

to live, and it was on their behalf that he felt thoroughly affronted by the ugly edifice of the hospital.

His thoughts returned to Jen. She had always been resolute in her support for his creative side, encouraging him when he doubted himself, constructively helping when things had looked so promising with *Cymbal*. Since the bands demise, Jen's entire position had changed. Matt had had a shot at stardom and it hadn't worked. Meanwhile, Jen's creative life had entirely expired. Since Callum's birth, she felt isolated. She was the first amongst their friends to have a baby and she felt trapped by childcare and, most crucially, the lack of cash. She also continued to be furious that Matt's pride prevented him calling his parents to ask for help. Friends would still call with invites, but childless, they had no conception of the planning required simply to leave the house, let alone join them in the pub at short notice. Spontaneity was easy when you had no kids. It was almost impossible once you did have them.

She'd taken the news of being pregnant again very badly. She tried to be upbeat and joyful, but it felt like a nail in the coffin of her creative life, of everything that she had understood to be 'Jen.' Matt also understood this, the very qualities that had so drawn him to Jen back in Northampton had been trampled by the life that they had led. In addition to being unrelentingly forgiving of his misdemeanors, she had been proud, stubborn, flirtatious and in essence, fun to be with. He didn't know where that Jen had gone, but he knew that the longer they stayed in a small flat, with no money, that the chances of her re-emerging, grew weaker and weaker.

Nonetheless, he wasn't prepared to turn his back on music, to cut his hair, wear a suit and go to work (realistically, working for her family remained his only option if he wanted anything other than a menial job). Surely that would merely mean that he and Jen just swapped places and that he became the square peg in the round hole, relentlessly commuting into a meaningless job for the rest of his life. Yes, it would bring money, but he knew loads of guys with money, doing jobs like that, and behind the veneer of success, he could smell the rank depression and hopelessness. He wanted the old Jen back, but he wasn't prepared to sacrifice himself. Yet.

Anyway, this was going to work. It had to.

He found himself driving down Fitzjohn's Avenue and spotted a parking space up ahead. Once parked, he jumped down the steps of number 77 and knocked on the door of the basement flat. The perspex plaque outside said 3P Management (Steve liked to joke that it was named after his first management commission cheque).

The door was opened by Crystal, Steve's rather dopey 16-year-old work experience girl ('free labour, mate'). She beamed hopefully at Matt as he swept past and turned left into Steve's office.
"Matthew, my man... you're early."

Drive-By Shouting

"Yes, needed to escape the domestic routine. Not a problem I hope?"
"No, this is a chance to have a chat before the others get here. I wanted to have a bit of a conversation with you anyway. Sit down; Crystal will get you a cup of tea." He nodded and mimed tea-drinking to Crystal who had appeared at the doorway.

Coombes spread his hands expansively: "So, to bring you up to speed, we're a whisker from getting Dougie to sign you to Oxy Records. But, he's slightly dragging his heels, because he still feels that the project lacks that one 'killer' song that'll break you on the radio. I've obviously explained that domestic airplay shouldn't be a problem, given the number of DJs I represent!" He grinned widely. "But I imagine he's thinking bigger than the UK, he's looking for that big worldwide hit, that un-ignorable, copper bottomed smash hit. If you can get that, you can release half a dozen lesser follow-ups and they'll still be hits. It's the one to wedge open the door that we need. And I have to say, I kind of agree with Doug. We still haven't found it."

"What about the Portastudio demos I did? I thought you liked them?"
"I did, I did. There's at least two singles there, but neither of them is the break through no brainer hit. That's what we need."
Matt looked (and felt) confused: "So, they're hit songs, but not big enough hits?"
"Exactly. What we need is something like that song, *Walk the Mile* from your first *Cymbal* album. Lovely upbeat feel and a really cracking chorus. And it's the

Drive-By Shouting

right direction for us too. That song really should have been a hit."

Matt joined in enthusiastically: "You're telling me it should. Apparently, according to Mike, the RGA radio plugger, it went to the Radio One playlist meeting, but got voted down at the last minute. We'd just had some crap reviews in *NME* and *Melody Maker,* who always hated us from the beginning. I think that played against us. Nobody was willing to champion us, so we got bumped off the list. I was really upset by that."
"Well that's show business. But you do have every right to have been upset. It was a great single."

Matt brightened suddenly: "But surely that's the answer, we just re-record *Walk the Mile,* and that's our hit!"
Steve shook his head: "That won't work. The song's associated with having failed once. But more importantly, and I'm kind of glad this has come up, it's already published. And one of the items on the agenda today is, publishing. One of my absolute requirements on this project is that all publishing goes through me. I made a mistake when we represented Michael Stonely. We took a nobody and through sheer hard work, we created a massive hit, but everybody else made the money. Once all of the record company costs were recouped, there was nothing left. But Bernie Taal, who wrote the song, he made a bleeding packet! When the big royalty payment hit, he sent me a big bunch of flowers, to say 'thanks.' The cheeky fucker!

Drive-By Shouting

Anyway, I'm already acting as de facto publisher, paying you all the salary, paying for demos, studios, home recording setups, and all the costs of pushing an unsigned project, it all costs a ton, so it needs to be virgin material, published by me, all the way. That's not a problem, I hope?" He stared sternly across the desk at Matt.

For his part, Matt was already aware that the key earnings in music came from the songwriting publishing and he could understand Steve's desire to maximise this, but it still made him feel uneasy. The music business was littered with stories of management and publishing being under the same roof and it was a fairly blatant conflict of interest. It was difficult for your manager to negotiate better terms with the publisher if they were one and the same person.

Matt decided to articulate his doubts: "Isn't it going to be difficult for *you*, the manager, to argue effectively on my behalf with *you*, the publisher? Don't you think?" Matt smiled meekly, but felt the point needed making. Across the table, Steve's already stern expression turned to ice. He spoke slowly.
"Matt, I like you and I think that you and I can work together and make a lot of money together. But let's be clear, these are my terms and they are not up for negotiation." He stared at Matt, allowing his words to hang in the room. In the silence, Matt felt the chill go through him.

Drive-By Shouting

Satisfied that the message had been received, Steve allowed a slight melting of his expression, "But look Matt, back to the song. No, we can't use *Walk the Mile*, but if you were to find yourself writing something very similar, <u>very</u> similar, with the same kind of feel and hook, I think we might be onto something."

Matt was aware that he was in uncharted territory with Steve and needed to keep on the right side of an invisible line. But he needed clarity: "You want me to rip off my own song?"
"I wouldn't put it that way, but I think you get my drift... It's what's needed..."
"But I co-wrote *Walk The Mile* with Gram Kane from *Cymbal*. He wouldn't be too happy."
"You'll obviously make it different enough to not get sued Matt, and we'll get a friendly musicologist to ensure that that's the case before we release it. Don't worry though; you're not responsible for Mr. Kane's feelings. This is about you. And your family." Steve stared at Matt once more, who squirmed in his chair.

"I'm a bit unsure Steve, this isn't really the way I work. It all seems a bit… I dunno, calculated?"
Steve stared at him, a faint disgust evident on his lip: "That's not the way you *work*?" He sighed. "The problem with you Matt is that you think of music as some sort of noble, artistic affair. When in fact, the music business is a dirty, grubby industry that operates in the gutter.
Pop music isn't all art and fuckin' poetry y'know? It's about scams, stunts and cons; it's about who emerges with the copyright, and what they can do to make that

Drive-By Shouting

copyright into a bankable asset! You can keep your airy fairy integrity shite; the history of music is littered with the dirty deeds done to get guys like you up the greasy pole. And you can either join them, or you can slide down with all the other losers. That's the choice for anyone in your shoes, and anyone who says otherwise is a liar or a fool. So, now, that's your choice." He stared squarely at Matt, "Give it a go Matt."

Matt understood. It was an instruction, not a request.

The doorbell rang and Matt heard Crystal shuffling along the corridor from the back office to welcome in the other guys, who had arrived en masse from West London. Steve walked past Matt to greet them in the hallway, leaving Matt to reflect on what had been said.

Drive-By Shouting

Chapter 15
Nine months later - BBC Elstree Studios 1993

Appearing on *Top of the Pops* for the second time, felt to Matt like one of the defining moments of his life. Yes, the playback was still tinny (and the volume too low) and yes, the rubber drum mats and cymbals still drowned out the music, making the whole miming experience very alien, but none of that mattered. He was here in his own right, fronting his own band and singing his own song.

The debut single by *Kensal Rise* had entered the chart at number three, an extraordinary impact after the short promo campaign. Steve's inroads into Radio One had guaranteed blanket coverage on the station, but equally impressive was the play-listing by Capital, Virgin and all the other big commercial stations. By the time of the industry only midweek chart, they were predicted number eleven, before the surge in sales following an appearance on Wogan had swept them into the top three.

The two-and-a-half minutes of miming flew by, but were long enough for Matt to notice the different reaction from the girls in the front row. He wasn't just

Drive-By Shouting

an anonymous hired hand, filling in the camera shot; he was the main attraction and he felt a hundred pairs of eyes focused almost exclusively on him. He was intoxicated, far more so than could be explained by the glass of champagne he'd swigged just before coming on.

The thin playback ended and the boom camera pulled up high and spun around to Simon Wood, once again hosting the show. Now off camera, Matt turned around and high-fived the band in turn, Clive's huge hand stinging him considerably more than the others. The hired-in backing group nodded in farewell as the four 'real' group members tripped off the stage, through a door and out into an ill-lit BBC corridor. Despite the anticlimactic setting, Matt was pulsing with adrenaline, unable to really comprehend that, finally, all the things he had dreamed of were becoming real.

They crowded back into their dressing room and started opening bottles, which had materialised while they were in the studio. Steve came in just as the corks started flying.
"Oh, I see you've found the extra champagne. Thought you boys might like something to come back to!!"

Half an hour later they headed down to the bar with all of the other acts. Once there and with more drinks in hand, Steve drew Matt to one side.
"Matt, I was watching you on the monitor tonight. You look terrific. I really think this band is going to be massive, but already, you're emerging as the star."

Drive-By Shouting

Matt swelled with pride. "Thanks Steve. That means a lot to me." He sensed that Steve's mood had turned serious, as he held Matt in one of his searching stares. "Matt. I think that you and I are in this for the long haul, yeah?" Matt wordlessly nodded his assent. "So we should have a pact. I'll give you total transparency on everything I do or view on your behalf, but, I expect total loyalty from you. No fucking off and thinking some other twat can manage you better. They can't."
"I know that Steve."
"So, we have a pact, yeah?"
Matt beamed back at him. "Absolutely. We're a good team Steve."
"Yes we are and we should stay that way, because, if we don't," Steve's eyes bored into Matt's; "I'll sue the bollocks off you anyway. Or worse..." He laughed and thumped Matt on the arm. Through his euphoric haze, Matt knew this was not a joke.

The previous year had gone better than anyone could have reasonably expected. Matt had dutifully reconstructed *Walk The Mile*. Keeping the tempo and structure essentially identical, but altering sufficient chords and melodic notes to make it different, he had emerged with a song which musicologists could testify was not a copyright infringement, but in feel and impact, *I Like Your Style*, was very similar to *Walk the Mile*. The whole process had made Matt very uncomfortable. The repeating bridge pattern and its distinctive chromatic bass part had remained and he was acutely aware of that section being a typically

Drive-By Shouting

'Gram' part. Matt had nonetheless focused on Steve's words "you need to be a bit selfish; this is about you and your family" and he'd pushed past his feelings of discomfort and done what was asked of him. He'd tried to help Gram in the past and been rebuffed; now he had to help himself.

The song had become the golden ticket. It had swung Doug Bowley at Oxy into panic mode, making him desperate to sign the band before someone else did. *I Like Your Style* became the centre piece of the whole project and, as sole writer, Matt naturally took lead vocals on the track, solidifying him as the focal point from the outset. The deal was tied up within weeks and a more generous regular salary from the record company advance replaced Steve's modest cash payments. It had all come good. And nothing could stop Matt now.

Drive-By Shouting

Chapter 16
Three years later - London 1996

Matt closed the front door and walked into the June sunshine. It was 11.50am and the sun made the road look like paradise. He turned out of Haslemere Road and down Crouch Hill towards the 'village' centre. A W7 bus laboured by, on its way up the steep hill and Matt was aware, as he so often was these days, that numerous young people had clocked him and (the big divide amongst fans) were either coolly pretending that they hadn't seen him, or were openly gawping at him. He regularly complained about the invasion of his private life and what a pain in the arse fans could be, but was still secretly thrilled that his mere presence could elicit such responses.

As he approached the pub, Gram suddenly appeared opposite him on the corner of Haringey Park.

Matt shouted. "Oi Gram! Knob-head!"

Three people sitting outside the corner cafe looked up in alarm. Gram, well used to the traditional greeting, stopped and turned, with his eyes raised in

Drive-By Shouting

disapproval. Gram crossed the road and the two men greeted each other while walking the 100 yards to the Haringey Arms, a surprisingly well preserved, small 'old man's pub' nestled next to The Church Recording Studios.

The pub was quiet and they took their pints out to a small table in the rear courtyard, nodding at the gaudy ceramic Bing Crosby bust as they passed by.
"So Grammy, another year older. Here's to us!" He extravagantly toasted Gram before taking a large swig from his pint.
"Yup, belated happy birthday to us. How long you home for this time?"
"Oh, just a week. Got back on Tuesday and slept solidly 'til Wednesday night. Or tried to! Jen doesn't seem to appreciate that I might not want to hang out with the kids on the first day after a tour. Especially after flying east. So that's been a bit of a bone of contention. Already! I've been home four days, but it's still pretty frosty."
"Sorry to hear that. I see Jen from time to time in the supermarket. She told me about the house. That must be nice Matt?"

The comment felt pointed, but Matt ignored any intended awkwardness: "It's nice for Jen. I've hardly been there. Obviously, she found it, got her dad to sort out all the legal and stuff and I came home a few months ago to a new house that I'd only seen in photos! Had to happen though, having two kids and a small flat was impossible. Anyway, I was home after the Australasian tour last year and it was hell, so I

Drive-By Shouting

agreed she should look for somewhere else. And as a few royalties had started to come in, it gave us the option."

"I imagine the PRS payments from *I Like Your Style* alone would be enough to buy a house!" Gram left a pregnant pause and looked directly at Matt. Matt refused to take the bait; this awkward moment came up most times he saw Gram nowadays. He would never directly refer to any impropriety around *I Like Your Style*, but instead mentioned it meaningfully.

Matt found his whole approach very passive aggressive and refused to fill in the gaps for Gram. If he didn't have the gumption to actually tackle him directly, then Matt wasn't prepared to assist him. He had mentally already prepared his defence and almost relished the opportunity to put the issue to bed, but he also knew Gram had too much pride to directly accusing of taking his song. So, as usual, he diverted him, smoothing over the awkward moment.

"No, while it's a good earner, it's not much better than some of the others. *Four Hands*, for instance, gets massive radio play in Germany, so that earns a lot. But yes, it's all meant that Jen could house hunt and that's improved things. Anyway, what about you? I take it you're still sharing with Colin?"

Gram, realizing that Matt was impervious to barbs about *I Like Your Style*, reluctantly allowed his indignation to subside and started filling Matt in with details of his flat sharing and Colin's strange ways. As

Drive-By Shouting

usual, Matt was only half listening. He reflected that he was bound to Gram in many ways, they had shared over 10 years of hopes and dreams before their pasts had so dramatically diverged and it was this history that he liked and valued. The song would, however, always be a sore point lying between them and he knew that it had rendered any genuine friendship to antiquity. He wished he could simply assign part of the song retrospectively to Gram. After all, he was now accumulating a lot of money from the entire catalogue of songs, but this would inevitably draw Steve, as publisher, into the fray and Steve simply wouldn't entertain it. ("What's he done to earn it? Has he got off planes jetlagged, toured constantly, worked his bollocks off? No he hasn't! He didn't write 'our' songs, so he can piss off! Stop being such a wuss Matt! You can't be sentimental in show business."). Matt brought himself back to the present to listen to the tail end of Grams account...

"... which is how he ended up in the predicament in the first place!"
"Who did?"
"Are you even listening to me Matt?"
"I'm sorry, vagued out there for a second, it's the jetlag."
Gram looked at him doubtfully: "Well anyway, in short, yes; Colin is still a weirdo."
"I dunno worse people to share a flat with. You should try Jen."
"Oh dear! Trouble at the mill? Is it really that bad?"

Drive-By Shouting

Matt rubbed his eyes wearily: "It's difficult. I'm away so much, which is what I always wanted, but it's like we're strangers each time I come back. We sort of have to re-meet each other and when you've got small kids demanding attention, it's hard to have a good time together."

"Well, that's not going to change in the near future."

"Actually, it might. Things are changing at quite a rate at the moment. Clive, of all the guys in the group, has got it into his head that he should have a solo career! He dropped it on us at the end of the US tour. I thought something was going on. He's been a bit distant, not really hanging out or sharing stuff with us. I mean, obviously his real music taste isn't what we do. All he ever listens to is R&B."

"Surely that's not a big deal if Clive leaves? I know he's popular with women but, and I'm sorry if I offend you, he's a bit of a crap singer!"

Matt gave a conspiratorial chuckle: "Ahem, I couldn't possibly comment! Suffice to say, his mic is always pretty low in the mix! No, it's not about the loss of him, it's more... I think it might be an opportunity. As you know, and *you* know probably better than most people, all of this is pretty much what I've always dreamt of: recording, touring, big hotels etc.. But, I'm truly knackered! I haven't stopped for three years, plus the three Cymbal years before that. I feel really burned out and if I carry on, I'm..." He looked earnestly at Gram, "I need you to keep this private. I'm probably going to end up divorced."

"So, things are that bad then?"

Drive-By Shouting

Matt looked down sadly: "They are. And I can't even blame her really. I'm so knackered whenever I see her, and even if she gets her Mum to take the kids for a week and comes to join us on tour, well, that's weird too. It's like joining the circus for a week. She doesn't like the atmosphere, the band doesn't like me being distracted and she ends up having her head filled with all sorts of ideas of what goes on when she's not there."
"And what does go on when she's not there?"
Matt shrugged: "The other guys aren't married, so there's no reason for them to hold back. So, Jen sees Clive copping off with somebody different every night and just sort of assumes I'm doing the same when she's not there." Matt found it odd that he had slipped into a confessional mode with, of all people, Gram. But it felt like the two of them were back in their Northampton lives, when they'd been truly close. It felt good to have somebody to talk to.

Despite himself, Gram was feeling the intimacy too: "And <u>are</u> you? Are you copping off with women when she's not there?"
Matt looked at him ruefully: "I'm not a saint Gram. I'm aware that I'm married and that I don't want to lose my kids. I'm nothing like the other guys in that respect. I'm comparatively very faithful."

Gram laughed out loud: "Only you could use an expression like that Matt! '*Comparatively* faithful', an interesting concept!"
"Okay I've had a couple of weak moments, but I don't make a habit of it. I shouldn't be saying any of this, but you know the rules; 'what goes on tour, stays on tour.'"

Drive-By Shouting

"Matt, it'll go no further. Honour amongst thieves! But anyway, surely Jen knows you by now. It's not as if you were entirely faithful back in Northampton or when we were in *Cymbal*. I thought she just turned a blind eye to it all?"

Matt rubbed his chin: "It's complicated. It's an unspoken thing between us. Yes, she knows that I was a bit liberal with my attentions in the past, but we're involved in a strange mutual delusion that none of that ever happened and that we've always been entirely faithful and loving. In truth, she has, but as you know, the same can't be said about me. It all sort of works when I'm at least living in the same city as her, but it gets a bit strained when we're apart. The thing is though Gram, even though I say that the kids can be a pain in the arse, I still look at them and they're completely amazing. I stood over Sophia's bed as she slept last night and watched her for about twenty minutes. She's like this perfect little miracle, a doll that *I* made. Even after all of the albums and getting to create stuff, in moments like that, you just feel that the very best thing you've ever done is the simple act of creating life. Which doesn't make sense? It's all so banal; any halfwit can have a kid. And, having toured Texas, I've seen the proof of that! But, in all seriousness, that's it in a nutshell; if I carry on I'll lose them, I know I will. And I don't know if I'm prepared to pay that price."

Gram found himself strangely moved. However hard he tried to be furious with Matt, he had a curious way of working his way under Gram's skin, of making him

Drive-By Shouting

care. Gram was also aware of the weakness in his own armour. When he coldly analysed it, despite his anger and bitterness at Matt's success (and his own relative failure), he remained reluctant to entirely fall out with Matt. Gram was starved of access to success and his only window onto it, was his 'friendship' with Matt. He was almost ashamed of the fact that knowing Matt gave him kudos. It was the one name he could drop casually, and for a man with low self-esteem, that was a hard habit to give up. Currently, this desire to have a famous friend outweighed his self-loathing of his need to have that. He looked across the table at Matt.

"So, you're leaving the band?"
"Well, not leaving. More, folding the band while it's ahead. I can take advantage of Clive going, so I can get off the merry-go-round and spend time at home. And hopefully repair my marriage."
"And then what? What you going to do to the rest of your life? Gardening?"
"Dunno, but if it's rock 'n' roll or the kids, and I really never thought I'd feel this way, but it's the kids who win."
"Strictly speaking Matt, it's not rock 'n' roll!" Gram grinned, unable to resist the spike. "You'll always be able to resume your career at the end of the pier one day!!"
"Well Gram, it may be hilariously naff to you, but 14 million people thought it was worth spending a tenner on in the record shop, so you won't find me apologising for being in *Kensal Rise.*"

Drive-By Shouting

He stared icily across the table and there was an awkward silence. Aware that he had lorded it over Gram, Matt sought to ameliorate as he verbally shifted gear: "So what about you Gram, are you playing?"
Gram shifted uncomfortably: "Of course. Still doing the crappy covers gigs and driving to pay the rent. But I'm writing with this really brilliant young girl, she looks like a doll and the stuff is really good. I figure that I'm getting a bit old to be the face of 'the act,' so I'm doing more of a background musical director, stroke, production role. I've got a couple of meetings lined up: A&M, Hit-and-Run Music, and a few others... I think we're in with a shout..."

Matt felt momentarily sad listening to Gram's latest project, knowing (as he suspected Gram did too) that he was unlikely to get signed to a record contract again. The moment had passed and Gram looked too much like what he was, a failed musician, clutching at straws.

"Well, hang on in there. When you have one, let me have a copy. If I come across the right person, I'll put it in their hands."

Gram brightened: "Would you? Because that would really help?" He continued to enthuse about the doll faced girl and Matt wondered how long a man could sustain himself on forlorn hope. Matt would, of course, never pass on a CD or cassette tape to anyone. Gram's stubborn nature would ensure that any attempt to give him a leg up would end in tears.

Drive-By Shouting

Despite Matt's anger and incredulity when Gram had turned down the *Top of the Pops* gigs with Jasminder (and look how that turned out), Matt had still felt motivated to try to lift Gram out of his situation one more time. Once *Kensal Rise*, the band's eponymous first album had been recorded, they had needed to put together a backing band for their first tour. Matt had once more lobbied Steve on Gram's behalf.

"Steve, I really think we should offer my old guitarist Gram Kane the guitar slot in the touring band."
"Why? You feeling guilty about the song? Because that's not a good enough reason."
"Steve, that's not the reason. It's because he's a fantastic guitarist. And, of course, it's because he's my mate."

Steve looked at him doubtfully: "Matt, the world is tipping over to one side with guitarists. Why complicate things by getting your mate in? You'll end up obligated to him and it's an unnecessary complication. We need to be able to hire and fire as circumstances dictate and this will make life difficult. Well, not for *me* it won't, but for you. Anyway, Tony Duncan is going to be musical director of the band, he's great, and he's got a whole roster of excellent guys."
"But Steve, if he works for us, this Tony guy, then surely if one of the acts wants a specific musician, then I'd have thought it's our decision?"

Steve looked at him for a couple of seconds, debating whether now was the time to assert his authority. He relented: "Okay Matt, I personally think this could

Drive-By Shouting

come back and bite you, but if you feel that strongly, then I'm not going to stand in your way. I'll talk to Tony and we can get your guy Gram to audition."
"He'll pass the audition no problem Steve; he's a really brilliant guitarist. Thanks for this, it means a lot."

Matt had been thrilled at the prospect of throwing a good chance Gram's way. He was pushing the boundaries of his relationship with Steve, but after all, he was the 'act' and it was important that he was able to share his success with his old friend. His guilty conscience was also weighing heavily on him. *I Like Your Style* hadn't been released yet, but this might smooth things over and avoid any unpleasantness when Gram heard it. Was it calculating, to place Gram in the role of employee, thereby neutering him? On balance, Matt didn't think so. It was just a leg up that Gram needed.

Gram, however, had seen things rather differently.
"You want me to come on board *after* you've recorded the album. To be a hired gun, playing somebody else's guitar parts, playing material I didn't write and although I haven't heard hardly any of it, I assume it's not exactly up my street? Matt was crestfallen that he was having to sell the opportunity to Gram.
"It's good stuff Gram and it's a really good chance? I've got to confess, I'm pretty amazed that this is your reaction! I honestly thought you'd be thrilled, especially after you said 'no' to the Jasminder /*Top of the Pops* thing. It's like there's no learning curve with you Gram. Because, surely you can see that doing these kinds of things means that you mix with the right

Drive-By Shouting

people? You just don't know where it might lead. I'm stunned."

Where the *Kensal Rise* job had led, was three years of touring the world playing increasingly larger venues, which had quickly become arenas. The original musicians had stayed with the band (with the exception of the first bass player who had graduated to playing with Tina Turner). After all of Matt's cajoling of Steve and twisting his arm to create the opportunity, Gram had once again shot himself in the foot with his total inflexibility. Returning to the present tense, Matt found Gram still talking about the doll girl.

"... and really, she's exactly the right age for it."

Matt suddenly wondered why he was here. He and Gram had polarised so much, that it was difficult for either of them to relate to the other. He had come to realise that the reason celebrities huddled together, was because it was only other celebs who could appreciate the way that your life changed. Gram had been the best mate he had ever had, but that was when they both had nothing and they were now leagues apart. Matt felt a shadow of depression descending over him and wanted to curtail Gram's doll monologue.

"So, you'll never guess who Steve is going out with?"
Gram looked bemused to be interrupted mid-flow, but was nevertheless intrigued: "Oh, I don't know, is it RuPaul?"
"No, it's definitely a heterosexual thing this. And probably your least favourite person in the world."

Drive-By Shouting

Gram looked perplexed: "I've got so many least favourite people, I'm spoiled for choice. If it isn't Margaret Thatcher or Madonna, then I'm stumped? Go on; put me out of my misery."
Matt grinned, banishing the spectre of depression now that they were engaging in some banter: "You won't believe it... He's only gone and started seeing... Kate Craw!"

Gram rocked backwards in horror, almost falling off his stool: "Whaaaat? That evil witch? Well, there's a marriage made in absolute hell."
"Funny you should say that. He's only been seeing her for about six weeks, but he confided in me that already he thinks she's the one." Gram looked agog at this: "Remind me never to confide in you, blabbermouth! But really? I know she's pretty, but what does he see in her? She's such a callous cow. Then again, I could ask 'what does she see in him?' Maybe they're both just impressed with how evil the other one is?" He smiled wickedly: "Bloody hell, they'd better not have kids. It'll be *Damien Omen One, Two and Three,* all rolled into one!"
Matt laughed despite himself: "The thing is, Steve wants me and Jen to meet up with the two of them for dinner. Apart from the frostiness between me and Jen at the moment, it'll be bloody odd having to be nice to Miss Craw, after all the crap she dealt us years ago. I suggested to Steve that I may not want to see her again, but he keeps saying that it's all water under the bridge and that it's important to him that we get along; that

two of the most important people in his life should like each other."
"Bloody hell! Rather you than me Matt."

Drive-By Shouting

Part 7

Double Chorus

Drive-By Shouting

Chapter 17
Summer 1999 - Crouch End

Kate awoke to the sound of her phone ringing. The lounge was dark, as dusk settled over North London. She reached for the phone, checked the caller and groggily answered.
"Hello..."
"Kate, are you okay? I hope you don't mind me calling, but I've been on tenterhooks all day and I figured he must have left by now."

Kate focused on her watch and saw it was 9:53pm: "Oh God, I'm sorry Gram. I fell asleep after Steve left. I must have been lying here for hours."
"You've been asleep! Bloody hell, I've been really worried; I thought you'd had to deal with Steve for all of this time."
"Sorry..."
"Do you want to be alone, or shall I pop round?"
"I'm not sure; I'm still a bit groggy. Give me ten and I'll call you back."
"Okay, but just tell me in a couple of words; is everything okay? Was it awful?"
She rubbed her eyes sleepily: "Yes, pretty awful. But it's done, and everyone can move on. Let me have a

Drive-By Shouting

shower and wake up a bit, and then we can speak in a few minutes."

Twenty minutes later, Kate carried her tea into the dark garden and dialed Gram. He answered straight away: "Hi."
"Hi Gram. I'm a bit more myself now. Sorry about earlier..."
"No problem."
"Listen, I'm a little less woozy, but I still feel a bit tender after today and I think I should just be alone, and let all this sink in tonight. So, do you mind if we don't talk much? I *do* want to have a chat with you, but maybe tomorrow? Let's meet up in the morning and talk properly then. If you're free, of course?"

Gram sounded disappointed: "Er, ok, if that's what you want. Before you go, did you tell Steve everything?"
Kate hesitated before answering: "Almost. He doesn't know about Matt. I just couldn't do that to him. He was upset enough when I asked for a divorce, so I wasn't prepared to twist the knife even further. But he does know about the baby and, although he's arguing against it, I think he knows that it's over between us. He'll be back for another try, I'm sure. After all, he's not somebody who likes to take 'no' for an answer."
"He still wants you back? Even with the baby?"
"Unbelievably, yes."
"Wow. Well, hat's off to him for that. But does he think it's anything to do with me? Should I be looking over my shoulder?"

Drive-By Shouting

"I told him categorically that there was nothing going on between you and me, but who knows what he believes?"
"Well then, I'd better keep my crack squad of private security guards watching my back then. Just in case!" Gram tried to sound casual, but he knew of Steve Coombes' reputation. He was not somebody you would choose to cross.

"I don't think that you need to worry, in fact, I'm sure you don't. I was very clear with him that you're blameless in all this." She had a sudden urge to be alone and free to think. "Listen Gram, we're drifting into a full conversation here and I'm still a bit all over the place about this. How about we firm up the arrangement and I see you tomorrow in Banners at eleven?"
"Okay, let's do that." Once more, he sounded disappointed. "Sorry, I realise that I'm drawing you into a chat here. Glad you're ok. See you tomorrow."

He reluctantly rang off and Kate sat in the dim light which bled out of the flat and onto the garden, nursing her cup of tea in her hands. Sounds of echoing laughter and tinny music drifted from a garden a couple of hundred yards away, mixing with a pair of dogs randomly barking at each other from separate ends of the road. Despite the distant noise, there was a stillness and sense of peace in the air, with a gentle breeze wafting through. She felt herself coming to and was inconveniently wide awake late in the evening.

Drive-By Shouting

By now in something of a whimsical mood, she went back into the flat and retrieved a box file of keepsakes and photographs from under her bed and took it back into the garden; reading letters and looking at photos in the dim light from the flat. She picked up a pack of photographs of her and Steve at the beach, roaming around Rye town centre, taken when he had courted her a few years ago. She had initially found him brash and rather pushier than she liked, he certainly didn't conform to her type. Gradually, however, he'd won her over. It was hard to resist a man who never tired of adoring you. He had been ridiculously generous, considerate and, she had really felt this, truly loving. For the first time in her life, she had put her fierce independence to one side and allowed herself the indulgence of being cared for, of being looked after. It had felt wonderful.

On a cold day in spring, he'd invited her down to his beach house near Rye, the ancient citadel town along the coast from Hastings. They'd driven down in a soft top Mercedes and arrived at a dusty potholed shingle road, which had crunched beneath them as they had bumped along past dilapidated bungalows and, in a couple of cases, disused train carriages which had been converted into strange little houses. It was an oddly chaotic and charming place; a quintessentially English encampment of random dwellings. Most were occupied by locals, but a few had been snapped up by Londoners as holiday homes, entranced by the cheap chic feel. They had rumbled around a couple of bends on the track, before parking in front of a rather more impressively maintained bungalow encased in black shiplap weather boarding. The garden was almost entirely shingle, with a few planting beds constructed out of old railway sleepers. Kate was instantly captivated by the place.

The interior had been gratifyingly spartan, in contrast to what she'd expected Steve to choose. There was no attempt to make the house impressive; it was simply an incredibly homely bolthole. Kate had instantly fallen in love with the place, with its log burning stove and path down to the shingle beach. Being there with Steve, Kate had felt more secure than at any time in her life and, she reflected now, it was that weekend that had begun the snowball which had grown into loving Steve and then marrying him. In retrospect, she had come to realise that who she had thought she was marrying, was a long way short of the full picture.

Over the past few years, the beach house had continued to be Kate's refuge from life, the place she could go to find herself, to think clearly and to rediscover what she really wanted. A sudden urge overcame her. She quickly packed a bag and dressed and within thirty minutes was steering her car through the quiet streets of Hackney, on her way to the coast.

By Friday, the therapeutic effects of the sea air had worked their magic and Kate felt able to project forward, to see her life in a positive light. Many people had questioned her decision to marry Steve, as she had questioned it herself. However, she had felt that the

Drive-By Shouting

security blanket that he wrapped around her was what she needed and, against the tide of the many doubting opinions, she had ploughed on. She realised now that, bruised from the brutal end of her previous relationship with David (the drummer with *The Feelers*), she had craved a sense of permanence, some substance in her life, and Steve had offered that. But, it had been a mistake. It was a relationship fuelled by his adoration of her, but not, in the brisk coastal light of day, by a passionate love in her. And since she'd seen beyond Steve's civilized façade to what really lay behind, there was no going back.

She had called Steve to explain that she had come away, partly out of politeness. Despite the cold legality of her co-owning the property through marriage, she still felt the need to ask permission to use the house; especially in the current circumstances. He had willingly consented (he had long ago grown bored with the house anyway, it had been Kate who had used it, almost exclusively, for the last two years) and he was clinging to a glimmer of hope that her spending time in their old stomping ground would lead her back to his arms. She gently reiterated that nothing had changed, that she still didn't want them to continue as husband and wife, but thought it best to let this realisation sink into him gently. Anyway, the upshot was she was in the place where she felt the happiest.

Having tired of dining on the meagre fare available from the local petrol station, she drove the three miles into Rye to stock up on provisions. She mentally composed recipes as she walked around the shop.

Drive-By Shouting

Despite the warm weather, she craved comfort food. The trolley was filled with more than she could possibly consume alone and the idea of a risotto for one made her feel suddenly lonely. As soon as she was outside the shop, she dialed Gram.

Once again, he answered almost instantly. "So, you haven't forgotten I exist then?"
"No, not at all. Like I said the other day, I'm sorry I blew out our breakfast. I just needed some headspace to sift through everything. But, it's all sifted now to the 'nth' degree. So..., I wondered if you fancied a trip to the seaside."
"When?"
"Well, *now*, I was thinking!"
"Er, no, I can't do that. I've got my gig at the Arsenal Tavern tonight."
Kate grimaced: "Ah, sorry, I forgot."
"And I've also become remarkably van-less since my little moment of forgetfulness at the Fleadh."
"Well, that's no problem really. You can take the train to Hastings and I'll pick you up. Why don't you come down tomorrow morning?"

He considered for a while: "I'd love to, but the thing is, I'm embarrassed to say that I'm a bit broke. Mind you I suppose I'll get some cash at the gig tonight though, so, yes, what the hell, let's go for it!"
"Okay that's brilliant! I'm looking forward to seeing you, just get yourself to Charing Cross, there are trains every half-hour. Call me when you know which one you're on, so I'll know when to get you from Hastings."

Drive-By Shouting

"Okay, sounds simple enough, and actually, now I think about it, it sounds brilliant! I'll probably get a train around 11-ish and I'll call you then."

"Gram, that's fantastic. You'll love it down here. It's really magical, and don't forget to bring your swimming trunks!"

"Really? With my legs?"

"Yes, really. And speaking of legs, break one tonight and we can speak in the morning. Bye!" She ended the call giggling and with a broad smile on her face and became aware of her elevated mood. Her friendship with Gram had been so unexpected and unlikely, but it seemed almost divine in its timing.

Saturday - East Sussex coast

At 12.59, the train rolled into a sunny Hastings station and Gram, incongruously dressed in his black jeans and leather jacket, stepped through the station, to find Kate in a yellow soft top Vauxhall Tigre, just outside. She was wearing her sunglasses, her blond tresses curling around her shoulders, looking for all the world like a '50s movie star. He waved and then somehow clambered over the door and lowered himself into the small car.

He looked at her askance and smiled: "I still can't believe you choose to drive this car, of all the ones you could have!"

Drive-By Shouting

"How dare you! She's beautiful! And yes, lovely to see you too." She patted his hand, shifted the gear and then moved off.
"So, we're at the seaside?" Gram took in the surroundings and the hot sunshine.
"Oh, don't be put off by Hastings. The old town's lovely, but this part's a bit of a shit-hole. But we'll be out of here in no time."
"Well, coming from the wastes of North London, it looks great to me. Bloody beautiful on the way down, by the way; green valleys and rolling hills everywhere. And the trains are the old-fashioned slam door type. I felt like I was on my way to Hogwarts! I didn't think they had those anymore?"
"I wouldn't know. I've never taken the train down here. I'm far too posh! But very glad you had a nice little nostalgia trip, dear boy!"

"You should do it. It's really lovely. Mind you, it might bring you too close for comfort to a certain Mr. Mann. The train stopped at Hurstwood and just sat there for 10 minutes, for no good reason. I felt like getting off and going round to smack him one. Except I don't know where he lives and I couldn't be arsed anyway, to be honest. And, I'm not meant to be doing those kind of things anymore!"
"Oh don't bother thinking about that creep on a day like today! You're on holiday..."

Kate felt elated, the sun on her back, the hills of Fairlight up ahead and after three days in solitary contemplation, nothing was going to dampen her mood today.

Drive-By Shouting

They spent the day swimming, talking and eating. The tide was in and the beach almost deserted, making Gram feel like they were shipwrecked on some distant island. London felt like another country. The sea had a bracing chill that made Kate draw her shoulders high around her ears, as she shrieked at each cold wave, laughing and grimacing in equal measure. Gram found her company thrilling.

The day ended with the two of them sitting on the covered wooden veranda at the front of the house. Gram sipped a beer and sank back on his chair, his feet up on the coffee table: "This is an extraordinary place Kate. I think I might marry Steve if I got to live here!"
"Well, if some of the rumours about my husband are true, he might have you!"

Gram tried to make out her expression in the dim light: "You seem very comfortable with that. The fact that you've married a guy that a lot of people think is, at the very least, bisexual. Didn't that make you wonder whether things were right?" When Kate didn't answer, he continued. "You don't mind me asking this do you? I'm not prying. I'm just... curious?"

Kate continued weighing up the question before eventually replying: "You're obviously not the only one to wonder about this, but, at the beginning, he was completely wonderful. Despite my initial reservations, because I too wasn't sure whether I was his love interest or his fag hag, he really won me over. His reputation is

Drive-By Shouting

as a pretty hard headed dealmaker, but he was kind, considerate and very loving to me. It just grew between us. I think I was also vulnerable. I'd just split up with David, you know, from *The Feelers*?"

"Yeah, I remember him. Bit of a wanker, if you don't mind me saying?"

She laughed: "I don't! He was! And so far as I know, he still is! Anyway, I was a bit all over the place at the end of that. And then, there was Steve, doing everything he could to make me feel good about myself. He actually brought me here and it was partly this place that swung me in his direction."

Gram looked over at Kate, "I hope you don't mind me asking about all this, but it's just that he always seemed such a strange choice for you. It was all very *Beauty and the Beast.*"

Kate shrugged in agreement: "Oh definitely, you're not the first to say that!" She suddenly looked perturbed. "I hope that doesn't sound conceited?"

Gram flashed her a warm smile and shook his head.

Reassured, she continued: "On so many levels, he wasn't my type. Like you say, he's the complete opposite of the pretty boys from bands that I'd dated before. But, he really did appear to be a big softy behind the mask."

Gram nodded: "But that's just it, even the mask is pretty scary. I don't know how much to believe, but if the rumours are true, he was a pretty heavyweight villain before he got into showbiz. You know someone who didn't really have boundaries, if you were unfortunate enough to cross him?" She remained

silent, so he continued, "And you've hinted, pretty strongly, that I could potentially be in trouble if he thought that I was involved with you. That doesn't make him sound like a pussycat."
Kate nodded as she listened. "You're right. I was very wary at the outset, because, obviously, I'd heard all of the rumours too. He categorically denied the stories though; he just said it was all nonsense. He also said that he never publicly denied any of it, because it gave him quite a big advantage in business to have people wanting to stay on the right side of him. And, he said it amused him to let people believe it all."
"And do you think that's true?"

Kate considered her answer carefully: "Well… I certainly believed him at the beginning…"
Gram looked up, his interest piqued: "And now?"
She eyed Gram keenly and assessed him, weighing up whether she should respond or not. Eventually she spoke: "This is not to be repeated, yeah?"
"No, I promise."

She continued to look at him intently: "I really mean it Gram. I need you to keep your word. I'm really putting my trust in you that anything I say will go no further, because, just a whisper about me doubting Steve could cause huge problems, and it would be me who would be drawn into it all." She held his gaze, which he matched as he answered her: "Kate, you can tell me. I promise to never betray your trust in me. Okay?"

"Okay, on that basis… Because the only other person

Drive-By Shouting

I've ever discussed this with is my sister, and I can trust her with my life, so don't let me down!" Seeing him nod in agreement, she continued, "I completely believed Steve at the outset and all the rumours were actually more a source of humour between us. You know, I'd joke that he could do away with anyone who was being obstructive; anyone who didn't give me a presenting role I wanted, or something like that. It was all so outlandish and so at odds with the life we were leading; living in Hampstead, hanging out with all the stars, with a few minor Royals thrown in, y'know? It was all very glamourous. So, the idea of Steve being an East End thug was just… Well, it was just farcical really.

But gradually…" She paused and grimaced; "I started to meet a few of his old 'associates,' you know, the guys from his past or, at least, I thought they were from his past. He normally kept them at arm's length, but eventually, after we'd been married for a while, he started letting a few of them come round to the house. And they were… Well, they were, frankly; *monsters*. Charming monsters, but still utterly terrifying when you looked past the smart suits."
"In what way?"
"It was just the way that they *were*. Because, you could tell that underneath all the money, under the veneer of respectability, they were basically just… just… *evil*. And I grew to increasingly realise that these were men who could, and would, do anything. And I mean *anything*."
"Such as?"

Drive-By Shouting

She looked at him solemnly: "I'm sure you can imagine. Pretty much anything; all the things that you wouldn't want to think about... It was then that I started looking at Steve in a different way. If these were his oldest associates or 'friends' even, then what did that say about him? Was he just more skilled at hiding it than them? I mean, you start to imagine all sorts…"
"Was it anything specific?"
"No, never. But it was the realisation that, if he was choosing to mix with these people, and it seemed that he was doing business with them too, then, in all probability, he had some of that… I don't know… some of that *horror* in him as well. And once I'd seen it, I couldn't un-see it. From that moment on, I think, in retrospect, that I began to distance myself from him. And in a strange way, it was mirrored in him too. I think he sensed that I'd seen through him."
"And did you ever feel threatened?"
"Oh God no, I'd have left a lot earlier! I'm not saying that! I'm certain he'd never harm me. And it was never anything overt; it was just a growing feeling that he wasn't who I'd thought he was. I never felt personally threatened, but, I wouldn't advise anyone else to make an enemy of him."

She sat back in her chair and threw up her arms, "Anyway, enough about all this. It's all conjecture anyway. It's all 'something and nothing' and based on no more than my gut feelings. But I still wouldn't want you to repeat this. Okay?" She anxiously studied Gram again.
"You have my word."

Drive-By Shouting

"C'mon, let's talk about something else." She stood up. "Another beer?"
Gram nodded and smiled in appreciation: "That would be excellent."

As Kate went through the house to the kitchen, Gram picked up Kate's tobacco sunburst Gibson J200 Montana Special, quietly marveling at how somebody who (by her own admission) could barely play owned such an impressive instrument. He pulled it across his lap and quietly picked out some familiar patterns while he reflected on Matt's situation, particularly in the light of all of this information about Steve Combes. He wondered if Matt realised quite how risky his predicament might be. He had been so busy worrying about the loss of his career; maybe he ought to be more worried about his safety?

Kate returned with a beer for Gram and rejoined him on the front veranda, listening appreciatively to his playing. Eventually, he felt slightly self-conscious about lapping up all of Kate's undivided attention, and stopped. He was unused to being noticed, and certainly unused to being properly appreciated. He felt the need to divert her.

"This place is just amazing Kate. I can understand why you love it so much."
"Yes, it's a special place."

She looked worried, as if their previous conversation had remained with her. "And, you have to remember that Steve spotted it and felt it was a special place, so

Drive-By Shouting

he's not all bad? I feel sort of dis-loyal, having said all of that stuff about Steve, because he's not just some one dimensional, cardboard cut-out villain. There's more to him than that. There had to be, or I wouldn't have been with him. And this place also reflected a side of him, this worn, hammered together place. Totally at odds with the power suited guy that the world sees." She sipped from her glass and briefly listened to the sound of the waves crashing on the beach, lost in thought. Eventually her attention returned to a patiently waiting Gram.

"When I think about it now, though, I think this place was just a phase for him. He hardly comes here anymore; it's become pretty much my personal plaything. I'm almost always here alone and I like it that way. Although, I do very much like having you here too. So, thank you for coming down. And it's great to hear that thing being played, it's a little bit wasted on me; I can only play three chords and none of them very well!"
"It's a pretty lovely guitar, how come you ended up with such a good one if you can't even play?"
"Well, that's Steve again. I only had to mention a passing interest in anything, and the best guitar, the best oil paints and easels, you name it, and it would turn up the next day. That's the other side of him. Very generous. He looks after the people in his circle very well. You feel very cared for..."

Gram stretched out on the chair and smiled: "I can imagine that's very seductive. We all need to be looked after sometimes. And actually, today has been a real

Drive-By Shouting

boost to me, so thank you for inviting me down. I haven't had a holiday in years, but one day down here has made me feel like a new man. Sitting on the beach this afternoon, looking at that vast horizon, I thought a lot about where I'd ended up and it's not where I thought I'd be. I'm really determined to change it all now. To change everything. And to that end, I'll be stopping at this beer. I'm sticking to a maximum of a couple of bottles a night. And I haven't touched dope since the Fleadh. I really want to go in a different direction."

"Well, I'm also determined to help you, because I can see that you've been a bit uncared for. I want you to put your proud Northerner shtick to one side. If you still think you've got something to offer as a producer and writer, then let's make it happen. I've got money, you've got the talent. And, at the risk of opening up our historical can of worms, I do kind of owe you one. It would make me feel good to help you."

Gram grimaced awkwardly: "Don't worry; the *history* is completely put to bed. But I'm still not sure it would make me feel good to have you financially backing me Kate. And I'm not just being stupidly proud for the sake of it. I'm also aware that, out of nowhere, you and I have become... quite close, you know, really good mates. I'm pretty uncomfortable with taking charity from you. It could really screw this up. Screw up the nice friendship that we've got."

"Well don't think of it as charity then. Think of it as a loan, or, as I said the other night, if you'd rather put it

Drive-By Shouting

in the music business parlance, an *advance*, repayable when you break through and make money. There's nothing remotely charitable about that! What do you actually need to get yourself up and running?"

Gram sat quietly, caught between his pride and a rising excitement that he may be able to actually change his life. Finally, he spoke: "Okay, if I was able to stop being pigheaded, I'd need a studio. A few months ago I went to a small business centre in Hornsey, where they have units available, but I just couldn't justify it at the time, but I think they're still empty. I'd need a mixing desk, all the cabling and some decent microphones. I know a guy who's selling the whole lot second-hand; it's all good gear and it'd be relatively cheap. However, the big-ticket item is that I would really need a stereo sampler, because that's where everything's going. Virtually all music will be made using those in a few years. I've been borrowing the hire units from Rox Rentals, but obviously that's now off-limits." He raised his eyebrows and grinned ironically. "Anyway, I've got really good at using them over the last couple of years, and used one on the *Blue Dolls* record that only you, in the whole world, thought was any good!"

"It was good. Actually, it was brilliant! Okay, so how much are we talking in cash terms?"

Gram started to mentally tot things up in his head: "Well... The industrial unit is £400 a month plus bills, but the big upfront costs are, I reckon I can get all of the gear from the guy who's selling for about fifteen grand, and the stereo sampler is about six thousand, I

Drive-By Shouting

could do with two of them, but could manage with one..."

"We'll manage with two, thank you! As George Michael says; if you're gonna do it, do it right! So, none of that is a problem financially. And what about the *Blue Dolls*, are they still around?"

"It was mainly Polly actually, the singer. The other girls were more window dressing really. It was her that I mostly worked with and developed. When I met her, she just looked like the perfect popstar; you know the way that some people have just got it, the *thing*? I'm still in touch with her; she's working in a shop, a bit disillusioned, obviously. It all looked so promising, and then, nothing. And now she's back serving customers instead of doing Top of the Pops. The usual story..."

"But would she be interested in trying again?" Gram noted that Kate sounded genuinely enthusiastic.

"Like a shot! But why? It didn't sell, and no one's interested…?"

"That's simply not true. *I'm* interested." She paused and thought for a moment. "Okay here's the deal. If your young starlet Polly is up for another crack at it, I'll be the manager. I'll finance the studio, give you the support that you need and, if the songs are as good as that CD you did, I'll get you a major record deal. How does that sound?"

Gram fought to sound measured in his answer; such was the rising thrill that was beginning to race through him. "Really? I mean, that would be brilliant, but

Drive-By Shouting

you're not a music manager. Is that something you think you can do, or even want to do, especially in your condition?"

"Gram, I'm pregnant, not ill! Think about it. I know 'everybody who's anybody' in the music business, plus, lots of TV and almost all of the music press. As they say, it's *who* you know, not what you know! So, far from this being charity, this is an investment, but with the added benefit that I'm helping a friend and that would feel good. But, genuinely, I'm not a fool. I wouldn't put my money into this if I didn't think that you were someone who's really talented and has masses of untapped potential. So, are you in?"

Gram found himself laughing as the full wave of excitement crashed through him. "You're bloody right I am!" His body tingled, and he felt truly happy for what he realized, was the first time in ages. "God Kate, I feel so happy about this. It's like a weight has been lifted off me! This is going to be brilliant and yes, I think you'd be the perfect manager too."

"So, when we get back to town, let's meet up with Polly and get her on board. Then let's make some brilliant records and, along the way, make lots of money! We need to drive back tomorrow so I can meet Steve on Monday morning, so why don't you give Polly a bell and let's see if she's around later in the day, or in the evening? That'll give me something to look forward to after another difficult session with Steve."

Drive-By Shouting

Gram propped up the Gibson and jumped up out of his chair excitedly, while reaching into his pocket. "No time like the present. I'll call her right now!"

Sunday morning - The beach

Shortly after 6am, Gram was awoken by the sunlight pouring through the cracks in the window shutters. After ten fruitless minutes, spent trying to coax himself back to sleep, he sat up, pulled on his jeans and shirt and tiptoed through the bungalow, to avoid waking Kate, who was gently snoring in the main bedroom. Once in the kitchen, he turned on the kettle before opening the back door, revealing the vast expanse of shingle that lay behind the house. The sun was too inviting for him to wait for his cup of tea, so he found his boots on the front porch and crunched down the shingle path at the front of the house and onto the beach.

The tide was in and, shielding his eyes from the bright glare reflecting off the water, he took in the vast expanse of horizon. Other than a solitary dog walker some 500 yards to his right, Gram had the beach to himself. He walked over to one of the wooden sea defence groynes and, finding a sunbaked dry section, sat down on the weather-beaten wood to drink in the view.

His mind wandered over the events of the past few weeks. He was genuinely surprised to find himself

Drive-By Shouting

viewing events that would previously have been personal disasters (losing the backline gear at the Fleadh festival, losing his job and his means of transport) as hugely positive changes in his life. His conversation with Kate on the porch the previous evening, had filled him with real hope, a feeling he had grown un-used to, since the demise of *Cymbal* and the slow fall to oblivion that he had undergone since. That the catalyst for this change, this injection of belief, should be, of all people, Kate Craw still astonished Gram. He had, with some justification (he thought), absolutely detested Kate. She had been vicious in her criticism of *Cymbal* and this had somehow been exacerbated by the fact that she was, undeniably beautiful.

When he'd first met Kate, Gram had been thoroughly intimidated by her. Despite her down to earth nature, he'd found her unapproachable; she was simply too perfect. He remembered their first meeting and how he'd immediately clammed up in her presence. He could barely believe that events had turned the way that they had, that she was on the cusp of representing him, or that he now thought so highly of her. It was thoroughly unexpected.

A thrill ran through Gram as he anticipated all of the possibilities with the *Blue Dolls*. Polly had sounded ecstatic when he had spoken to her and more than a little star-struck to hear that Kate Craw was interested in managing her. Like Gram, any doubt about Kate's experience was swept away by the sheer intoxication of somebody, *anybody*, saying that they like you, they

Drive-By Shouting

value what you do, and that they believe in you. The boost that such a small and simple validation could inject was profound and it was coursing through Gram as he breathed in the sea air and let the morning sun pour itself into him. He felt glad to be alive and that he had plenty to live for. He was acutely aware of how alien these feelings were to him.

Later, after Kate had joined him for a bracing morning swim, the two of them had ambled around Rye, Gram marveling at the medieval beauty of the old town citadel, with its cobbled streets and ancient houses. It was unbelievably quaint. They lunched at The Mermaid, interrupted twice by people seeking Kate's autograph ("it always happens more out in the sticks," she explained, "in London, no one gives a toss if you're famous or not. Celebrities are ten-a-penny up there!").

Kate suggested they leave soon after lunch, in order to avoid the London bound traffic and by 3pm they were reluctantly trundling up the A21. After a few minutes of silent contemplation, Gram spoke: "I'm glad you're kind of sorted with Steve now, but doesn't it piss you off that our mutual friend Matt is getting off scot free? That he gets to keep his happy family, his wonderful career, to manipulate everyone else, while staying safe in his cosseted world? Whilst you are, quite literally, left holding the baby. Doesn't that piss you off?"

She kept her eyes on the road while thinking about this: "Yes, it does piss me off, but, without completely destroying Steve, I can't see how I can make Matt account for his behaviour." They drove on before Gram

Drive-By Shouting

broke the silence a minute later: "Bizarre coincidence though, that he ends up living halfway between your beach house and London?"

Kate shrugged: "It's not a coincidence. Soon after I started seeing Steve, Matt and the *lovely* Jen came down with us to the beach house for a long weekend. They loved it there, so when they started thinking about moving out of London, they gravitated in this direction. They realised that going all the way to the coast every day was too far, but maybe by being somewhere near Tunbridge Wells, I think they thought they could have the best of both worlds. You can be in London in under an hour or at the beach in 45 minutes. So, no, it's not a coincidence."

They continued in silence, apart from the wind noise. Suddenly, Kate chuckled to herself, Gram turned to look at her.
"What's amusing you so much?"
"You're right. I don't see why he should get off scot free. At the very least, he should be made to feel uncomfortable. So, shall we have a bit of fun at his expense?"

Drive-By Shouting

Chapter 18
Hurstwood - Sunday afternoon

Matt reached across for the bottle and replenished his glass. Around the table sat their guests for lunch, all enjoying the alfresco feast at the large table down on the pool terrace. Matt surveyed the scene. He, Jen and their well-heeled local friends, enjoying a languid sun-drenched day in the most beautiful surroundings. It was a glorious picture, the appreciation of which was almost entirely marred by the turmoil in Matt's head.

He sank the contents of his newly filled glass in an attempt to quell the rising terror within him. It was now five days since Steve Coombes had visited him at the *'Live at 10!'* studios and he still hadn't received a return call, despite leaving three voicemail messages for him on his mobile phone. He had eventually called Vanessa at the office, to ask if Steve was okay. She'd merely hinted that Steve was *out of sorts* and a bit upset, but that she was sure he'd call back very soon. Obviously, neither Kate nor Gram would communicate with him either and so, into this information vacuum, Matt was creating the perfect cocktail of terror, vacillating between believing that no

Drive-By Shouting

news is good news (surely Steve would have hunted him down if he had learned the truth) to expecting a metaphorical hammer blow to strike at any moment, throwing his entire life into total turmoil. He reached instinctively for the bottle once more.

"Seriously Matt, you should move quickly on this. The whole tech stock market is going crazy. Getting in now will see you multiply your investment tens of times. Or even hundreds! It's really going to be that big. Surely you'd be interested in at least looking at it?" Matt sat in silence, absorbed in his personal horror story. He became aware of his sleeve being tugged.

"Matt, Matt. Stop being so bloody dozy! Greg's been waiting for you to answer and you're off in dreamland. Sorry Greg, I think it's his age!" Jen laughed nervously before turning to Matt: "I think we should look seriously at what Greg's saying Matt, don't you?"

Matt brought himself to attention: "Sorry Greg, really sorry… I just drifted off a bit, probably drunk more than I should have today."
"I'll say!" Jen shot him a mock angry look, that Matt knew also contained the genuine emotion. Matt returned his gaze to Greg: "I still don't get why everyone is so fired up about this dotcom stuff. Why is everyone piling into buying shares? What's the big deal?"

"Oh Matt. It's going to change the world!" Greg spread his hands expansively. "Everything we do is going to change. We won't be going to the shops in a few years,

Drive-By Shouting

we'll just buy everything on the World Wide Web and get it all delivered. It'll revolutionise the whole world."

Matt looked perplexed: "What's so special about that? My friend's mums all had Littlewoods catalogues when I was a kid, which did pretty much the same thing, and nobody's rushing to buy shares in that!"

"Yeah, but Matt, this won't just be a couple of mums. It will be absolutely everyone! Everybody in the world. And it's the operators who establish themselves now, who'll conquer the world and own it! Like, for instance, there's this start-up, WooWoo.com, they're into women's fashion and they're going to eventually be the biggest supplier of women's clothing on the planet. The world and their wife will buy from them. I mean everyone's wife who has money, that is! They'll all buy their clothes on the Internet and they'll do it at WooWoo.com. Mark my words. This is the gold rush!"

Matt wearily rubbed the back of his neck: "I just don't agree. Any time I've tried to get onto this World Wide Web thing, it's crap! Everything takes hours. Who's going to bother their arse going through all that? Waiting for stuff to load onto their computer?"

Greg grinned conspiratorially: "But that's just it Matt. All the techies are saying that that's the thing that's going to change, and soon. All the web stuff is going to get fast, really fast! And when it does, that's when all this tech stock will rocket in value. Listen Matt, I hardly ever recommend stock to friends, the last thing I want is for some stock to go bad and then I end up with an

Drive-By Shouting

angry mate. But really, this is different. Even Sally and I have gone big on this, because when it comes good, I reckon we'll be sitting on stock worth millions. Tens of millions."

His interest piqued, Matt began to perk up: "What, really? *Tens* of millions?"
"Yes. You'd never have to work again. And you wouldn't be answerable to anyone, because nobody can touch you when you've got that much."
Matt nodded: "Okay Greg, now I get it. I mean, it does sound a bit too good to be true, but I guess if anyone knows about this, *you* do. How much of an investment would get you that kind of return? You know, tens of millions?"

"I'd go in with everything you've got Matt. But I don't know, one mill, maybe a couple of million? You wouldn't even have to bother your arse presenting telly programmes then! You could just sail around the Med on your yacht and do whatever you want."

Matt quickly projected himself into this scenario and liked what he saw. All of his current anxiety was centred on his overreliance on Steve Coombes' goodwill. Even if he rode through this terrible situation, he was always going to be vulnerable, given Steve's volatility. Even with his PRS royalties and TV money, he and Jen just seemed to spend everything that came in, refitting the pool house, relaying the tennis court, managing the land, the list of expenses was endless. What he needed was what Bob Geldof called 'Fuck You Money,' to insulate him from disaster if all his income fell away. And this certainly sounded like the route to get there.

"Okay Greg, I'll give you your due; you've gone quite a long way towards convincing me. This does sound interesting. Really interesting! I'll see what I can do to raise some cash and then, let's talk a bit more. But obviously, let's do it when I'm not quite so pissed, that would be helpful!" He felt his tongue struggling slightly with the words, as the cumulative effect of a full day's drinking began to slow him. He leaned forward and clinked glasses with Greg before raising the glass to his lips, intending to drain it once more. He stopped short as Jen grabbed his forearm tightly and hissed angrily: "What the hell! Matt, did you invite them?"

He followed her gaze up the sloping lawn towards the house and saw, a hundred yards away and strolling nonchalantly towards them, Kate, her arm linked in Gram's. Greg, having also followed Jen's alarmed gaze, turned to view them. "Wow, it's that Kate Craw girl! How cool Matty boy, Hurstwood's becoming celebrity central!" He slapped Matt's arm and in a slightly lowered voice said lasciviously, "God, she's a looker, isn't she?"

By now, Gram and Kate were twenty yards away and within earshot. Jen rose from her chair and, after summoning as much sincerity as she could muster, greeted them.
"Kate, darling, how lovely to see you again. And you too, obviously, Gram." She swept around the table and

Drive-By Shouting

air-kissed Kate, before awkwardly squeezing Gram's arm and grinning inanely at them both.
"So, you decided to pop in? Bit of a way from North London!"

Kate smiled sweetly, despite the obvious insincerity of the welcome. "Well, we were down at the beach house and..."
"Oh the beach house, how lovely!" Jen's rictus grin made her face ache.
"Yes. And on the way back, we saw the sign to Hurstwood and just thought: 'Hey, let's be spontaneous and pop in.' I hope it's not inconvenient, because I see now that you've got a bit of a gathering going on. Sorry to intrude." Kate was already regretting the whole idea and had tried to abort the visit in the front-driveway, but Gram had been determined to go ahead. She had a bad feeling about the whole enterprise.
Jen was flapping: "Oh no, no, not at all! You're so welcome! We finished lunch some time ago, but you know, how lovely, you can join us for a drink." Jen turned to face Matt. "Can't they darling? Join us for a drink?"
Matt sat stunned in his chair.

Jen blustered to cover the awkwardness of the impasse: "Oh, ignore Matthew guys! He's obviously too pissed to speak! Hey everyone! This is Kate and Gram. Old friends of ours. And this is..." She swept her hand to signify the whole table, "and this is, well; everyone! Hah hah!"

Drive-By Shouting

Kate walked reluctantly around the table being introduced to all of the guests, while Gram remained standing opposite Matt, looking on impassively at Kate, waving and nodding as each lunch guest was introduced.

"So, grab a seat at least and let's get you a drink!" Jen fussed around the table picking up clean glasses. Kate decided that the game had gone far enough and held up her hands in apology. "Actually Jen, we really were just popping in as we were passing, and I can see that our timing is a bit off, you guys are obviously in the middle of a session. So, I think we'll just get going. I mean it's not like I can drink anyway!" She immediately realised her mistake.

"Why's that?" Jen cocked her head and looked at her, and then Gram.
Kate, thinking quickly, raised her car keys: "Because, I'm driving, obviously! So, anyway, sorry to disturb you, but we'll just get going, eh, Gram?" Suddenly desperate to get away from the scene, she turned to go, but Gram remained rooted to the spot, staring at the ashen faced Matt.
"Nice house you have Matt. Very big and impressive. Haven't you done well? Talent really pays, eh?"
"That's a funny thing to say Gram?" Jen trilled nervously, as Gram continued to stare at Matt, still sitting mutely in the chair.

Abruptly, Matt levered himself up, feeling suddenly sober, as adrenaline and fear flushed through him. He could feel his heart beating wildly in his chest.

Drive-By Shouting

"Jen, look after our guests. I'll just walk the guys to their car, so we can catch up a bit." He sounded angry and Jen looked to him askance, rather confused by his sudden animation: "Oh, okay, if you want. Well, if you must go, nice to see you Kate, same with you Gram." They exchanged waved farewells with the lunch party and started up the lawn towards the house. They walked in an expectant silence until they were about fifty yards up the slope, when Matt, in a furious sotto voce, hissed at them: "What the fuck do you think you're doing? You pair of bastards!" Gram moved protectively to switch places with Kate to be nearest to Matt. He spoke calmly: "Calm down Matt. It's about time that you realized that there are ramifications when you decide to just *use* people."

Matt angrily retorted: "What you mean by that? What have you told Steve? I need to know."
Ignoring the questions, Gram replied testily: "You've got away with being a complete twat for far too long Matt. So, a little bit of dis-comfort will be good for your soul."

They had reached the house and Kate began to walk briskly around the side, evidently keen to escape the scene that had unravelled out of her control; and desperately regretting that she hadn't succeeded in stopping before it was too late. Gram, however, grabbed her hand and steered her back through the open French doors into the large kitchen and diner with its atrium roof and large furnished area beyond.

Drive-By Shouting

Gram briefly took in the grandeur of the vast room, before turning and addressing Matt sarcastically: "Well Matt, this *is* impressive!" Matt ignored him and turned away to speak imploringly to Kate: "Tell me what you've told Steve. Please?" Gram moved between them.
"Don't think you can just try to intimidate Kate while I'm here." He stared aggressively at Matt.

Sensing, through his fearful haze, that he was going to get no help from either party, Matt switched back to straight anger: "Well, if you're not going to tell me, then just fuck off out of my house, both of you! How fucking dare you just turn up unannounced? What the fuck are you playing at?"

Gram looked at him mockingly: "Oh how ironic! You leave endless messages for both of us, but when we drop in for a chat, we're not welcome. How strange!"
Matt's face turned puce with rage: "Because you haven't come here to tell me any of the things I need to know, have you? You've come to play with me; it's all a fucking game to you!" Matt swayed and steadied himself, holding onto the kitchen island unit. Gram laughed: "Look at you Matt, quivering at the prospect of all this being taken away. Of all your ill-gotten gains falling out of your hands." He sneered at him.

"What the fuck is wrong with you Gram? I've lost count of the number of times I've tried to lift you out of the gutter, but it was your own pigheaded ignorance that kept you there. It wasn't ever anything that I did, whatever you may think."

Drive-By Shouting

"Well, you stole my song, for starters."
"Oh, for fuck's sake...The usual blame game. You've obviously decided that you hate me and that everything that's wrong with your life is my fault, but the truth is everything that's shit in your life, is your own doing. You're the problem, not me! You rode on my coat tails for years, but couldn't take advantage of it, because... you're a loser!" Matt finally started to feel powerful, asserting himself over Gram. He watched as Kate gripped Gram's jacket and turned him to face her. "Please Gram, this is awful, can we just go?" Gram registered the imploring look on Kate's face and nodded. Wordlessly, he started to follow her out.

Sensing a victory of sorts, Matt's braggadocio got the better of him and he addressed Gram's departing form mockingly: "Yeah, that's right Gram; just do what you're told! Just look at you now; still the obedient puppy. You're a fucking loser!" Matt swayed and grinned provocatively, his temporary sober-state abandoning him. He was unable to resist a parting shot. "Still wanting to drink my dregs? My sloppy seconds!"

At this, Gram's self-control collapsed and, before Kate could intervene to stop him, he marched back towards Matt. His punch was so hard and fast, that Matt, already slow and unsteady, simply collapsed on the floor, clutching his face. He screamed up at them.
"Get out of my house, you fucking bastards!"
"What's the hell is going on?" A startled Jen appeared at the French doors. She took in the scene; Matt on the floor, drunk and bleeding from his nose. Kate, looking

Drive-By Shouting

shocked and wishing she was anywhere but there, and Gram; fist clenched, standing triumphantly over her stricken husband.

"What are you all doing? Everyone can hear you screaming down at the pool! What the hell is this all about?" Gram turned to look at her and then back at the prone Matt, his frightened ashen face once more in evidence beneath the smeared blood.
"Well, go on Matt. Why don't you tell her?" They stared at each other in silence, before Gram grabbed Kate's hand and swept her through the house, unsure of which way was out. Kate took over and pointed "It's this way." She shouted over her shoulder; "Jen, I'm so sorry about this. I'm so sorry about everything..."

Once outside the house, Kate tore her hand out of Gram's grasp and turned to face him, red faced and angry: "Gram, why did you do that? I can't believe what just happened! That was... that was... completely over the top!" With his anger now beginning to subside, Gram nodded: "Yeah, I'm sorry Kate. But, after what he just said, he did deserve it... The red mist just came over me."
"You could have just ignored it and done as I'd asked, and just left."
"No, I couldn't. I've had years of feeling discounted and second-best, being made to feel shit by him. And then seeing how he's living, like a fucking king! It all just boiled over."
"But to do it when I was there? That was horrible and completely selfish. That wasn't the plan!"

Drive-By Shouting

He shuffled awkwardly: "But there wasn't a plan, was there? It was a spontaneous idea of high jinks. It was just 'let's go and poke the bear to see what happens.' And when we did, it was just inevitable that it would all kick off like that."

Kate looked up at him furiously: "No it wasn't. It wasn't inevitable at all. I just wanted to shake him up. To make him feel something, just a little of all the crap that's going on, that's all. I didn't want him punched!"
"What was I supposed to do, when he said those things?"
"Walk away, like an adult! And I didn't want Jen witnessing it all!

"Well, that's his problem. And anyway, he'll smooth it over as usual. Whatever shit he makes up, she'll lap it up; that's a very well-worn script, so don't worry about that! And, from the look of terror on his face when we arrived, I think you can rest assured that he is definitely 'feeling the pressure.' He's terrified. I don't think I've ever seen him so scared. So let's not fall out about it; after all, he's the common enemy. Let's just get in the car and get out of here, eh?"

They both climbed into the car and headed towards Matt's gates. They drove down the twisting Sussex lanes in silence, Kate stern and focused on the road ahead. After a few minutes she spoke in a clipped, stern tone.
"Gram. You shouldn't have done that. That was too much. I can't believe that I opened up about Steve and my fears that he had something dark and possibly

Drive-By Shouting

violent in him. And then you go and do that! I can't believe you pushed it so far. That was horrible!"
Gram breathed deeply, a calm returning to him: "I know. I went too far. And I'm sorry I did that in front of you. I'm not like that. I'm not really a violent guy. So in terms of you, I'm really sorry it happened. But, in terms of me, *that's* been coming for a long, long time."

"But that's just the problem Gram. That was all about *you*; all about you deciding that today was when you wanted to settle *your* grievances. Never mind that you've told me about all the numerous times that you sat and had a quiet drink with him over the years without calling him up for his behaviour. It had to be *today* that your volcano blew its top? It had to be about you and him." She slowed down and pulled the car to the side of the road and turned to face him. Gram squirmed in his seat, but eventually met her eye defiantly: "Actually, what set me off was him insulting you, that stuff he said was completely insulting. All about drinking his dregs and the rest. It was disgusting."

"That wasn't you sticking up for me! That was you reacting like a Neanderthal to being called a loser. Don't try to twist this into you defending my honour. Because we both know that it was all about your alpha male shit! Please don't insult me with your knight in shining armour routine.

Gram seethed as he considered this. When he spoke, he was calm: "Actually Kate, it was probably a bit of both. I was offended on your behalf by what he said,

Drive-By Shouting

but yes, he also said all the things I knew he'd always thought about me too. He thinks he's superior to me and that I've just tried to ride on his coat-tails, although, actually, everything he knows about songwriting, he learned from *me*! Fundamentally, you're new to this whole thing Kate, but I'm not. Yes, Matt's stuffed it to you over the past couple of months, quite literally, as it happens," he noticed Kate flinch at this, "but he's been doing it to me for years!"

"That still doesn't excuse your behaviour to him! All of that happened because you provoked him with what he stood to lose. He just retaliated."

Gram felt his temper rising again: "For fucks sake Kate! What's really going on here? You seem incredibly bothered that Matt got hurt. Is it that actually, a bit of you is still hoping that he'll decide to leave Jen? To join you in Paradise? Is that what this is all about? You're actually pissed off that I ruined the scene in your head; where he sees you, wishes he could be with you and starts to yearn for a new start? Is that what you thought would happen today? Because you seem ridiculously concerned about him getting punched!"

"What?" Kate was incredulous. "How could you even *think* that? After all the things I've told you. You think I want *him*?"

"Well, maybe you do, because you're stupidly angry about me giving him a smack. And one that was long overdue. Yes, that's it, isn't it? I'm just here to make him jealous, aren't I?"

Kate stared at him, mouth agape: "You fucking moron. You have no idea! I wouldn't touch him with a barge pole."

Drive-By Shouting

"Well, you're having his baby. So you're obviously not *that* disgusted by him!"
Kate slapped his face and glared angrily at him. Gram rubbed his red cheek and replied testily: "Oh, I see; violence is okay if it's you handing it out? You fucking hypocrite!"

She flushed with anger: "Get out!"
"What?"
"Get out of my car!"
Gram looked ahead at the deserted tree-lined lane and the fields rising into the distance. "Don't be stupid Kate. We're in the middle of nowhere!"

Kate, fuming, considered for a while, before turning the ignition back on and driving off, angrily spitting out words at him: "Don't say a fucking word! I have nothing to say to you. Nothing!"

His face still stinging, Gram concurred and stared angrily out of the window.

Ninety minutes later - North London

Kate turned the corner into Drylands Road and pulled up outside Gram's flat. They had driven in an awkward silence for over an hour and a half. The energy fizzing off Kate had been sufficient to deter Gram from initiating any conversation. His anger had fully subsided and switched into a deep regret, and Gram now simply wanted to repair the damage. Kate

Drive-By Shouting

switched off the engine and continued to stare straight ahead.

"Kate. I really fucked up, didn't I?" He turned his head to look at her. She silently ran her tongue across the front of her top row of teeth and continued to stare directly ahead through the windscreen.

"I'm afraid I can't talk about it Gram. I'm really hurt and angry about what you did. And even angrier about what you said. Especially after all the things I told you. So, can you please get out of my car?" She maintained her forward gaze.
"Kate, I'm sorry... Can we just talk about this?"
"Just get out please."

Realising the futility of trying to pressure her into a response, he awkwardly and reluctantly got out of the car. He held the passenger door open and bent down to eye-level.
"Shall I call you tomorrow? When you've had a chance to calm down?"
"Please shut the door."
He paused until Kate turned to look at him. This time, there was no mistaking the barely suppressed fury in her staccato voice.
"Just close the fucking door!"

He had only just done so, when the engine sprang to life and she swiftly pulled away, leaving Gram to watch the tailgate disappear around the corner.

Drive-By Shouting

Chapter 19
Tuesday - Two days later

At just after 11am, the doorbell rang. Kate paused, a deep presentiment of who was at the door throwing her into a momentary paralysis. The bell rang again and, mind made up, she opened the door. As she had predicted, Gram stood outside, trying to look nonchalant despite his evident nervousness. He looked at her earnestly.
"I thought we should talk?"

Ignoring the proffered bunch of flowers, she replied: "You'd better come in," before turning and walking ahead of him. He followed her through the flat and into the lounge, trying to read her mood. At least she'd invited him in. She sat and gestured to the armchair opposite. She watched him intently as he took a seat and Gram realised that he would be required to initiate the conversation, as Kate's pride obviously precluded her from doing so.
"I've had a shit couple of days Kate. I shouldn't have said what I said. I'm sorry about what happened as well. I acted like a thug. I'm really, really not like that. And I know that's hard to believe after the past couple

Drive-By Shouting

of weeks, but I'm not. I just boiled over; but that's it, it's over. I promise you, I'll never behave like that again." Kate remained impassive and he felt obliged to carry on. "And I'm especially sorry that I did that after you'd told me about Steve's 'dark' side. I don't know what came over me. Well, I do, utterly selfish stupidity. I was lancing the boil, but I know my timing couldn't have been worse. It was utterly selfish."

She sat in silence, determined to mine the awkwardness of the moment. Gram surmised that this was a form of punishment. Eventually, her face softened a little.
"Do you really think that I want to be with Matt and that I'm just using you?"
"No, I don't! I was just angry. It was the red mist. I was lashing out saying irrational stuff. I'm sorry."

Again, she paused before speaking: "I felt very betrayed by you saying that stuff. All the more so, to hear it coming from you. I thought you understood what I think about Matt and how this situation that I'm in," she gestured to her midriff, "is not what I would ever have wanted. I thought you understood me?"
Gram looked at her plaintively: "I *think* I do Kate, but, I just don't know what we're doing here. I mean, what is this? I start hanging out with someone I had previously thought of as my mortal enemy. Who I then find out, that I really like? That I *really* like." He looked directly at her. She returned the stare unflinchingly as he continued. "I realise that I want to spend all of my time with her. I realise that I think about her all the time; but all the while, she's having a baby by someone

Drive-By Shouting

else. And it's actually by someone I detest, and who I realise, belatedly I admit, that I've detested for a long time. I know that this is now 'make or break' for us, because if we can't sort this out, then…." He mustered his courage. "So, I'm just going to be honest with you and lay my cards on the table. The main thing that tipped me over the edge wasn't his big house, or him stealing the song, or him slighting me. All of that matters; but I've lived with that crap for years. What brought it all to a head was the thought that he, of all people, had been anywhere near you. I was basically, insanely jealous. Because he doesn't deserve you."

He thought he noticed the hint of a smile on Kate's face, but it was gone before he could fully register it. "So, I just don't know what we're doing here Kate. Are we just the 'We Hate Matt Mann Club?' Or..." He paused, "or, what exactly are we?"

Kate closed her eyes and thought. After a while, she raised her head to look at Gram.
"I met with Steve again yesterday."
Gram looked at her in bewilderment: "Yes, I know you did, but that doesn't really answer my question?"
"Bear with me. As you'd expect, it was difficult. I know we talked about him being a hard man, but he does have a vulnerable side. And I seem to do nothing but cause him pain." She looked down sadly. "But anyway, he's reluctantly agreed to start moving towards divorce. I think he hopes that if he's co-operative, I'll look kindly on him and maybe relent. Obviously though, that's never going to happen." She paused again, trying

Drive-By Shouting

to formulate her words. "He still thinks that, actually, I'm seeing you and that you're the father of my baby."

Gram looked sadly at his hands and blew out his cheeks, before Kate continued.
"And the thing is Gram... I realised that while he was saying it... and while I was thinking how angry I was with you... I realized that I wished it was true. I wish this *was* your baby."
Gram's gaze darted back to her and they locked eyes across the coffee table.

She continued; "I'm in a very fucked up place Gram. My marriage has broken down irretrievably, I'm accidentally pregnant by a married man who I realise is far, far less than what I thought he was and then, when all this shit has happened, I get to know you."
Their eyes remained locked on each other as she spoke.
"And, the bottom line is, I wish this baby was yours." She forced a nervous smile. "And if me saying this frightens you off, then so be it. But it has to be said."

Gram remained glued to his seat, his mind whirring: "Christ Kate, we're doing everything the wrong way around here! We haven't so much as kissed each other; yet here we are, facing each other, having a heartfelt 'truth' session. So..."

He rose and moved round the coffee table before kneeling at her feet, taking her hands into his. "The last couple of days have been hell for me Kate. Thinking that it was all over, that we'd never speak again. And it made me realise..." He gulped as he mustered his courage, "What it made me realise is this; I think I love you. Well, actually, I'm pretty certain. I *do* love you. I can't stop thinking about you. I want to be with you all the time and thinking I'd lost you just felt like the worst thing ever." He squeezed her hands and smiled. "But..." His face grew suddenly solemn, "I can't pretend that the pregnancy isn't a factor. And that being with you, you know? That *this* isn't going to be an issue? Assuming you want me?" He looked into her eyes.

"So you love me, but at the same time, you don't?"
"I'm not saying that. What I am saying is, I do love you, but I can't guarantee how things are going to go. It's a big ask, accepting you having a baby by... by *him*. And I'm scared of getting in too deep and then letting you down." Gram felt a sudden tug somewhere deep in his chest and froze. He'd been setting out the terms of engagement, but Kate had said nothing; she was an island.

As he knelt before her in supplication, he had the odd sensation that he was turning to stone; frozen forever like some medieval knight, offering his doomed and worthless heart. He tried to talk, but the paralysis that gripped his chest was spreading. His throat was dry and all he could manage was a word, a single word. "Kate?"

She slid off the chair onto her knees and faced him. "Honestly, I don't know what I want. Yes, I *may* love you; but it could, you know… it could just be hormonal? I'm so 'all over the place' at the moment, that I don't know what to trust. And I'm also acutely

Drive-By Shouting

aware that I have a pattern, and that pattern has led me to make bad choices in the past. I'm scared of repeating that again. But... I do know that I feel better when you're around."
Gram took her in his arms and pulled her towards him. She buried her head in his neck and hugged him tightly. A muffled voice emerged, "I'm so sorry about our fight as well Gram. I've been really upset since Sunday." He felt her hot breath on his neck and held her tightly. She lifted her head to look at him. "You're right, of course; this is pretty intense for people who've never even kissed." She beamed at him. "Let's remedy that eh?"

Her eyes locked onto Gram's and she slowly moved up towards him until their lips met. Gram's eyes closed as he felt the plump softness of her lips. Their tongues briefly touched in an electric moment, but it was an essentially chaste kiss, with no suggestion that it was a precursor to anything else. She pulled back to look at him again.

"So, what are we going to do?"
"Let's go with the flow and then see how we get on. How does that sound?"
She smiled. "Okay, I'm happy with that. I'm not asking for anything Gram. I'm not in any position to demand commitment or anything like that, but you make me happy. And just being with you makes everything seem better."
"I know; I feel exactly the same. I think you're amazing."

Drive-By Shouting

She stood up, still holding his hand. "Come with me..." She silently led him through the flat and into the front bedroom and drew him down onto the neatly folded bed.
"We're not here to do anything, so there's no pressure. I just want you to hold me." She folded her arms around him and hugged him tightly.

Two hours later

Gram opened his eyes. After a moment's acclimatisation, he reminded himself of where he was. He lay, half covered under a thin summer duvet, studying the shapes in the curtain fabric, trying to find the repeat pattern on a seemingly random design. He glanced to the side and saw that he was alone in the bed. The bedding smelt like lemons and sunshine, rather unlike his own; and he rolled luxuriously on the sheet to look at the ceiling and the patterns of the reflecting light. After a few minutes of dreamy contemplation, the door opened and Kate, hair unkempt and dressed in a thin silk dressing gown, nudged open the door and entered the room, a mug in each hand.
"Thought you'd want tea?"

Gram rubbed his eyes and stretched out a hand. "Lovely. I'm struggling to wake up here. What time is it?"

Drive-By Shouting

"Nearly two! You went out like a light; fast asleep in no time at all. Well, nearly no time!" She flashed him an ironic smile.
"Sorry, I haven't really slept for the last two nights. What with all the crap rattling round my head. Because, I really thought I'd blown it." He shuffled up the bed and sat upright against the headboard, allowing Kate to sit on the side of the mattress. Sipping his tea, he dreamily focused on her.

"You okay? You know, about everything?" He gestured to the bed with his thumb.
She smiled shyly. "More than okay. I haven't felt this good for months. Well, apart from down at the beach, with you. That was pretty lovely too."
"I know. I feel the same." He reached and interlinked his free hand with hers and softly caressed it with his thumb.
"Are we good now?"

Kate beamed a smile at him: "I should hope so, after that! But yes, we're better than good. We're fucking ace!" She grinned before a slight shadow crossed her smile. "And you? Are *you* okay with all this? Given the baggage?"

Gram paused and thought for a moment. "I can't pretend that it's not an issue; but if it's a choice between having you, baby on board and all, or not having you at all, then it's a no-brainer. You're the most brilliant person I've ever known and I know that I *have* to be with you. I just need to work on small details like, you know, raging jealousy!"

Drive-By Shouting

She squeezed his hand tightly: "You've nothing to be jealous of Gram. You're superior in every way to him. A hundred times more of a man."
Gram allowed himself a small smile of satisfaction: "Flattery will get you absolutely everywhere!"
"It's not flattery, it's true." She gripped his hand tightly once more. "Now, enough about love, flowers and what a stud you are. When am I going to meet Polly so we can get going?"

Gram raised his eyebrows delightedly: "You still want to go ahead with all that? It's not too complicated now that we're, you know, together?"
"All the more so"
"Well, I did call her yesterday and made an excuse, because I thought, you know, the plan was off after we had our row. But she's still very keen, obviously."
"Call her. Let's get the ball rolling."
"Okay. My phone's in my jacket in the lounge. Would you get it please? I'm a bit, well; naked."

She grinned back at him: "It's a little late for shyness Gram! But don't worry; I'll get it for you my Little Prince! However, before we push on with all of this, I do have one stipulation: you told me you were signing on. Yes?"

Embarrassment immediately washed over Gram's face: "Yes, I'm rather ashamed to say, I am."
She waited for him to raise his eyes and looked at him directly: "Well, I want you to go there today. And I want you to sign off, because it's doing nothing for your self-esteem."

Drive-By Shouting

He looked at her dubiously: "I'm not proud of being on the dole, Kate, but just swapping from it to being a kept man isn't going to bolster my self-esteem."

"We've already discussed this Gram. You won't be a kept man. I'll call my guy at Harbottle and Lewis and get him to draw up a formal contract. That way, you'll have the security that, whatever happens between us romantically, you're on a guaranteed wage. It's not charity, it's an advance against royalties, it's business… We're going to make great music together, and a lot of money together, but I need you to feel good about yourself. And signing on isn't the way to achieve that."

Gram continued to look thoughtfully at her: "Kate, I do want this. I really do. But I'm afraid it'll screw things up between us."
"You being on the dole and feeling downtrodden is the only thing that could possibly screw things up Gram! You're a fabulous, talented guy. But having a grinding few years, signing on, shifting equipment, that's robbing you of all of your confidence. And, professionally speaking, I need a happening guy to write, produce and steer this project. So, it's a deal breaker for me. Let's sort out the contract and get you signed off at the Job Centre.
I signed on after my A-levels for a bleak couple of months and I don't think I've ever felt more crap about myself. Being condescended to, queuing in that horrible place, full of desperate people. So, let's just cross that bridge and make some money together, eh?" She squeezed his hand tightly in affirmation. "Come on Gram! This is going to happen. Are you in?"

Drive-By Shouting

Gram felt an enormous unburdening, as he once more projected an alternative future, one free of incessant poverty or dodging around for cash gigs and discounted supermarket food. Feeling almost lightheaded, he answered: "It's a deal. I'll go there today."

Kate beamed and crawled up the bed, placing her cup on the sideboard. "Good! Let's get the real Gram back up and running, eh? But, before you go..." She bowed her head, her hair forming a blonde curtain around their faces and lowered herself to kiss him, her tongue instantly seeking out his.

Drive-By Shouting

Chapter 20
Dean Street, London – The Groucho Club

Once out of the taxi, it took all of Matt's acting ability to continue his portrayal of a successful, carefree and rich young man, as he dragged his queasy mass up Greek Street. After days of silence, he had finally been called by Vanessa from Steve's office and invited (or was it summoned?) to join him for lunch after that morning's show had ended. His probing of Vanessa had not done much to reassure him ("no, Steve didn't want to speak to him," "yes, he was still looking upset").

He had exited the taxi early to give himself some thinking time, but, as he turned into Old Compton Street, he was aware that Dean Street was fast approaching. He mentally rehearsed the possible outcomes of the meeting, if Kate had named him, he was heading into the most horrific showdown and his career was over. If she hadn't, he remained hanging on the hook, vulnerable, and anticipating the day when the dam broke and Kate revealed all.

Either way, after weeks of turmoil, he had decided that things had to change. He could no longer afford to be

Drive-By Shouting

so over reliant on Steve Coombes' goodwill. To have his whole life and happiness resting in Steve's hands was simply unbearable.

Re-energised by Greg's enthusiasm, he had called the investment banker and following the conversation, started liquidating whatever assets he could, quickly moving to sell two of the cars and, with Jen's blessing, put the holiday house in Devon on the market. He needed cash to invest. Greg had reinforced their conversation from the Sunday gathering (before it had turned into the horror show with Kate and Gram) and Matt was now fully convinced that he needed the real tangible wealth that could only be got from investment. And the dot-com explosion was "guaranteed to deliver."

He gingerly touched his chin, still throbbing from Gram's punch ('what a coward' he thought, 'hitting a guy when he was pissed…'). He had taken to leaving the studio make-up partly in place, to cover the discolouration that was still forming around the affected area. His cheek and gums still throbbed angrily and he drew his fingers away, partly in a wincing realisation that the area was still tender, and partly out of recognition that continually touching it would disturb the thin layer of make-up. He reached the lobby of Groucho's and paused, mustering the courage to enter. Bolstered by the broad smile of the attractive girl on reception, he pushed open the doors into the bar and turned right, en route to the restaurant beyond. It was only when he drew close to the opening that he spied Steve, staring miserably at the tablecloth

Drive-By Shouting

in front of him. Matt paused again for courage, before striding over to the table with as much confidence as he could manufacture. Steve sensed his arrival and looked up, a strange detached look on his face. He gestured to the chair opposite.

"Matt. Glad you could make it." His tone was neutral and his mood, once again, was difficult to determine. Matt couldn't decide if it was suppressed rage or general unhappiness that he was viewing. He swallowed hard and forced himself to maintain his veneer of confidence. "Steve, I've been trying to reach you since last week. What's going on?"

Steve leaned back in his chair with his arms folded. "What's going on? Fucking everything is going on!" He eyed Matt keenly. "But, I think you know that already, so I imagine you can tell me what's going on in some considerable detail. Nice make-up, by the way."

Matt fought hard to disguise his alarm, desperately trying to formulate some sort of response, but before he could reply, Steve continued, "I hear you had an altercation with that shit of a mate of yours. Sticking up for me, were you?"
Matt's mind whirred in confusion: "What do you…? Who told you?"
"Kate. Says she and mateyboy dropped into your house on the way back from Rye. And that you got into a row with him. Looks like he caught you with a haymaker. Did you at least land one on him?"

Drive-By Shouting

A glimmer of hope and possibility occurred to Matt. Was he off the hook? Had he got away with it? "I'm ashamed to say I didn't manage to return the punch. I was a bit pissed actually."
Steve shrugged. "Shame. Still, interesting to hear you'd stood up to him. Kate thinks I'm a mug. Says she's not actually seeing him. That he's 'just a friend.' But you obviously find that as unbelievable as I do, don't you? Despite your protestations last week. I presume you know all about the baby?"

Feeling the sweat pricking the back of his collar, Matt feigned surprise: "Baby? What baby?"
"Turns out my lovely wife is *up the dufi*. Despite the fact that it can't be mine, 'cos I fire blanks. Mind you, it'd have to have been an Immaculate Conception anyway, as I haven't been near her in, well, a year or probably more." He gave Matt a strange look. "So the kid is definitely not mine." In terror of incriminating himself in any way, Matt remained silent. Steve looked at him again: "The thing is, I offered to take the kid on. To be his Dad, and everything. But... but she's determined to be with that guy. And all the while she's claiming it's not even his! What kind of bullshit is that? If it's not his, then whose is it?" The question hung in the air, until Matt half spluttered:
"Well, it must be his. Doesn't make sense for it to be anybody else's."
Steve nodded, but then held Matt in a stern gaze: "So, anyway, this has all been going on behind my back. So, how long have you known?"
"About what?"

Drive-By Shouting

"About the fucking affair! The baby, everything! I presume that's why you had a rumble with him?"

Matt's mind raced: "Yeah, that's er..., well, I didn't know until…, until I bumped into them backstage at The Fleadh a couple of weeks ago. And, I wasn't certain then. They said they'd just bumped into each other, but then, when they turned up at mine on Sunday, well, that was confirmation. So, I went at him."
"So, that's when you found out about the kid?"
"No, no... I didn't know about that 'til you just told me. No, I was just totally outraged at them turning up at my house, acting like a couple, knowing how I am with you, how close we are, you know?"

Steve sipped his Budvar and looked at Matt impassively: "Well, there you go Matt. It's at times like this that you find out who your real friends are."

Despite Steve's words, Matt felt a deeply uncomfortable sense of menace emanating from his manager. He wanted to move beyond this impasse.
"Listen Steve, it all sounds like a shit situation. But, hopefully, you'll pull through, and you know, all this crap will pass."
"Yeah, it's crap. But it will pass..." Steve looked away and quietly took in the busy room, before appearing to mentally change gear. "So Matt, there's something that I need to discuss with you." His tone once more alarmed Matt. "I need to talk to you professionally and, y'know, it's unfortunate to have to spring this on you, but I fly back to the States tomorrow, and I thought you should know this before I went."

Drive-By Shouting

Matt's alarm was once more in overdrive: "What is it?"
"Well, it's not what you want to hear, I'm afraid. They want to make a change at *Live at 10!* Kris Boyd, you know the big cheese at ITV daytime, he's not happy with the..." Steve made mock quotation signs with his raised fingers, "chemistry' between you and Faith Lerner and, as you know, it's kind of *her* show. So I'm afraid it has to be you that gets moved on."

Matt sat stunned: "I don't fucking believe it! On top of all the other things that are going on, this is the last thing I need."
Steve studied him closely, "Why, Matt, what else is going on?"
Matt rapidly covered his tracks, "It's just stuff that's going on at home. You know Jen, marriage, stuff..." He sought to divert Steve. "Is Faith Lerner behind this? Is it her who is agitating for the change? Because I've chummied up to her like there's no tomorrow."

"Nah, it's not her, she likes you, says you're a sweet guy. No, it's coming from upstairs. They just want to change the dynamic, a fresh face. And, I do also have to tell you this; there were a couple of remarks about you looking a bit *worse for wear* over the last couple of months. Suggestions that you looked like you'd had a skin-full. A few whispers to that effect have been coming out of production. Is any of that true?"
"For God's sake, that's all lies! Complete lies! The bastards..." He shook his head bitterly as he looked around the room.
"Yeah, crap news, I know..."

Drive-By Shouting

Matt, not for the first time recently, felt as if his stomach was in freefall: "Jesus Steve, that's shocking timing. We're nearly at the end of this run and I've only got another four or five weeks' money left. And my living expenses are, as you know, ridiculously high. I was relying on them keeping me on. I had no reason to suspect that they wouldn't re-new. Fucking hell!"
"Yeah, it's shit timing, but, you know, you've still got your Super Channel gig every week?"
"Steve, that's barely two grand a month! I only do that because I like doing something musically based. That won't even cover my staff bill at home!" Matt stared intently into the distance, his mind racing, desperately seeking a solution. "Listen, I don't like to ask Steve, but are you in a position to sub me at all? Just for a bit, 'til it improves?" He looked hopefully at Steve.

Steve spread his hands and grimaced: "I'm afraid not Matt. I'm potentially about to lose fifty per cent of everything I own to my lovely wife. Otherwise, of course, I'd love to help, but at the moment, I just can't. Bad timing."

Panic began to rise in Matt's chest: "Christ Steve. This is bad. I just didn't see it coming, so I haven't got anything put by. Do you think I could maybe get back to singing? Could we get a deal? Would that boost things?"

Steve slowly shook his head: "Honestly? I think you missed the boat. I mean Clive is going great guns, as you know, but he came right off the back of the band, so the timing was right. You're over three years out of

Drive-By Shouting

the band and things have moved on. I mean, I can ask around, but I'm not sure how far we'd get. And I doubt there'd be much cash initially."

"God, I can't even rely on my PRS royalties; they're erratic at the best of times, but they've really started to drop off. Every quarter is less than the last."

Steve shrugged: "Well, yeah, the further you get from being in an active band, the less you get played on the radio and then the royalties really drop-off. But, you know, they'll settle into a nice low-level income, even so."

"Yes, but Steve, I don't live like that!"

"I know, I know. But something else will come along, I'm sure. And in the meantime, Box Office USA is re-commissioning *Manhattan Cafe* for a fourth season. So that'll give the royalties a little boost." Steve rubbed his chin and ruminated. "Of course, there may be a way that you could raise money off the back of that?"

"How so?"

"Well, maybe there's the option of a 'buyout'. Rather than waiting to see what royalties you get over the years."

"Really, that's an option? How much?"

"Well, I don't know. They offered it last time they re-commissioned and it might be worth considering now. I mean, how much longer can it run? This'll be the fourth series and there's only so much mileage you can get out of a sitcom. I can't imagine it'll get shown much in the future, so maybe now is the time to take the money and run?"

"How much money? For me, specifically?"

Drive-By Shouting

Steve ruminated for a moment: "I'm not sure. They haven't actually offered it this time, but I seem to remember it was a few hundred thousand last time out. I'm not sure, exactly," Steve suddenly brightened. "And if they're not in the market, then maybe *that's* a way that I could help you out? If I'm buying an asset, then that might be something I can find the finance for. Yeah, maybe I can look at the numbers if no-one else is buying. Maybe *I* could do a deal with you?"

Matt's thoughts raced ahead, as he calculated the potential returns if this sum was invested in the Dotcom shares: "But, if I could get half a million after tax, well, I think I might go for that. Maybe even less if its cash now, rather than waiting. Bird in the hand and all that? I think you're right. It can't run forever and if they're offering something now, or if you are, it might good sense to take it."

Steve nodded, "Okay, I'll look into it and come back to you. I'm not promising anything, and you might find it's a lower sum than you're imagining, but I'll get you a figure and then it's up to you."

"Good. Because that might just make everything all right."

Ninety minutes later, Matt boarded the train at Charing Cross, relieved to not meet anybody he knew and to find an empty six seater compartment in first-class, he was in no mood for idle chat. As the train pulled out, his thoughts returned again to the conversation with Steve and the terrible news about *Live at 10!*

Drive-By Shouting

On the one hand, he appeared to have avoided one potential landmine, Steve was still in the dark about him and Kate, but he had been completely blindsided by developments at *Live at 10!* He'd done absolutely everything to ingratiate himself to everyone there, and for what? The bastards had dropped him anyway.

He cracked open the first of the premixed gin and tonics that he'd picked up at the station and downed it in one go. The fizz made his stomach tingle when it hit, briefly soothing the mass that seem to boil and bubble, churning away. He realised he'd have to tell Jen all the bad news on his return and immediately reached into the carrier bag for another tin.

Part 8

Coda

Drive-By Shouting

Chapter 21
Ten years later - London 2009

Gram paid the taxi driver and turned to face the row of neat terraced houses. He identified the correct one and knocked on the door. He fought to look composed and confident when it was opened by a tall, gaunt man wearing a sling on his left arm. Matt Mann extended his right hand in greeting.
"Gram. It's been a long time..." Gram warily took his hand and accepted the invitation to go into the house. It had indeed been a long time and Gram was still unsure of how this meeting would proceed.

Three days earlier, Gram had been standing on the deck at the (by now, extensively expanded) beach house at Rye, when Colin had called out of the blue. Kate had observed him pacing up and down, trying to guess at the identity of the caller, but, even without knowing, had clearly detected that rather mixed news was being conveyed. As soon as the call was terminated, he had turned to her.

Drive-By Shouting

"That was Colin. Pretty bad news about Matt. Well… depending upon your viewpoint."
"What's happened?"
"Well, he's okay apparently, but he was involved in an accident; he fell off a cliff. Sounds quite badly hurt."
"What! A cliff?!"
"Yes, apparently he was a shooting a pilot for some TV show."
Kate breathed deeply and absorbed the news, analyzing how she felt about it. "Ok… right… Well, I'm sorry to hear that. Not something you'd wish on anyone; even him. What's the prognosis?"

"They're not sure yet. Colin says he'll let me know when he's heard more."
Kate considered this for a moment. "So he'll probably be ok? Colin didn't say he was at death's door or anything?"
"No, he thinks he'll be ok. He's got a few broken bones; but it can all be fixed."
"Even so, not a nice thing to happen to anyone. Even Matt Mann."
"Yes, I'm surprised by the fact that I was so, sort of *concerned* to hear it." Gram rubbed his chin and looked out to sea. "I couldn't have imagined all those years ago that I would care one way or the other about what happened to Matt. But I'm surprisingly sorry to hear this."
She nodded. "I know; me too. But, he's been out of our lives so long, that I really don't feel any rancour anymore."

Drive-By Shouting

And it was true. Matt had been almost entirely absent. In terror of his status of *father of the child* being revealed, he had readily agreed to all of Gram and Kate's terms. There had been no contact, no interference or objection to Gram being registered as Ellen's father. And, henceforth, the paths of their lives had diverged wildly.

The *Blue Dolls* project had been astonishingly successful and was still going strong, with Polly regularly gracing the covers of magazines and, more beneficially to Gram and Kate, continuing to sell records and receive solid airplay of all of the material composed with Gram. But, even before they had secured a record deal, fate had created an opportunity for Gram to change his life.

Sitting with Kate, in the office of Dave Bassant, A&R Director at BLG, they had almost got to the point of concluding a deal for Polly and the *Blue Dolls* project, when Bassant had had a light-bulb moment. He had just allowed the first demo version of *Slightly Unsightly* to end, when a thought occurred to him.

"That's really good. Great vocals and, I have to say, a really nice production job. It's excellent stuff Gram. Which gives me an idea...?" He got up and pulled a press photo from his filing cabinet. "We're doing a new band, '*White Herons'* with, you know, Ryan Shaw and Jedski from *UnderClub*?" He handed the photo to Gram, "and it's going to be great – y'know, all the good bits of the old Madchester rave scene, but updated, so it's really *relevant...* But... the thing is..." he eyed Gram

Drive-By Shouting

keenly, "They're a bit *tricky* to work with. And I've been having a few issues with producers. They've been holed up in a residential studio in Wales, y'know; *Rockfield?* But... they have certain predilections and both Colin Laing and Paul Norman have walked off the project. There's no doubting that they can be a bit... naughty; but I can't help thinking that Colin & Paul are being a tad prissy. So, anyway, the bottom line is this; we're in a bit of an impasse with producers. And... listening to your stuff and all that lovely vibe you're getting, well, it might be a good fit." He grinned and looked hopefully at Kate and Gram. "So, I don't suppose you'd fancy having a go with them? You'd be doing me a really big favour."

Gram could barely believe his ears. Three months after handing back his van keys to Rox Rentals, he was the writer and producer of the *Blue Dolls*, who were about to be signed to a major record label. And now, he was being offered the chance to produce an album with established artists (albeit troubled ones), also for a major label. He just about managed to keep his cool and manufacture a nonchalant reply, "Well, I'd certainly like to give it a go."

What had followed was three weeks of barely controlled mayhem in the Welsh hills. It soon became apparent that both Ryan and Jedski were raging drug addicts and any attempt at working with them was nigh-on impossible. However, Gram wasn't prepared to let the opportunity pass him by. And so, rather than walk away from a fully funded three weeks of studio

Drive-By Shouting

time, he'd simply written and recorded twelve full backing tracks and decided to work 'around' the drugs.

He'd spotted that the combination of drink and drugs meant that Ryan (ostensibly the singer) spent about sixteen hours out of each twenty-four, either comatose or insensible. However, at around 9 or 10pm on most evenings, the cocktail of drink and drugs produced an 'eye of the storm,' where he tended to be relatively lucid and energetic for up to an hour, before his less attractive side re-emerged. So, every night for eight days, Gram and Chris, the recording engineer, set up a vocal mike and steered Ryan into the booth with instructions to "do something."

"Worra you want me to sing, kiddo?"
"Just make something up. Whatever comes into your head."
"Whoa! You're fucking mad you, maaan...!"

What Ryan produced rarely related to the track, in terms of either tempo or pitch. But, with judicious use of a sampler and an auto tuner, Gram managed to compile the shouted rants into something usable. Despite the unconventional approach, it had worked, and Dave Bassant had gratefully taken delivery of the master tapes seven weeks later, leaving Gram free to go straight into preproduction and recording with Polly and the *Blue Dolls*.

Ten months later (and still barely more than a year since the Fleadh debacle), Gram had been the producer and co-writer on two top five UK albums with Ryan's

Drive-By Shouting

band, *White Herons*, starting to make headway in the US charts.

As if this professional success wasn't enough, Gram's personal life had also shifted monumentally. He had legally adopted Ellen, his wife Kate's beautiful daughter, whom he readily and willingly accepted as his child. Two further children (Dylan and Thom), and a steady succession of moderately 'hit' albums later, Gram was a different man from the downtrodden failure of eight years previously. He was fit, tanned and wealthy, dividing his time between the Sussex coast, the flat in Crouch End and the family's house in Provence.

It was this entirely rebooted Gram who followed a limping Matt into the small kitchen diner at the back of the terraced house in Waterloo. Despite his success, Gram had an awareness that he had continued to relate that success to Matt. He realised that he had felt deprived of their annual birthday meet-ups, of his opportunity to bask in the glow of everything that had happened, the cessation of their meet-ups had occurred at the very moment that the seesaw had shifted, leaving him feeling slightly cheated. Despite his trepidation, he'd been looking forward to this.

"Tea? Coffee? Beer?"
"A bit early for beer thanks. Tea would be good."
Matt switched on the kettle and turned, propping himself against the kitchen worktop. Gram took in Matt's louche frame and confessed to himself, despite the plaster cast, the fading yellowed bruises and the

additional ten years of wear and tear, he was still a good-looking bastard.

"You're looking a bit thin Matt."
"No kidding Sherlock!" He smiled, making Gram feel more at ease. "Yup, I spent years keeping an eye on my waistline, but instantly dropped a stone on my new *special* hospital diet. So I suppose there's an upside to everything!"

"All joking aside Matt, are you okay?"
"Oh, this?" He gestured to his bandaged body. "It all got blown a bit out of proportion actually. It was a TV pilot for a new reality show, where they dump a bunch of people on a remote Scottish island and see how they cope. They needed some people with a bit of TV experience to give it a dry run and the money was ok, so I grabbed it. Bloody stupid thing to do in retrospect, given that I'm not exactly your outdoors type! We were on this freezing bloody island and the light was starting to fade. So, rather than walk miles over some hills, we decided to take a shortcut. We were edging around some steep rocks, when I slipped.
I actually fell thirty feet, and it all looked great on the camera footage, where I just disappeared out of shot with a scream! Bloody shame it's not even for broadcast; it was all pretty dramatic. But, actually, I was pretty lucky. It could have gone really badly. I landed on my rucksack, and it pretty much cushioned the fall. And, although the broken arm and ribs were bad enough, I still got off lightly; compared to what could have happened. The sun always shines on the righteous, eh?

Drive-By Shouting

My new agent thought it would be good to get me back in the papers; for the first time in years!" He smirked wryly. "But I think she overdid it a bit, I've had people thinking that I genuinely nearly pegged it! Still, it all helps with the insurance claim; that'll come in very handy!"
"Yeah, at first Colin made it sound like you were at death's door. Still, good to see you're ok, and even when I found out it wasn't that serious, I thought, well, we may as well meet up anyway." Gram sat awkwardly, not really sure how to press ahead after such a long break in their contact and a strange tension filled the air.

Matt broke the silence. "Listen Gram. I'm really glad you've come to see me, even if the reason for the visit was this stupid accident. I know we had lots of reasons to fall out years ago, but I'm really pleased to see you. You look well. You look successful!"
Gram, relieved by the direction that Matt had steered the conversation, replied warmly, "Thank you. Yeah, it's good to see you too. There's a lot of water under the bridge.

To be honest, this does all feel a bit weird after so long. I can't pretend that I wished you well eight or nine years ago, and the last time I saw you, in your kitchen at Hurstwood! Well, that was obviously not something I'm proud of" He looked across warily at Matt. "But we do go back a long way and, despite our differences then; I was y'know, concerned to hear that you'd been hurt."

Drive-By Shouting

"Sometimes it takes a bit of an 'event' to build bridges." Matt turned and added milk to the two cups and passed one to Gram, before awkwardly maneuvering himself to sit opposite him at the kitchen table.

"The fact is, Gram, I'm not the same person that I was ten years ago. I did things, and made decisions then, that I wouldn't dream of doing now. But it happened, I did do those things and now I have to live with the consequences. I can't undo everything, but anyway, it's actually good to see you again – despite my bloody nose last time around!" He smiled and Gram nodded in acknowledgement.

"So, anyway Gram, enough about my personality transplant. You've done some nice work over the last few years. I've seen your name crop up on some decent albums, with some really good production, as I would have expected, obviously. You've done well Gram." He looked approvingly across the table and Gram was taken aback by just how thrilled he felt to receive this affirmation.

"Thank you. It's all gone better than I could have dreamt really. As you'd probably guess, it's almost all down to Kate rather than me." He studied Matt to gauge his reaction to Kate's name. He merely smiled in agreement.

"I'm really pleased that you and Kate have been so good together. Obviously I haven't seen you, but I hear through the grapevine and I've read a few of Kate's interviews in the press; she's done bloody well with the books eh? How many has she written now?"

"Five. And another just about to come out."

Drive-By Shouting

"Yeah, you really look like a good team."

"We are. I feel incredibly fortunate." He paused, before willing himself to tackle the most awkward issue between them. "I, or rather both of us actually, have appreciated the fact that you've stuck to your word about Ellen. We all know that, biologically at least, you're her father, but I don't feel like that at all. She feels a hundred per cent my daughter. Not just legally, but really mine, in terms of what she means to me. I love all three of the kids the same, but... but, I appreciate that you've left us to it and not tried to make contact. I obviously want, well, I insist actually, that it all stays the same, but... I still want you to know that she's brilliant. A beautiful, healthy and very, very happy little girl."

Sadness fell over Matt's face: "It hasn't been easy, knowing that I have a child out there. But I've never even met her, so that perhaps makes it slightly better. I imagine it'd be harder if I'd got to see her, got to know what she's like. Does she know about me?"

Gram answered firmly: "No. And we don't currently have any plans to tell her." He held Matt in a stern gaze.

"Don't worry Gram; I'm not going to rock the boat. In many ways, I'm pleased that she's got you as a dad. Despite everything that's happened, I still know that you're a decent guy. I still think of you as my friend."

Matt looked across the table with an intensity that Gram found unnerving; it had been years since they'd been this honest with one another. He felt his resolution softening and he took out his iPhone.

"Okay, on the basis that we completely understand each other and that the status quo is remaining firmly

Drive-By Shouting

in place?" He looked at Matt and waited for the nod of agreement, which was supplied. "Here are a couple of photos of her." He handed the phone to Matt. "Scroll forward; there are five or six nice ones of her and the boys."

Matt sat and silently scrolled through the photos, pausing to zoom in on a couple. "She's lovely. Looks just like Kate..." He returned the phone to Gram. "Don't worry Gram. I won't rock the boat. I have enough trouble seeing Callum and Sophia, without sticking my oar into *your* family. So, I know the score. I'll keep my distance."

Gram smiled, pleased that such an accord, one that it seemed so unlikely a few years ago, was now so easily achieved.
"So, what, you don't see much of your kids?"
Matt grimaced: "Nah, I mean, Callum occasionally disobeys his mother and takes a train up here, but Sophia is right under her thumb, so I almost never see her."
"That must be hard?"
"It is. But, they've had their minds twisted by Jen continually dripping poison in their ears. So it's only to be expected."
"Yes, I heard about the split. It sounded messy. Sorry."
"I'm not." Matt laughed bitterly and shook his head, "Jen turned out to be a right money grabbing bitch."
Gram smiled wryly: "What happened?"
"Oh Christ... Everything happened! It's a rambling story, but if you're interested?"
"I am. I was there from the beginning, so tell me."

Drive-By Shouting

Matt stretched back on his chair and studied his hands: "Okay, you asked for it... It all started to go wrong when I got dropped from *Live at 10!* That just came right out of the blue, and I suddenly stopped earning ninety per cent of my income, which is a bad enough thing to happen under any circumstances. However, this also coincided with me taking the worst advice of my life, selling the house in Devon and, really stupidly, most of my song publishing rights, to Steve Coombes, as it happens, for what turned out to be far less than their real value. In retrospect, I think he took advantage of me there. But, I guess I volunteered for it, so I've got to accept my share of blame. And this was all so I could invest in Dotcom stock, all of the shares that I was assured *couldn't fail.*"

"Ahh. That's not good..."
Matt raised his eyebrows: "Too fucking right it wasn't! I ploughed over a million into WooWoo.com and a few months later, it became the first really big casualty of the 2000 crash. I lost everything, except the house in Hurstwood and this place, thank God! With almost no money coming in and mortgages to pay, it was a horror story. The worst thing was I was always tantalisingly close to getting a big TV gig that would have pulled us out of the mire. But just when it seemed I was about to get the job, it was like an invisible hand just cut the strings and I fell away again, like some sort of discarded puppet." He shook his head sadly, reliving the disappointment of the time.

"Anyway, after the endless pattern of last-minute rejections dragged on for over a year, and with us not able to pay the mortgage, Jen suddenly announces that she wants a divorce! And to cap it all, it's so that she can shack up with my dear old friend Greg Knowles, the bastard who gave all the crap investment advice in the first place!" He looked at Gram. "You met him briefly, when you popped in to punch me?" He smiled to reassure Gram, "Anyway, I found out later that they'd been *having it off* for a couple of years. And now, he lives in my house and acts as 'daddy' to my kids. Nice eh?"

"Did you come out of it with anything?"

"A bit. It turned out that *Greg the Cock* had moved all his money out of the dotcom stock, just in time to save his own arse, but nobody else's! So, he had plenty of cash to buy me out of my half of the Hurstwood house and I used most of it to pay off the mortgage on this place. Then, the rest just kind of dribbled away, as I continued to nearly get job after job. I was always in pole position and then the rug would get pulled at the last minute. After a few years, it was obvious that it was all over with TV; nobody would touch me with a bargepole. So, it's been pretty hand-to-mouth ever since."

"And what about your parents? Couldn't they help?"

"Oh, that's a whole other world of pain! You never met my dad did you? He was always away from home. I mean, always! Turns out, the reason for that was that he had another family in Solihull! And then, to cap it all, he went bust, which is how the truth came out really. Suddenly, when the money ran out, all of his

Drive-By Shouting

secrets emerged. Now, my mum lives in a crappy little cottage that leaks, in the middle of nowhere. So, no. No help available there."

"Bloody hell... Poor woman..." Gram had a mental picture of the icy, stuck-up Mrs. Mann, living in vastly reduced circumstances. It was oddly unsatisfying. "So, what are you living on?"
"Bits and pieces. I do guest appearances on daytime shows. Reviewing new record releases and stuff like that. Crap money, but just enough to keep me going. Plus, I get a few grand a year from what publishing I did manage to retain. So, I get by..." Matt rubbed his thin face with his uninjured hand, the weariness of the last decade etched deep into his brow. He rallied slightly as he projected an imagined future.

"I'm keeping an eye on all those 80's revival shows. They're massive now, so I guess it's only a matter of time before there's a demand for a Nineties version, and *Kensal Rise* could get some work on those? Obviously, it would have to be without Clive; he certainly wouldn't lower himself to be involved with anything like that. He's far too big time... Who'd have predicted that eh?"
"Yeah, extraordinary that." Gram laughed. "Because, so far as I can hear, he still can't sing for toffee!"

"You don't need to tell me that! He was only brought in to the band to look good and I still can't believe that he's had this enormous career, and that people think he's the real deal! You know, he only went and won an

Drive-By Shouting

Ivor Novello award for 'Best Song - Musically and Lyrically' last month?"

"Yes, I know. I was at the awards."

"Well, you can probably spot that he couldn't write his way out of a paper bag! He's only on the writing credits because Steve Coombes insists that he gets a royalty, he didn't actually write a note of the song. He doesn't write any of them. He couldn't!"

Gram smiled wryly: "Yeah, I had sort of assumed that was the case."

Matt shrugged: "So, anyway, that's the state of play. If I can get through this crap okay and look normal again," he raised his eyes and gestured to the cast and the lingering bruising, "then maybe we can get a few gigs, with or without Clive."

"And TV? Is anything possible there, y'know, new agent and everything?"

"No, not really. Well, so far as anything mainstream is concerned, anyway, it looks like I'm only good for cheapo productions. I did finally change agent a few years ago, once Steve Coombes became completely uncontactable and distant. Completely impossible to speak to, actually, he didn't want to know me once things got difficult; he seemed to find failure disgusting, like it was contagious or something. But Anne, my new agent, she does manage to get a few corporate gigs and small appearances, but nothing noteworthy." Matt paused and rubbed his eyes. "I still just don't understand how it all went so wrong. I mean, I know I screwed up my finances and made some bad investments, but it's the fact that TV also simultaneously went so completely crap. How every

Drive-By Shouting

really positive screen test or meeting would turn to shit at the last minute? It really was weird like I was cursed or something!"

Gram looked at him thoughtfully: "Do you really not know what happened Matt?"
Matt stared back intently: "What do you mean? Do you know something?"
Gram looked away and shifted uncomfortably, weighing up his heavy burden of knowledge. He considered for a while before looking once more at Matt: "I'm not sure whether I should tell you this, but I think from what you've told me, you've suffered enough."
"Go on?" Matt's taut face was now entirely focused on Gram's.
"I've only just found this out myself Matt." He twisted awkwardly on the chair again as he weighed up the justification for going further. He looked at Matt's pained expression and couldn't help but contrast it with the face of the charismatic nineteen year old he'd met so many years earlier. Gram knew what relentless rejection did to a man and, almost despite himself, felt a sudden affinity with Matt.

He resolved to tell him. "Ok, you need to know this… I'm afraid that I was as *in the dark* as you about all this, until last week. It was only when Kate and I talked about your accident and, I have to admit, it only really came up when we started talking about your, y'know, fall from prominence; how, one minute you're everywhere, on the telly, in magazines, and the next, you'd disappeared! It was only while I was wondering

Drive-By Shouting

out loud about all that, that Kate finally told me what'd been going on. About what had actually happened."
Matt's face was stony: "And what *had* happened?"

Gram drew a deep breath. "I had always believed that you'd been kept out of all the Kate and Steve divorce stuff. But..."
Matt's face instantly flushed with alarm: "Are you saying he *knew* all along? That Steve knew?"
Gram bit the bullet. "Yes."

He allowed this to sink in, before elaborating further: "When Kate asked for the divorce, she said that Steve started making veiled threats about what he was going to have done to me, because, obviously, he thought I was Ellen's father. So, eventually, and under intense pressure," he glanced at Matt's stricken face, "it was under real, *real* pressure, that Kate told Steve the truth. But she made him swear that he wasn't allowed to harm you in any way. She made him give an unbreakable promise that you wouldn't be hurt."

"No, not physically! But, fuck me; the bastard has made me pay in other ways!" Matt threw up his good arm, his face red and angry. "Christ, he's played me for years! It was him all along, wasn't it? It was *him* cutting the strings. Actually setting me up, just so he could make me fall!" Matt's eyes blazed with fury. "And the bastard also managed to manoeuvre me into selling my song's on the cheap..." He angrily and awkwardly levered himself up and hobbled to the sink, resting his right hand on the worktop and staring out of the window.

Drive-By Shouting

Gram already knew that telling Matt had been a monumental mistake. He spoke quietly in an attempt to defuse some of the anger.

"Matt, I'm sorry to be the one to tell you this, but I think you've probably been through enough. And that you'd want to at least know why everything went so badly?" When Matt didn't answer, Gram looked up to see his thin frame shaking as he supported himself on the worktop. A small stifled sob escaped and Gram realised that Matt was trying, unsuccessfully, to hide the fact that he was shaking, and weeping with rage.

Gram arose noisily, the wooden chair squeaking violently against the tiled floor. He started to move over to Matt. "Matt, are you okay?"

"Just leave me, would you?" He turned to face Gram, his face contorted in distressed fury. "Really, please just leave me." He wiped his sleeve across his eyes before spinning around and angrily jabbing a finger in Gram's direction. "Your fucking wife dropped me in the shit for no good reason. She destroyed my life, because she didn't have the fucking intelligence to just make something up? Anything! She could have invented some mystery guy, some fling, but no, she had to destroy me!"

Gram recoiled, startled by Matt's change of tone. He sensed a change to the air in the room, with an electric charge now crackling around the two of them. "Look Matt, this really isn't Kate's fault; she had no choice. She tried to deflect him, but Steve's not a fool. You, of all people know that. He knew that she wasn't the type

Drive-By Shouting

to just pick up some guy and certainly not to get pregnant by some stranger. She did *try* to divert him, but he was relentless? He just kept saying that there was something she wasn't telling him, because me being with her, without me actually being the father, didn't stack up; unless there was some other undisclosed element. She says he can smell a lie from a mile away and there wasn't any way she could pull the wool over his eyes."

"Bollocks. She'd lied to him before, she could have lied again! She chose to drop me in the shit, and save herself and *you*, of course." Matt snarled at Gram. "And as for her not being the type to pick up some guy and tell big, fat lies, how would you know? You knew fuck all about her until you grabbed onto her coat-tails."

Still reeling from the sudden and alarming change of atmosphere between the two of them, Gram stared angrily back: "Oh, we're back to me needing to hang on to someone's coat-tails again, are we? So, all the blather about how well I'd done was just soft soap? Just the usual Matt Mann smoothy bullshit! All that crap about how you'd changed, how you're not the same person. That's all shit, as usual. You haven't changed at all! And now you're back on your usual track of insulting me and also insulting my wife? Kate saved you from a far worse fate because, whether you know it or not, Steve Coombes has the capacity to do just about anything! You got off lightly and that's entirely thanks to Kate."
"Bullshit! She was just saving her own arse. Your wife's a fucking bitch."

Drive-By Shouting

The insult hung in the air between them as Gram stared silently and furiously back at Matt. After ten years of keeping his temper firmly in check, Gram was inwardly appalled at how close he was to losing it once again. It had only taken twenty-five minutes in Matt's company to undo him. Quickly calming himself, he spoke slowly: "I came here today because, firstly, I'd heard that you'd been hurt, and also, I thought that there was a glimmer of hope that you'd changed. That there may have been a chance to put the past to bed. But I can see that you're still the same narcissistic wanker that you always were; still obsessed with yourself and incapable of seeing your own role in your downfall. So, Steve played you and fucked you over? Yes! But wouldn't you do the same in his shoes? It's always someone else's fault with you, isn't it? I don't know why I fell for the crap and came here today; why I even bothered being concerned.

"I'll tell you why you came... For my approval. You came because you're a sad little man with a sad little life who's been obsessed with me from the minute we met."

Gram gasped: "What! Obsessed? With what?"

"Me. You're obsessed, and have been from the minute we met. Following me around like some lame puppy. Wanting to *be* me, wanting what I had, wanting to fuck my girlfriend. Christ, you used to creep Jen out, the way you sat there, puppy eyed, like you were about to burst into tears at any moment, stealing sad glances. And then, you acted like some jilted lover when I left the band, like I'd broken your fucking heart because I didn't want to play for fifty quid every Friday night. And Kate Craw. Bloody hell, Kate! Finally, here you

are, pretending to be my daughter's dad! Why don't you admit it Gram, you're the saddest fuck in town? Or, should I call you by your real name. I mean, what is it? Can you even remember who you were before you met me?"
He triumphantly took in the sight of Gram, stunned into silence, before continuing.
"You're fucking obsessed with me, that's why you're here. But just fuck off now and go back to your sad, smug existence with your whore of a wife. All of this is *her* fault, and it changes everything!"

Finally spurred into action, Gram's eyes bored into Matt's. "If you ever call Kate that again, I'll fucking rip your head off." He discovered that he was clenching his fists, but knew immediately that he would prove unable to strike someone in a plaster cast, whatever the provocation. "I'll tell you what Mann; I'm just going to leave, before I do something I'll regret." He turned to leave.
"Yes, just get out, but don't think this is the end of it."
Gram spun around to face Matt. "Meaning what?"
"Meaning, don't think you can go back to your cosy family and rest easy. All the nice chat stuff earlier. Forget it! Now I know that she screwed me over and offered me up to save her own arse, it's time for payback. Starting with this; I'll be contacting my daughter. Let's talk custody!"
Gram pointed an angry finger at Matt's face. "If you so much as *try* to contact her, I'll break you." He glared at Matt to reinforce the point. "And if you cared about her or about anyone other than yourself, you'd know that *you're* the last thing she needs, having a twat like you

Drive-By Shouting

come into her life? She's nine years old! She's a little kid! And she doesn't need you messing with her head. Because you've got nothing to give anyone Matt, nothing! Because it's all used up on yourself, you selfish bastard."

He continued to jab a finger at Matt's nose. "Mark my words. If you try to contact her, I'll finish what's left of you. And I'll also tell Steve Coombes that his promise to Kate no longer applies, that he's free to do what he wants to you. He'll be pleased about that because, even now, I'm pretty sure he'd like to send some of his 'associates' around to visit you." Gram was pleased to see a brief moment of panic cross Matt's face. "I'm not joking. If we hear from you and certainly if Ellen hears from, or even *about* you, we'll contact Steve Coombes. And, if the gloves are off, he'll come for you, big time. You won't know who they are, or when they're coming, but he's got some pretty vicious people in his little gang. So good luck with that, looking over your shoulder forever... You won't get a second warning; stay away!"

"You sad sack, back in the playground unable to fight your own fights, hiding behind Coombes." He gave a derisory snort; "Get out of my house!"

Gram was stunned into silence. He turned and strode through the terrace, slamming the door on the way out. His heart thumped in his chest as he re-traced the chaotic course of the conversation, while he strode down the street, furious with himself for divulging Kate's secret; once again falling for the Mann charm, until the mask had slipped and the Matt Mann of old

Drive-By Shouting

had re-appeared. He found Kate's contact on his mobile phone, but thought better of calling. This was a conversation he needed to have in person.

Whittlesey Street - Waterloo

Hearing the front door slam to announce Gram's departure, Matt finally snapped, flinging a mug furiously against the wall. He winced and held his injured shoulder before sitting back down on the wooden chair, his feet crunching on a broken chunk of pottery.

He stared at his hands, spread awkwardly on the wooden table, and felt the anger pulse through him. The jumbled disappointments and let downs of the previous nine years began to slot logically into place, and he could visualise the giant hand of Steve Coombes orchestrating the whole sorry saga. His anger slowly morphed into a detached contemplation. In a strange way, it was almost comforting to be able to finally make sense of what had previously been a fog of regret and self-recrimination: 'Had he been too casual? Too serious? Overly friendly? Just what had turned each opportunity so suddenly sour?'

Now, he finally understood, he'd never stood a chance. The merest whisper from the mighty Steve Coombes had seen him marginalised. Now that he saw things clearly, he realised that, in all of the let-downs, the job had almost always gone to an alternative client of Steve's, always to somebody that Matt knew well, just

Drive-By Shouting

to twist the knife. And, as for the few jobs that *had* gone outside of his client list, well, Steve had obviously hated him sufficiently to allow some other agent to collect the management commission on those occasions.

The more he thought about it, the more he felt Steve's behaviour to be entirely predictable and, strangely, appropriate. Of course Steve hated him, he'd been his friend and confidant, and he'd taken Matt off the rock 'n' roll scrapheap and opened doors for him. And in return, Matt had seduced his wife and got her pregnant. But the torture of the past decade? Anything would have been preferable to that. A dawning awareness came over him. Resistance seemed futile. He had spent the last nine years desperately trying to clamber back up the greasy pole, to regain some sort of success, but his cards had been marked all along. It had all been over long ago, and everybody else had known it. He'd just failed to receive the memo.

An idea quickly formed in Matt's mind. He'd struggled against the tide for far too long. If the world had no further use for him, then no striving on his part was going to change that. He stood up decisively and walked gingerly through the tiny house and levered himself up the stairs, his commitment growing with each step.

Drive-By Shouting

Later that day - the beach, near Rye

Gram opened the door to the beach house and called out a 'Hello.' Kate appeared in the doorway, looking pleasantly surprised to see him.
"You're back? I thought you were staying in town tonight?"
Gram shrugged: "Changed my mind."
"You should have called. We'd have made more pasta." She gestured to Sarah, the housemaid, and the empty pots by the sink, before noticing that Gram's face was etched with worry. She cocked her head to one side in query.

He took the cue: "I didn't want to have this conversation on the phone, get your coat, let's have a walk along the beach; I can sense three sets of ears listening in here?" He turned to look through the open doorway to the TV lounge to see, as he had presumed, all three kids eavesdropping, fascinated to see Dad nursing a secret concern. He blew sad kisses to the children and walked back out of the house. Kate picked up a jacket and joined him outside on the front deck. She took his hand as they walked down the steps towards the beach.

Back inside the house, Sarah, the housemaid, immersed a dirty pot into the sink full of soapy water, whilst she observed the two of them through the glass doors. They'd stopped and were facing each other on the path that led down to the beach; and she could see that Gram looked tense.

Drive-By Shouting

He reached out to Kate, placing his hands on her shoulders. Sarah had stopped scrubbing the pot; she knew bad news when she saw it. Kate lurched back a step, pushing Gram's hands away as she staggered away, before sinking to her knees. Sarah could see that she was sobbing.

She was busy making sense of the unfolding drama, when she became aware that she'd been joined by Thom, the youngest boy, who was also watching the action through the glass.
"Sarah? Why is my Mummy crying?"
She reached down and picked up the four year old, hugging him to her: "I've no idea sweetie. Maybe she stubbed her toe, eh?" She started back towards the TV room. "Let's leave Daddy to look after her and we'll go and watch TV with the others hey?" Thom gazed over Sarah's shoulder as he was carried along, and briefly saw his mother place her head in her hands and sink into a crumpled heap on the sand, before he was carried through the doorway to be with the other children.

Drive-By Shouting

Chapter 22
Fifteen days later – The beach, near Rye.

Gram heard the answerphone kick in again, just as it had done on all of his calls to Matt's phone over the preceding four days. The atmosphere had been fraught in the house over the previous fortnight, but the complete silence from Matt had eventually led to a thawing of the frosty air, as Kate saw it as an indication that they were going to be left alone, and they had finally arrived at an uneasy truce. Increasingly, however, the total absence of news was causing Gram's anxiety to grow.

He was still perched on the side of the bed, staring at the phone screen, when Kate emerged from the en-suite bathroom, rubbing her wet hair with a towel.

"No luck?"
"No, nothing. No answer, no voicemail message, but now it says his mailbox is full, so I can't even leave another message." He looked up at her. "Something's happened…"
"Like what?"

Drive-By Shouting

He looked intently at her: "You know what I mean. Like I told you; he was very upset when I left him. I thought it was all raging anger and fury, but maybe it was more inward looking than that?"
"You still think he's capable of doing something stupid?"
"I don't know. Isn't everybody, if they're provoked?"
She looked at him impassively: "I think that Matt Mann has far too much self-regard to ever stoop to harming himself. I think you're worrying unnecessarily. You should just enjoy the peace, bad news usually travels fast. So, I think we'd have heard if anything had happened?"

"I know, I'm probably being overdramatic. It's the uncertainty that's doing my head in, the not knowing. So anyway, I'm going to go back up there today and see him, just to make sure. I want certainty for us and, despite everything; I'd still hate to think that anything I'd said had pushed him too far. Silly, I know, after all the stunts he's pulled. I'm too bloody soft sometimes."

Kate shrugged indifferently: "Well, I suppose that it's unlikely that you could make things any worse Gram?" She gave him a reproachful glance, and he, once again, avoided her eye in regret. "Anyway, I doubt anything's wrong; he's probably just sulking. But if you're that worried, you should go. Personally I'm just pleased that he's stayed away. Beyond that, I don't care too much; I've wasted too much time worrying about this already."
Gram got up and walked over to his chest of drawers. "You're right, and obviously, my main concern is that

Drive-By Shouting

he leaves us in peace. But, just to be on the safe side, I'll take the train up this morning. Just for some peace of mind."

Later that day – Waterloo

Gram turned the corner at the White Hart pub and walked up past the bleak terraced houses that comprised Whittlesey Street. For the second time in a couple of weeks he reflected on how like a Victorian prison the houses looked. Reaching his destination, he rapped on Matt's front door. The door remained closed. After a minute he knocked again, but this time significantly harder. He stepped back and looked up at the bedroom windows, just in time to see the curtain fall back into place. He shouted up; "Matt! Matt!"

While he was strangely relieved to see signs of life, he was annoyed to find that the door remained resolutely shut. He hammered on it once more, before bending down and opening the letterbox to shout through. "I know you're in there so just open the door!" Through his small peephole, he saw movement on the stairs within, as a pair of bare legs descended the stairs. He stood up to face the door in anticipation of it opening. Abruptly, the door swung open and a tall, 30-something stranger, with a towel wrapped around his waist and water dripping from his hair, faced him angrily: "What's your problem mate? I was in the fuckin' bath!"

Drive-By Shouting

Gram recoiled on the pavement and quickly double checked to confirm that he had knocked on the correct door. He had. "Sorry! Sorry, I thought you were Matt." Gram reeled in confusion. "Is he in?"
The man's demeanour remained angry. "Who the fuck's Matt?"
"What? Matt Mann, of course. He lives here."

The angry bather turned and shouted up the stairs: "Oi, Julie…! Julie! Who'd you get this place from?" A muffled voice sounded from inside the house, and the man continued a dialogue with its owner, "Well, I don't bleedin' know! It's a geezer asking about some Matt bloke?" He turned to glare at Gram, as he was joined by a bedraggled looking woman in her late twenties. "You deal with him. I'm bloody soaking." He flashed one more menacing look at Gram, before departing, leaving Gram to look intently at the woman, with her crumpled dressing gown pulled clumsily around her.

She sensed his eye critically evaluating her: "Yeah, sorry, we was, er… asleep…" Gram ignored her embarrassment: "Yes, I'm sorry to disturb you. I'm just a bit confused. Are you a friend of Matt's or something? Or his girlfriend?"
She gave him an alarmed look: "No! I'm with Pete. You just met him!" She continued to stare indignantly at him. "If you mean the bloke what lived here, this Matt guy? Well, I never dealt with him. He's gone."
"Gone? Gone where?"
"I dunno. It was all very quick. We was looking for a place to rent; me and Pete, that is. And this came up

Drive-By Shouting

all of a sudden, so we took it. I never spoke to this Matt bloke; the neighbour said he was off the telly, but I never saw him on it. Anyway, the house was all done through the lady what works at the lettings office. But, there's some post here to your friend." She reached over to the internal window sill and retrieved a few envelopes. "Mister M. Mann. Is that him?"

Gram nodded in assent and she continued. "Well, they said that all the post was being redirected, but these ones was already 'ere. So anyway, I don't know where your friend is. Sorry."

Gram's mind reeled once more. On the one hand this very probably meant that Matt was okay and that he hadn't done anything to harm himself. But giving up his base, the terraced house, seemed rash, and Gram immediately felt concerned at what Matt's next move might be. He looked once more at the woman: "Listen, I'm really sorry to have disturbed you, and your boyfriend, but before I go do you happen to have the number for the letting agent? I could maybe ask them where my friend is."

She brightened at the question: "Oh, you don't need no number. Just go round the corner," she pointed towards the end of the road, "and up the top to Stamford Street. Turn right and they're a couple of doors along. Called *Brampton's* and the lady is Kylie. She's 'oo we dealt with."

Gram thanked the woman and turned to follow her directions. Arriving at the estate agent's office, he asked for Kylie and was surprised to be pointed in the direction of a desk at the rear of the office, where what appeared to be a child was staring intently at a computer screen, intermittently stabbing the keyboard with her fingers.

She looked up and greeted him effusively, enunciating each word like someone who had only recently learned to speak: "Good morning sir and what can I help you with? Is you looking for somewhere to live?" Gram inwardly groaned, before wincing and feeling like a grammar snob. He leaned forward with his hands on the back of the chair and addressed her: "No, I'm sorry, I'm not a renter. I'm actually enquiring about my friend who has recently hired out his house around the corner, Matt Mann?"

The smile evaporated as the anticipated commission disappeared. She maintained her overly officious tone, but this time with an added note of coldness. "Yes, Mister Mann is one of our landlords. How can I help?"
"Where is he?"
"I'm afraid that I cannot tell you that sir. He was very particular that he didn't want to be contacted."
Gram looked perplexed. "But you must know where he is? You pay him his rent, I presume?"
"Er, yes, but that goes into a bank account. And I'm afraid that we can't disclose private information about our clients and Mr. Mann was very, er, particular, like I said that he didn't want to be contacted by anyone." She seemed delighted by the opportunity to be so obstructive, as if it conferred an exalted status upon her, and Gram sensed that there would be no further information forthcoming.

Drive-By Shouting

"Okay, I understand you can't give me contact details, but... just before I go, how did he seem to you? Did he seem okay? Happy? Sad?"
She looked confused: "I really don't know sir. I only met the gentleman once. The second time he just dropped off the keys when I was out. So I just don't know."

Gram considered this, before standing upright: "Well, thanks anyway..."
She gave a triumphant cold smile as Gram turned to leave. Before he reached the door, the other occupant of the office, a plump forty-something woman in a badly fitting business suit, piped up.
"Scuse me sir? I couldn't help but overhear, are you looking for Matt Mann?" Gram brightened as he turned to face her.
"Yes. Did you meet him?"
"Yes. I was here when he brought the keys in. I was thrilled! I've always been a fan. What a handsome man! Mind you, he's not well, is he, since the accident? Looked very tired, but still, he's lovely!" She drifted into a brief reverie, as she recalled Matt's visit. "I tried telling young Kylie who he was, but kids eh? Don't know who anyone is these days! But I think he's wonderful, a proper star! Terrible shame that he's not still singing. I told him that. I couldn't believe that he'd been living just round the corner all this time! I've got all the CDs and I used to love him on the telly. I used to watch every morning when the kids were younger. And now he's gone..." she looked genuinely glassy eyed and Gram briefly worried that she may actually weep.

Drive-By Shouting

He steered her back to his mission: "Did he seem okay to you?"
The woman brightened: "Oh, like I said, he didn't look well, the poor love, y'know? Since he had that terrible accident. But he seemed okay in himself, yes. Actually, he said he felt like he knew where he was going for the first time in ages, something like that, anyway. Are you like, big friends with him?"
Gram considered this momentarily: "Sort of. We go back a long way."
"Well, you're very lucky, being friends with a big star like that!"

Gram forced a patient smile for the woman's benefit.
"Did he say *where* he was going?"
"No, just that he was happy to be going away."
"And that's it?"
"Yes. Shame really. I'd like to have been friends with him. A lovely, handsome man. I told all my friends, but some of them didn't believe I'd actually met him. You know, after years of being such a big fan, some of them actually thought that I'd just made it up!"

Gram thanked the woman and left, managing a wry half-smile at the thought of Matt thoroughly enjoying being recognised by the woman. He imagined that it was a belated moment of affirmation for Matt; somebody, somewhere, still loved him.
He walked out onto Stamford Street and fumbled in his pocket for the phone. Kate answered quickly: "And?"
"And… he's gone. He's rented out his house and disappeared. With instructions not to give out his

Drive-By Shouting

contact details to anyone."
"Really? How bizarre."
"Yes, it is. I don't know if I feel relieved or worried."

Kate paused for thought: "I think we just need to let him be. If he wants to go off, well, that's his business. Let it go Gram. I don't think he's going to rear his head and bother us. And if he does, well, we'll deal with it. I got sick of him having power over us a long time ago. It's not a big deal anymore, so whatever he does, or doesn't do, we'll cope fine."
"You're probably right, as usual. At least it doesn't look like he's done himself in. And anyway, he's been gone for a week or so now, without bothering us. On balance, I'm probably more relieved than concerned. Just glad I didn't tip him over the edge or anything. I know I'm being pathetic, it's not like he deserves to have anyone checking up on him."
"No."
"And, y'know, I'm still sorry. I wish I could undo it. I've really learned my lesson. I'll keep my big mouth shut from now on."
"That would be best."
There was an awkward silence, as Gram struggled for yet another way to apologise. This wasn't going to go away quickly.
Eventually Kate spoke: "But I suppose it says something about you that you've even bothered. But now, you need to just let it go. The sun's shining; the kids all want to go swimming. Come home, eh?"
She sounded like she was forcing herself to say the right thing, to be conciliatory, but Gram knew that the betrayal was still lodged between them.

Drive-By Shouting

He answered sheepishly: "Yeah, I'm on my way…"

As he walked down Stamford Street, he hoped that it would be possible to get their marriage back to where it had been before he'd blurted everything out to Matt. He still smarted as he recalled the conversation at the beach, and his horror at what the disclosure had done to Kate. He deeply regretted hurting her, but was also tormented by some of her comments, which felt as raw now, as when she had uttered them. Her angry response had run on a loop through his head for the last two weeks: "You just couldn't resist could you? It wasn't enough for you to *know* what had happened, you had to let *him* know that you knew. You just wanted to finally feel superior to him. That was so *small*… you're such a petty man." His guilt at betraying her trust had made the previous two weeks almost unbearable, but it was her words ('petty' and 'small'), and the accompanying look, that haunted him still.

As he walked, he reflected on how he still had to pinch himself occasionally, not quite able to believe how *this* had become his life. He was under no illusion that, without Kate's intervention, he would probably still be a dope-smoking, angry van driver, marking time in a dead-end job. Existing rather than living.
His unlikely relationship with Kate had turned his entire life around and it chilled him to imagine life without her. She had seen something in him, that even *he* had stopped believing was there, and had cared enough to prise it out of him. He felt that, in a sense, she'd saved his life. He wondered if he'd blown it.

Drive-By Shouting

Sixty-five minutes later

Sitting in the sun drenched train carriage, Gram stared out of the window, as the rolling green fields raced past him. After lacerating himself again for letting Kate down, he allowed the effects of his can of Stella Artois to sooth him, before settling his thoughts on Matt Mann.

Matt's sudden departure was unexpected, but the fact that he had gone quietly and without disrupting his family, particularly Ellen, gave a level of comfort to Gram. Feeling a slight beer-buzz, he sat in the sunlight and drifted into a reminiscence of a mid-80's trip that he and Matt had taken during a late summer recess from Polytechnic.

They had taken cheap flights to Athens, found their way to Piraeus and jumped on the first boat that was leaving the port. Having studied the boat's numerous island drop-offs, they'd flicked through Matt's ancient borrowed copy of the Berlitz travel guide to the Greek islands and decided to disembark on Mykonos, assuming that the reference to 'the gayest island in the Aegean' was a quaint 1950's use of the word. They were disabused of this notion very soon after arriving. They were plunged into a hedonistic nightlife of gay & trans clubs, with Matt happily taking advantage of the company of numerous disappointed straight women, who, like them, had accidently ended up on the island. All of Gram's prurient Northern apprehensions were

Drive-By Shouting

entirely washed aside by Matt's enthusiasm for the endless clubs, parties and nudist beaches. Within a couple of days, everybody seemed to know (and love) Matt. He effortlessly slipped into the scene, carrying a slightly startled Gram in his wake. It had been a cementing experience for their early friendship, as they rolled around the island, existing on whatever leftover bread and olive oil they could liberate from open-air restaurant tables, before the waiters cleared up after the diners had departed.

Gram recalled one particularly drunk and debauched night, highlighted by the two of them racing chaotically over the rooftops of houses with two crates of stolen beer, closely pursued by the angry Greek bar proprietors. They had narrowly escaped, hiding in a darkened courtyard, desperately suppressing their panting breath for fear of detection. He drifted into the memory of the two of them lying drunk on the beach a little later, laughing hysterically at their triumph. He pictured Matt, feeling the love of the whole island, and declaring expansively: "This is the life Gram! When it all goes tits up for me and, let's be clear, it will, obviously! Then, this is where you'll find me..." he gesticulated drunkenly, "I'll be here, enjoying the sun, the sea and the total love of the people! All of them!" Gram remembered Matt's youthful face, filled with confidence and optimism. It was the face of a man who knew exactly where he was going and who wasn't going to let anyone stand in his way. He wanted to hate Matt, but there always remained a grain of affection, and if he confessed the truth, a part of Gram actually missed him. Despite everything that had gone wrong between

Drive-By Shouting

the two of them since, and even despite Matt's recent veiled threats, it was with a strangely fond nostalgia that he looked back on Matt at the age of twenty-one. He hoped that somehow he'd found his way back to that time. Maybe even to that place.

Part 9

Fade Out

Drive-By Shouting

Chapter 23
Six days previously – Hampstead, North London

Intrigued to hear his doorbell ringing at such a late hour, and on such an unexpectedly damp and squally summer night, Steve Coombes first checked the security spy-hole, before opening the door to a windswept and emaciated Matt Mann, who stood dripping on his doorstep. He hesitated, having not seen him for over four years, and his appearance had certainly altered, before composing himself.
"Well Matt, this is unexpected. To what do I owe this unannounced visit?" His tone was cool and unwelcoming.
Matt gave him a meaningful stare: "I think you know what this is about Steve."
Steve held his gaze: "I'm not sure that I do. You'd better come in."

He directed Matt through the wide tiled hallway towards the kitchen at the rear of the house, observing Matt's slight limp, before mechanically handing him a towel as they entered. Steve eyed Matt without warmth.
"So, Matt, why are you here? I heard about your argument with a cliff-face; you look like shit, by the way."

Drive-By Shouting

Matt mopped his wet face and considered this for a while before replying. "Yes, nice to see you too." He tossed the wet towel onto the kitchen island and leaned back against a cabinet, steadily eyeing Coombes. After an uncomfortably long silence, he eventually spoke: "So… I've found out the truth about the rather nasty game that you've played with me over the last few years. I hope it kept you entertained, dangling job after job in front of me, and all the while, making sure that they all came to naught?"

Steve stared back impassively, silent and belligerent.

Matt continued: "So, you decided to play politics and manoeuvre me, rather than just confronting me? And I don't mean sending your hired thugs, I mean *you*. Why couldn't you just come out with it and we could have talked about it, one to another? Why couldn't you just be a man about it? Not hide behind your hard-men or do the sneaky back-hand stuff; but just talk to me? Instead you acted like a fucking devious coward!"

A snarl had spread across Steve's face, his steely eyes boring into Matt's: "If I'd '*been a man*' about it, trust me, you wouldn't be walking around! You've got Kate to thank for that. It's only her that's kept you alive! If I hadn't had to give her my word, I'd have done things differently; *very* differently. You got off lightly."

Matt snapped back at him: "And I'm supposed to be grateful for that? That instead of tackling what had happened straight on, that you inflicted death by a thousand cuts. That you slowly tortured me. You destroyed my life. You took away everything I ever cared about!"

Drive-By Shouting

Steve's grimace evolved into a twisted smile: "Yeah, I did, didn't I! And it was one of the most satisfying experiences of my life. Even more so, because you didn't have a clue, did you? You thick bastard! But, I only destroyed your life after you'd done exactly the same thing to me! I let you into my life and you utterly ruined my happiness. You took away the woman I truly loved and all the while, pretended to be my friend. You backstabbing bastard! So yes, I played with you and dangled you like some pathetic toy. It was fucking enjoyable, actually! And it was no more than an eye for an eye."

"No it wasn't!" Matt's eyes bulged with indignation. "Yes, I made a mistake with Kate, I can accept that. I shouldn't have done it, but sometimes stuff just happens without anyone planning it. But that marriage was over anyway. If it hadn't been me, it would have been somebody else."

"But it *wasn't* somebody else, was it? It was *you*!" Steve spat the words out. "After everything I'd done for you. After I'd lifted you off the shit heap and given you access to all the things you wanted. I *made* you!" His face was red with rage.

Matt sneered back at him: "Bollocks you did! I think you'll find that actually, I was an *accident waiting to happen*. You didn't *make* me, you just happened along and saw my potential at the right time. You saw someone with innate charisma and thought you'd jump on the bandwagon and make some money. That's all!"

"You arrogant prick!" Steve laughed derisively, his head thrown back in contempt. "If I didn't *make* you,

Drive-By Shouting

then why was it so fucking easy to *break* you? Eh? Where was your 'innate charisma,' then? When producer after producer happily dropped you from every project? You were just another arsehole to them…
You like to kid yourself that you're special, don't you? But you're just one of a million smarmy bastards who think that charm will get you everywhere. But you're nothing. Nothing! I could throw a stick and hit twenty more just like you, in any street in London."

He saw Matt start to wilt under the onslaught. "But out of all the big headed tossers out there, I picked you. And you betrayed me like nobody has ever betrayed me before. And you were not going to be allowed to get away with that!" He stared at Matt with unconcealed malice.

Matt rallied to his own defence: "So why not have this conversation back then? Why not just get it out there, rather than torturing me for so long?"
"Conversation? I didn't want a fucking conversation! You forget who you're dealing with. I didn't want to talk to you then and I don't want to talk to you now! I just wanted to crush you, to break you, to make you feel as small and useless as you really are."
"You fucking bastard." Matt shook his head slowly as he stared back at Coombes. "But that's it, the fun's over. I'm leaving. I may look like shit, just as you say," he gestured to himself, "but I've been discharged now, so there's nothing holding me here anymore. So, you'll have to find someone else to torture, because I'm not hanging around in this country full of wankers, just so

Drive-By Shouting

that you can get your rocks off, sticking pins in my doll. I'm going where you and your thugs can't touch me. Where your fucking cowardly scheming can't fuck my life up any more. Because that's what you are. Take away all your East End pals, all of your psychopath 'associates,' and what's left? A spineless coward!"

Steve moved around the island close to Matt, his eyes bulging with fury: "Don't you call me a fucking coward, you piece of shit!"
Matt smirked defiantly: "Why, what are you going to do, big man? You've sworn your promise to your beloved Kate, so just fuck off with your empty threats."

Steve turned and reached into the kitchen drawer, before looking calmly at Matt:
"You think that'll keep you safe, some promise I made years ago?" He waved a large kitchen knife in the air. "You come here, shouting your stupid mouth off and think I don't have the balls to finish you off? You've no idea what you're dealing with..."

But, to Steve's consternation, he observed that Matt was not perturbed. In fact, he looked amused, which deeply unsettled him.
Matt smiled triumphantly: "But that's just the point Steve...I have *every* idea of what I'm dealing with. I know *exactly* what you're like. I'm one of the few people who do. Not even Kate knew what you were *really* like."
"What the fuck are you on about?"

Drive-By Shouting

Seeming to ignore him, Matt continued: "And the only other person who really knew what you were like is Vanessa."

A small kernel of concern was growing inside Steve: "So what, that bitch hasn't worked for me for five years. What's she got to do with anything?"
Matt smiled confidently again, throwing Steve further off-balance: "Yeah that's right. Vanessa. Your lovely old PA. But isn't she doing well now? The head of the literary division at *Grant Bowen Associates*; who'd have thought it eh? We've been in touch for a few months now… you see, some people still like me. I've been writing an autobiography, at her insistence…"
Steve laughed out loud: "You must be kidding? Who the fuck wants to read about your sad, washed-up life?"
"But that's just it. Once I found out about your little games with me, I had an epiphany, a real moment of clarity. I realized that all of the bits that I'd been editing out, well, that's where all the *juice* is. Those are the real page turners, the cold facts about Steve Coombes! All the stuff about you that I didn't think I could use. Well, it turns out I can! It'll be a massive best seller, especially with all the PR we'll get when you get arrested, when you go to trial, when they strip you of your MBE. And you can forget the knighthood you've spent years working on. That's a goner once this stuff comes out. *Dynamite*! That's what they're calling it at Grant Bowen! Who's gonna give a knighthood to a thug, a petty swindler and a tax avoider, eh? And then there are your young male friends. Well, they were *very* young, weren't they? What's that you used to tell me

Drive-By Shouting

Steve?" Matt grinned, "Ah, that's it; '*You can't buy that kind of publicity.*"

Matt quietly enjoyed the concern now tracing its way across Steve's face. He warmed to his theme.
"There were a few dates I was unsure of, but Vanessa's memory was amazing! And my! She's good on the figures. No love lost there, eh?" He saw Steve visibly slump as he realised what was happening. Matt looked at the knife, still held in Coombes' hand. "I'd put that down if I were you, there are a couple of things you definitely need to know before you start doing anything stupid…" Something about Matt's confidence in the face of the kitchen knife, demoralised Coombes, and he paused, before placing it on the counter.
"So, anyway, back to my autobiography. Now; it's *really* interesting. Because *you're* on so many pages. All the dirty deals, all the shit you pulled the secret bank accounts…"

Steve's face fell further, before he abruptly looked up:
"So, what's to stop me picking this knife up again."
"Well, absolutely nothing, But, then again, if I'm not home by 11pm, the scripts are absolutely everywhere, and Vanessa's got her copies"
"Oh, I can shut that bitch up…"
"Yeah, but not all of the other copies. You don't think I'd come here without insurance? At one minute past 11pm, it goes live; you don't own everyone in the media you know…"
The two men stared at each other in silence, until Matt eventually spoke.

Drive-By Shouting

"So, Steve, despite your cupboard full of knives, it's actually *your* life that's in *my* hands... Funny eh?"

Steve stared at Matt, hatred pouring out of him: "So what do you want, you shit?"
"It's not *what* I want, it's *how much*." He left a silence and stared impassively at Coombes. "I've done the numbers and there's a figure that would see me about right, it would compensate me for the loss of earnings from my autobiography and of course the serialisations, the interviews, TV appearances... Fuck me, there could be a screenplay! Then there's the songwriting royalties you swindled me out of. And there's also a bit for Vanessa; although frankly, she hates you so much that she'd probably be doing this for free. What did she call it...? Ah yes, *community service*!"
He calmly observed Steve. The mask had slipped and Matt could clearly see fear on his face.

"So here's what's going to happen. You'll pay four million right now, *tonight*, with me watching, so there are no *misunderstanding*s. And don't pretend that you don't have access to the money. I spent a *lot* of time in your office, and Vanessa spent even more time there, and there's always at least twice that much sitting in your nice offshore accounts. So let's get over to your computer and make this happen."
"And then what? You just blackmail me forever?"
"No, you'll never hear from me again, and all of the copies of the manuscript will disappear. All bar one, of course. I'll always have insurance, just in case anything should ever happen to me. But once you've made

Drive-By Shouting

payment, I give you my word, if you leave me alone, I'll never bother you again. Just make the payment and I'll leave. Then, you never have to deal with me again.

In thirty-six hours you're to contact Vanessa. Not a minute before 11am on Thursday. This is *not* an opportunity for you to see if you can intimidate Vanessa, so don't even try; unless you want to invalidate our arrangement? But, after thirty-six hours, once we're certain that the funds are intact and you haven't done anything underhand, you're to call her. She'll confirm that the payment has gone to plan, and will arrange for all of the manuscript copies and notes to be returned to you. After that, you can do what you like with it all. So let's open your laptop, sort the transfer and then I can be on my way."

Hatred and fury pouring from his eyes, Coombes seemed rooted to the spot, calculating all of the permutations that he could imagine, but he knew when he'd been outflanked. He dutifully turned and walked over to his desk.

Matt's arm ached, the painkillers had worn off, and even the adrenaline of facing down his own personal ogre was not sufficiently masking the throb, which was traversing his arm and working its way across his left shoulder. He slipped his hand into his jacket pocket and felt the reassuring shape of his passport. He had somehow kept a lid on his fear; he knew more than anyone that the stories about Steve Coombes were true. Just ten more minutes of self-control was all that he needed.

Drive-By Shouting

Thursday morning.

Steve Coombes had never taken kindly to losing money and had consequently spent the last two days in a foul mood. He had paced the floor of his kitchen, willing the clock to tick around to 11am. Unable to handle the tension, he'd got into his car and was aimlessly driving around North London. The money was bad enough, but the real source of stress was the knowledge that all of that material, all of that *dirt*, was out there, waiting to ruin him. He could ride out the four million, he had plenty more where that came from, but the public shame if all of the *stuff* came out, *that* would be too much to bear. After all the stunts he'd pulled, he knew how much fun the press would have in publicly whipping him. Getting on their high horses, like they hadn't been *in it* with him, up to their necks! He'd spent years building his veneer of respectability, he certainly wasn't going to let it be wrecked by Matt Mann, or that back-stabbing bitch Vanessa.

The moment his car clock ticked onto 11am, he angrily pressed the call button. After 2 rings it was answered.
"Good morning, *Grant Bowen*, how can I help you?"
"Put me through to Vanessa."
"Who's calling please?"
Steve's irritation was boiling up, he wanted to swipe the receptionist aside.
"Steve Fucking Coombes. Now put me through!"
There was a long pause, then a click.

Drive-By Shouting

"Hello Steve, interesting new name you've got!" she sounded icy. "What do you want?"

"Yeah, all right Vanessa, you bitch. You know exactly why I'm calling. I want the stuff immediately, you get that? The courier is downstairs in your reception now, so pack up your little fun bag and then we're all done."

"Steve? Is that you?"
"Who the fuck else are you blackmailing, of course it's fucking me!"
There was a pause on the line: "Sorry Steve, what are you talking about?"
"About Matt fucking Mann, of course."
"Matt Mann? Why? I haven't spoken to Matt in years…didn't he have a terrible accident? Actually, I think somebody said he nearly died…"

But Steve had stopped listening. He instantly understood. He pressed the 'Call End' button on his phone and tossed it onto the seat. His grip tightened around the soft cream leather of the steering wheel and he had the sensation that he was spinning out of control on a fairground Waltzer.

He turned the car onto the North Circular and accelerated wildly down the slip road, nearly careering into the left side of a black Mercedes as it approached from the nearside lane. Startled, the driver looked across in alarm to see what looked like a florid faced ex-boxer crammed behind the wheel of a Ferrari. He looked like a bear in a shrinking cage. The windows were down and even above the roar of the engine and

Drive-By Shouting

the screech of the brakes, he could hear the guttural howl that came from the depths of the demented driver. "Fuuuuuuccccckkkkkkk...."

Drive-By Shouting

About the author:

Drive-By Shouting is the new novel by broadcaster, songwriter and now author, Mark Chase.

Liverpool born, Chase has been a TV presenter on a variety of shows, including; *The Survivors Guide, Sextalk* (both C4), *Breakfast Time, Going Live!* (BBC1), *Wideangle, Country File* (ITV) and *Toyah & Chase* (VH-1). On radio, he has hosted BBC 5Live's *After Hours* and *The Chase is On.*

Behind the scenes, he has worked as a producer on both *Comic Relief* & *Sport Aid* and has written for a number of publications including *Esquire, the NME, Melody Maker, Maxim* and *Red.*

Mark was the leader of the notorious 90's band *World of Leather*, who released two albums and numerous singles through Sony Records. They toured extensively in the UK and Europe and sold respectably in Japan & Scandinavia, whilst skilfully avoiding the UK charts.

Drive-By Shouting

Prior to this, Chase had been a successful session musician & session singer, working with numerous artists including *Belinda Carlisle, Taylor Dayne, Big Trouble & John Barrowman.*

He lives in East Sussex with his wife, Jacqueline, and their four children.